PRICE SIXPENCE

MACKENZIE'S
GUIDE
TO
INVERNESS
NAIRN
AND THE
HIGHLANDS:
Historical,
Descriptive and Pictorial.

INVERNESS: MELVEN BROTHERS.
1901.

THE HIGHLAND RAILWAY.

BY	**TOURS**	BY
ROCK,	FOR THE	**RIVER,**
WOOD,		**LOCH,**
and	**HOLIDAYS**	**and**
GLEN.		**SEA.**

The Direct Route to INVERNESS and NORTH OF SCOTLAND is Via DUNKELD.

Leaving **Perth** the Line runs by **Dunkeld** through the far-famed **Pass of Killiecrankie,** skirting the **Deer Forest of Atholl,** over the **Grampians,** and through **Strathspey,** affording magnificent glimpses of **Ben Macdhui** and the **Cairngorms,** on to **Kingussie** and **Aviemore.** From Aviemore a new and direct Line to Inverness, traversing scenery of the grandest description, has been constructed, shortening the time on the journey by an hour. By the old route the Line runs past the ancient Towns of **Forres** (where the traveller can diverge and visit **Elgin,** with its magnificent Cathedral) and **Nairn,** "The Brighton of the North," to **Inverness,** the **Capital o: the Highlands.** Parties staying at Inverness can have a choice selection of Tours at Reduced Fares. (See Tours for 1901 at end of descriptive matter in the Handbook.)

From INVERNESS Northwards

the Line skirts the Beauly Firth to **Muir of Ord** (from whence a Branch Line has recently been opened to **Fortrose**) on to **Dingwall,** from which point the traveller can visit the far-famed **Strathpeffer Spa,** "The Harrogate of the North," or proceed through grand and striking scenery to **Kyle of Lochalsh,** and thence by Steamer to the **Isle of Skye** and the **Outer Hebrides,** visiting on the route **Loch Maree** and **Gairloch,** or proceed North through **Ross, Sutherland,** and **Caithness** to **Thurso** and **Wick,** visiting **John o' Groat's House,** and thence by steamer to the **Orkney** and **Shetland Isles.**

The whole Route affords an ever-varying succession of the most Picturesque Scenery, and the **Finest Shooting and Fishing in Scotland.**

Tourist Tickets are issued from the principal Stations in England and Scotland by this Route, along which there is now increased Hotel and Lodging accommodation.

For full particulars as to Trains, Through Carriages, Tours, Fares, Steamer and Coach Connections, &c., apply to Mr T. McEWEN, TRAFFIC MANAGER, INVERNESS, or the respective Station Masters.

INVERNESS. **T. A. WILSON, General Manager.**

N.B.—Passengers when Booking should ask for Tickets by the Highland Route **via Dunkeld**

Great North of Scotland Railway Company.

SEASIDE AND GOLFING RESORT,

CRUDEN BAY

(30 MILES BY RAIL FROM ABERDEEN.)

FINE, Hard, Sandy Beach over two miles long, exceptionally well adapted for Sea Bathing and Promenading. Bracing and very healthy climate.

The Rock Scenery in the neighbourhood is most attractive, the famous Bullers O' Buchan being about two miles from the Hotel.

The **Golf Course** of Eighteen Holes, laid out by the Railway Company, is pronounced by prominent Golfers to be one of the best in the Kingdom.

A Ladies' Golf Course of Nine Holes

has also been formed.

Cruden Bay Hotel

(Owned and Managed by the Great North of Scotland Railway Company.)

Bowling

   Greens,

Tennis

   Courts,

Croquet

   Lawns.

Bathing.

Boating.

Fishing.

This large and handsome Hotel occupies a charming site, and overlooks the Bay of Cruden.

Abundant supply of pure water. Perfect sanitation. Electrically lighted. Lift.

Electric tramway for visitors and luggage between the Railway Station and the Hotel.

Postal and Telegraph Office; Established, Episcopal, United Free and Congregational Churches within easy walking distances.

Trains between Aberdeen and Cruden Bay at convenient hours.

Address enquiries to the **Manager**, Cruden Bay Hotel, Port Erroll, Aberdeenshire.

MACKENZIE'S

GUIDE TO INVERNESS, NAIRN

AND THE

HIGHLANDS:

HISTORICAL, DESCRIPTIVE, AND PICTORIAL,

WITH

*PLAN OF INVERNESS AND TOURIST MAP
OF SCOTLAND.*

——o——

VERY MUCH EXTENDED AND IMPROVED
FOR SEASON 1901.

——o——

BY

ALEXANDER MACKENZIE, M.J.I.,

Author of the History of the Mackenzies ; of the Macdonalds and
Lords of the Isles ; of the Camerons ; of the Macleods ; of the
Mathesons ; of the Chisholms ; of the Frasers ; of the
Highland Clearances ; the Prophecies of the
Brahan Seer, &c.

INVERNESS AND NAIRN : MELVEN BROTHERS.

1901.

LIST OF ILLUSTRATIONS.

INVERNESS CAB FARES.

(Copied from Bye-Laws for the Regulation of Cab Fares.)

Between the EXCHANGE, HIGH STREET, and the

	S. D.		S. D.
Approach Road to Daviot House..	5 0	Lunatic Asylum Porter's Lodge....	2 0
Artillery Battery, by Rose Street..	1 0	Muirtown Bridge and Hotel........	1 0
Bridge over Muckovie Burn......	3 0	Ness Islands.................	1 0
Braerannoch House..............	1 0	Opposite Bunchrew House	3 0
Clachnaharry Village, West End...	1 6	Opposite Dochgarroch House......	4 0
Culloden Tile Works..............	4 0	Steamboat Wharf, Muirtown......	1 0
Culduthel Wood.................	4 0	Thornbush Pier.	1 0
Culcabock Village...............	1 0	Tomnahurich Cemetery (Entrance	
Entrance to Raigmore House......	1 0	* Gate)	1 0
Culloden Moor....................	6 0	Top of Cemetery.................	1 6
Holm Mills	1 6	From the Exchange and Back, by	
Kessock Ferry...................	1 6	Millburn, Longman, and Shore	4 0

FARES BY DISTANCE.—One mile or under, 1s ; and 6d for every additional half-mile or part thereof. Return Journey, half-fare additional.

When the fare going is 1s, Carriage shall wait ten minutes; when 1s 6d, fifteen minutes ; when 2s or upwards, twenty minutes ; if detained longer, a charge of 6d for every additional twenty minutes or part thereof.

FARES BY TIME.—MAKING CALLS, SHOPPING, ETC.—1s for first half hour, and 6d for every additional quarter.

FOR AN AIRING INTO THE COUNTRY.—8s for first hour, and 2s 6d for each succeeding hour.

From midnight till 5 a.m., Double Fare. From 5 to 8 a.m., Fare and a half.

Sea Locks

Thornbush Brewery

School
Lock
Stations
Clachnaharry
Post Office
Melrose Pillar
1434
Lescrip
Knockgur

HIGHLAND RAILWAY

MUIRTOWN BASIN

MERKIN

Scorguie

Muirtown Ho.

Militia Depôt

Madras School

Tweed Mills

Muirtown Br.

Muirtown Hotel

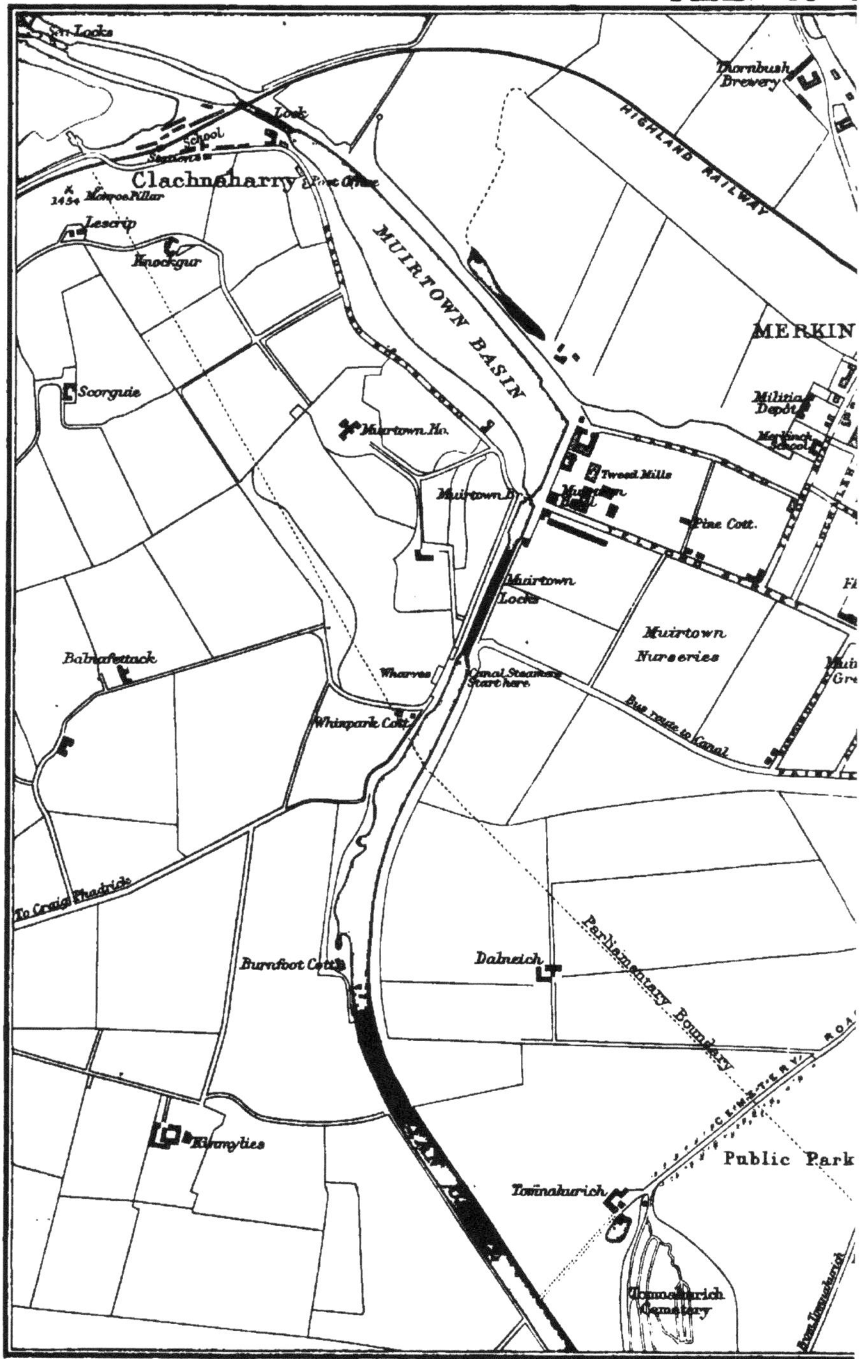

Pine Cott.

Muirtown Locks

Fi

Balnafettack

Muirtown
Nurseries

Muir
Gre

Wharves

Canal Steamers
Start here

Bus route to Canal

Whinpark Cott.

To Craig Phadrick

Burnfoot Cott.

Dalneich

Parliamentary Boundary

Kinmylies

CEMETERY ROA

Public Park

Tomnahurich

Tomnahurich
Cemetery

To Torvean

Scale of

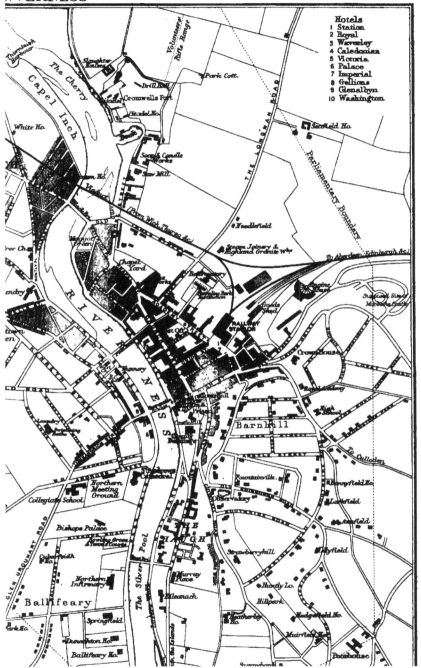

Hotels
1 Station
2 Royal
3 Waverley
4 Caledonian
5 Victoria
6 Palace
7 Imperial
8 Gellions
9 Glenalbyn
10 Washington

CONTENTS.

INVERNESS.

THE HIGHLANDS.

CONTENTS.

Royal Hotel,
INVERNESS.

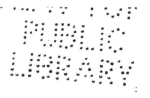

GUIDE TO INVERNESS

AND

THE HIGHLANDS:

HISTORICAL AND DESCRIPTIVE.

PROGRESS IN RECENT YEARS.

INVERNESS, the Capital of the Highlands, in 1645 had a population of only 2400; in 1798 of 5107; in 1831 of 9663. In 1861 it went up to 12,509, and in 1891 to 19,214, an increase of nearly 7000 in thirty years. During the last three decades, in the early part of which, mainly from 1861 to 1871, railway communication had been opened up with the north and south, the town progressed at a rate previously unknown, and situated, as it is, in the most central position both for water and railway communication, it is destined in the near future to become one of the most important towns in Scotland. In addition to the population resident within the Municipal boundary already stated, the suburbs—which practically form a portion of the town, and all of which have come into existence and grown up during the last thirty years—the inhabitants number between fifteen hundred and two thousand. There is a proposal on foot at present to bring all these within the Burgh boundary, in which case the town of Inverness will show a population almost double what it had a generation ago.

But the increase of mere population is proportionally insignificant when compared with the increase in the general prosperity of the Burgh. Before the advent of the Highland Railway, Inverness was a poor place. In 1851, it had only 1701 inhabited houses as against 2519 in 1881 and 4312 in 1891. And while the annual value of the real property of the Burgh in 1851 was only £23,603 (nearly £5000 less than it was in 1815), the annual value in 1891 was £92,446. The Corporation revenue in 1851 mainly consisted of the rents and feu duties of the Common Good, and amounted to £3800. In 1891 the revenue of the Town Council and Police Commissioners from all sources amounted to £27,869. These figures indicate a great advance in the material prosperity of the burgh, felt to be largely due to the Highland Railway system, and especially to the location of its works and head offices in Inverness. At present there are nearly 900 people employed in the town in connection with the Highland Railway, of whom about 800 are artisans. The amount paid in wages and salaries each year is above £60,000, of which over £50,000 or £1000 a week goes to the artisan class.

The buildings in Inverness and its suburbs cover more than three times the ground covered by buildings in 1855, and the superior class of houses now in vogue cannot be compared with those in existence then. The stagnation of Inverness prior to the introduction of railways is illustrated by a statement in the New Statistical Account of the burgh and parish published in 1845, and compiled by the minister of the parish with the assistance of Mr George Anderson, solicitor, Inverness, one of the writers of the "Guide to the Highlands." At that time the proportion of unmarried females above 20 years of age to unmarried

NOTE—.Revenue in 1901—£36,709 4s 11d.

From]   **Inverness Market Cross in 1726.**   [Burt.

males of the same age was about four to one, a state of things no doubt brought about by the want of employment in the burgh then for its male population.

In 1847 the number of Parliamentary electors in the town of Inverness was 507, the total in the four burghs forming the Inverness District being 918. Of these voters there were 51 in Fortrose, 118 in Nairn, and 142 in Forres. The number of Parliamentary electors in Inverness in 1891 was 2543. The Municipal constituency in the Burgh in 1847 was 416, divided as follows :—First Ward, 133 ; Second Ward, 129 ; Third Ward, 154. In 1891 the voters numbered 3101, made up of 1260 in the First Ward ; 901 in the Second Ward ; and 940 in the Third Ward.

In 1875 Parliamentary power was obtained to purchase the undertaking of the old Inverness Water and Gas Company, and immediately afterwards a supply of fresh water was introduced by gravitation—the original total cost of both being about £100,000. Within the past few years an arterial system of drainage has been laid down on both sides of the river at a total cost of £10,000, while at the same time several of the leading thoroughfares have been laid down with granite cubes, and the foot-paths re-paved with Caithness flags.

HISTORY AND CHRONOLOGY.

Inverness is a Royal Burgh, governed by a Provost, four Bailies, a Dean of Guild, a Treasurer, and fourteen Councillors. Its early annals are shrouded in the mists of antiquity, so that it is impossible to say when it was first founded. The early Scottish historians agree that it existed before the Christian era, Boethius saying that it "was founded by Evenus II. the fourteenth King of Scotland," who died 60 years before Christ. Buchanan concurs, while in Burns' Chronology we are told that "Evenus was a good king ; he made Inverness and Inverlochy market towns 60 years before Christ." These statements have been disputed

NOTE.—The Constituency in 1900 was 3580.

by modern historians; but it seems established that Inver-
ness was at a very early period the Capital of the ancient
Province of Moravia or Moray—which extended from the
Spey in the east to the watershed of the present County of
Ross in the west, and from Loch Lochy in the south to
the Kyles of Sutherland in the north. It was "the seat of
the Pictish Government," and it is said "that Gaelic was the
only language and tartan the only dress at that Court."
Druid Temple, two miles and a half to the south of the
Town, and the vitrified fort, the remains of which are
still distinctly traceable on the top of Craig Phadruig,
sufficiently prove that Inverness was a centre of importance
in the days of Druidism and hill forts. At Bona, a few
miles to the west of the town, are traces of a Roman
fort—"an oblong square, rounded at the corners and
encircled with an irregular ditch," to which more detailed
reference will be made later on.

We are told by Adamnan that Columba, the first Christian
missionary to the Highlands, visited Inverness in 565 for
the purpose of converting Brudeus II., the Pictish monarch
of that day, who had his seat at Inverness, to Christianity.
"Brude in his pride had shut the gates against the holy
man, but the saint, by the sign of the cross, and knocking
at it, caused it to fly open of its own accord. Columba and
his companions then entered; the king with those around
him advanced and met them, and received the saint with
due respect, and ever after king Brude honoured him."
The saint is said to have performed wonderful miracles in
Inverness during his visit in the way of casting out evil
spirits and defeating the king's seers and wise men. He
held several conferences with men of position on that occasion and converted many of them. The Pictish and Scottish
Kingdoms were in 843 united under the rule of Kenneth
MacAlpine, and Inverness lost the distinction of being a
Capital. The town is supposed to have been the scene of
King Duncan's murder by Macbeth. Macbeth's castle is

said to have stood upon the Crown, and a circular plot of ground, railed in and planted with trees. behind Victoria Terrace, is pointed out as its site. Bellenden, the translator of Boethius, referring to this point says—" Makbeth, be persuasion of his wife, gaderit his friendis to ane counsall at Innernes, quhare King Duncane happinit to be for the time. And because he fand sufficient opportunite, be support of Banquho and otheris his friendis, he slew King Duncane, the VII. yeir of his regne." Shakespeare adopts this version. In 1056 Malcolm Ceanmore, in revenge of his father's murder, destroyed the building in which it is said to have occurred, and raised another castle of his own, overlooking the river, on the present Castle Hill.

In the 12th century Inverness received its present arms under the following circumstances. Richard I. of England required a subsidy from William I. of Scotland—William the Lion—to assist in fitting out an expedition in the time of the Crusades to the Holy Land. Inverness contributed so liberally that as a special mark of his appreciation William made a grant of arms to the town with the crucifix in the centre supported as at the present day with the elephant and camel on either side.

It has been maintained by some that a charter was granted to the town by Malcolm III. Of this no authentic record exists ; but it is certain that a Royal Castle existed on the "Auld Castle Hill" before the time of Malcolm Ceanmore. In the reign of David I., 1124-53, Inverness was constituted a Royal Burgh and the headquarters of a Sheriff, whose jurisdiction extended over the whole of the North of Scotland. The place was then described " *Loca Capitali per totum Regnum*," or one of the Capitals or chief places of the Kingdom. In 1161 Malcolm IV. visited the town, and in 1163 he made Shaw Macduff, who was called " Mac-an-Toisich," or son of the Thane, hereditary constable of the Castle as a reward for great services rendered by him in suppressing a rebellion which had broken out in Moray; hence the name of Mackintosh.

William the Lion, who reigned from 1165 to 1215, and who had granted four charters to the town, visited Inverness in 1196. By the second of these, granted in 1180, he undertakes to make a fosse or ditch round the burgh on condition that the inhabitants shall "enclose the town within the fosse by good palings." They did so, and some of the "palings" were in existence as late as 1689. By his last charter this king continues all the privileges secured by the earlier one granted by David I., and establishes a weekly market to be held in the burgh in all time coming "on the Sabbath day in every week." Charters were also granted by Alexander II. (who visited Inverness in 1219, 1220, 1222, 1228-29, and in 1236), in 1217 and 1237, on which latter occasion a previous grant of the lands of Merkinch was confirmed to the burgesses, by a charter granted during that visit. In 1233 the same king endowed a monastery of Grey Friars in the town. At the Reformation the lands connected therewith were converted into a glebe, and the site of the Church into a burying place. A fragment of a pillar still standing in the midst of the graves is the only remnant of the monastery that now remains. Alexander III. granted a charter in 1250. He afterwards visited the town in 1260 and 1263, in which latter year he ratified the Annual of Norway at Inverness.

In 1229 Gillespick MacScourlane burnt the town, spoiled the adjacent Crown lands, and put to the sword all who would not acknowledge him as their sovereign. For this crime he and his two sons were afterwards put to death.

At this early period the burgh was noted for shipbuilding, and its reputation extended to foreign countries. Tytler informs us that in 1249, Hugh de Chastillion, Earl of St. Paul, one of the richest and most powerful of the French barons, consented to accompany Louis the IX. to the Crusades, and that the ship, which was to have borne him and his vassals to the Holy Land, was built, by his orders, at Inverness. Paris, the historian, refers to the same fact, and says, "this Count Hugh built a handsome ship at Inverness." Other foreigners repeat the statement. In 1280 a French Count who was ship-wrecked in the Orkneys had a large ship built for him at Inverness to take the place of the ship he had lost.

In 1263 Alexander III. came to Inverness, when he ordered a new pallisade to be erected round the Castle. From the Chamberlain's accounts the cost of this additional defence only amounted to £1 18s 9d, while the expenses of a wardrobe, with a double wooden roof, built within the stronghold, is put down in the same accounts at £7 19s.

The Castle of Inverness was recovered from the Cummings of Badenoch by Edward I., in 1303, after which it was stormed and taken by Robert Bruce, who in 1325 directed a precept to the Sheriff of Inverness to do full and speedy justice at the suit of the burgesses against all invading their privileges by buying or selling in prejudice of them and of the liberties of the burgh.

In 1369 David II., who in November of that year came north to Inverness to punish the Lord of the Isles, granted a charter confirming the rights of the burgesses to the lands of Drakies, and to the tolls and petty customs of the town. The same King was again at Inverness in 1380, and also in 1382, when he granted various other charters to the burgh.

In 1400 Donald of the Isles approached the town and threatened to give it to the flames unless it was ransomed by a large sum. The Provost, pretending to agree to his terms, sent the Island chief as part of the ransom a quantity of spirits, of which he and his followers partook so liberally that they soon became helplessly drunk. The Provost, followed by the citizens, taking advantage of the intoxicated state of the enemy, advanced upon them, sword in hand, on the north side of Kessock Ferry, and "put the whole to indiscriminate slaughter," except Donald him-self who managed to escape. In 1410 the Island chief on his way to Harlaw, fully revenged himself upon the inhabitants by burning the town and the oak bridge, described as "one of the finest in the Kingdom." Shortly after this James I. caused the Castle to be strengthened, when it was again placed under the governorship of Mac-kintosh. In 1412 there is an entry of a payment by the king to Alexander, Earl of Mar, for outlays and labour during the war against the Lord of the Isles, and among other items is one of £100 for lime which the earl had used in the reconstruction of a fortalice at Inverness.

In 1427 James I. visited the burgh, attended by his Parliament, on which occasion he held a Court in the Castle, to which all the northern chiefs and barons were summoned, when several of them were treacherously put to death; and among others, Alexander, third Lord of the Isles, was imprisoned for twelve months. After the Island Lord regained his liberty he collected 10.000 of his followers, and again burnt the town. He at the same time laid siege to the Castle, but failed to take it. In 1449, his son and successor, John of the Isles, seized the Castles of Inverness, Urquhart, and Ruthven, and in 1455, Donald Balloch took Inverness by surprise, plundered it, and burnt t to the ground.

James I. was again in Inverness in 1428, when he granted another charter to the burgh, dated the 28th of August in that year.

In 1457 James II., who was in Inverness on the 12th of October, confirmed all rights, privileges, liberties, and infeftments granted by his predecessors, by a charter dated at Edinburgh ten days later, on the 22nd of the same month.

In 1458 there is an entry in the Exchequer Rolls of James II. for oak planks, iron, wages of workmen, carpenters, lead for the roof, lime, seven locks, and

various other repairs to the Castle. There is also another
item of £18 9s od paid to Alexander Flemyng for work
and repairs done inside the building, and for a fort round
the walls thereof, by command of the king. In 1462 John,
Lord of the Isles, obtained possession of the stronghold.

In 1464 James III. visited the town and resided for some
days in the Castle, on which occasion he granted it
a new Royal Charter, ratifying and confirming all its
predecessors. He granted another on the 16th of
May 1474.

James IV. was in Inverness in November 1493. In 1499
he was again in the town, when he attended divine service
in a Chapel which stood on the Green of Muirtown, afterwards called the "King's Chapel," but now, as well as
a small burying-ground attached to it, covered over with
houses. Two years later, in 1501, he is referred to as
having been ferried from Inverness to Chanonry. The
same year the town was again given to the flames, by
Donald Dubh, son of Angus Og of the Isles, who claimed
the island Lordship.

In 1508 the Earl of Huntly became heritable Sheriff of
the County and keeper of the Castle, which he retained,
with a short interval during which possession was obtained
of it by the Regent Murray, until 1629, when he gave up
both offices for a compensation of £2500. According to
the *History of the Macdonalds*, "power was given to him
(Huntly) to add to the fortifications ; and he was at the
same time bound, at his own expense, to build upon the
Castle Hill of Inverness, a hall of stone and lime upon
vaults. This hall was to be 100 feet in length, 30 feet in
breadth, and the same in height ; it was to have a slated
roof, and to it were to be attached a kitchen and chapel of
proper size." This Castle, built in 1508, appears to have
continued in existence, though in a ruinous condition, down
to 1726, when it was repaired and extended by General
Wade. It was on the model of the old baronial keeps,

with four storeys, high pitched roof and turrets, and crow-
stepped gables. It was occupied by the clans in 1639, when
it suffered greatly, for we are told that they broke up the
doors, gates and windows, spoiled the pleasant plenishing
and rich library of books which it contained, "and brocht
all to nocht within that house, inferior to few in the
kingdom for decorment," or decoration.   On Huntly's
resignation in 1629 both the offices held by him were
conferred upon Sir Robert Gordon for life.

In 1514 all previous charters in favour of the burgh were
confirmed by James V.

The first Protestant minister, Mr Thomas Howieson, was
appointed to the town and parish in 1578. In 1638 it
became necessary to have a second charge, and in 1643,
a third, for preaching in Gaelic to a Highland and Irish
regiment then stationed in Inverness. The minister of the
third charge, however, was not permanently settled until 1766.

In July 1555, the Queen Regent, Mary of Guise, visited
the town, when she held several courts in the Castle, "for
the punishment of caterans and political offenders."

In 1562 the unfortunate Queen Mary came to Inverness
and remained for several days. Her Majesty was denied
access to the Castle by the followers of Lord Alexander
Gordon ; but the Mackintoshes, the Frasers, and the
Munroes, coming to her aid, the stronghold was taken,
the deputy-governor hanged, and his head exposed on the
top of the Castle. Shortly before she was dethroned, in
1567, Mary granted a charter to the burgh "in favour of
divine worship, and of the ministers of God's word, and of
the Hospital."

In 1587 James VI., being then of lawful age, ratified
Queen Mary's Charter, and in 1588 confirmed it by another.
In 1589 Master Oliver Coult was elected by the Magistrates
as the first Law Agent for the town, at a salary of sixty
pounds Scots. In the same year James VI. granted to
the Provost and Magistrates powers of Justiciary : and

in 1591 the same king granted the "Golden Charter of the Burgh" which ratifies all previous rights, and grants new lands and privileges, many of which have since been lost, such as the right of pasture, peats, fuel, and turf, on Craig Phadruig, Caiplich, Daviot, and Bogbain; the right of ferrying on Lochness; the right to exact petty customs from all the towns and villages north as far as Wick; and as a trading monopoly in all places between the burgh and Tarbet Ness. This monarch, however, never visited the town; nor did, we believe, any of his Royal successors, until the advent of her present Majesty, who has honoured it on more than one occasion during her gracious reign.

In 1613 steps were taken for repairing and upholding the existing bridge at an estimated cost of 3000 merks Scots. The town authorities agreed to find a third of this amount, the remainder to be raised by a tax on the lands. In 1620 the bridge was carried away by a flood. In 1624 it was replaced, Grant of Glenmoriston supplying the timber for £1000 Scots. It is described as "the weakest that ever straddled over so strong a stream." It stood, however, for fifty years after this repair.

In 1625 Duncan Forbes, Provost of Inverness, and a successful merchant, purchased, from Mackintosh of Mackintosh, the lands of Culloden, and became the founder of the present family.

In 1640 a woman from Morayshire, Margaret Cowie, opened a school in the town, and this was considered such an interference with the rights of the parish schoolmaster that the Magistrates passed a resolution that she "should not be allowed to teach *beyond the Proverbs!*"

In 1644 the Castle was repaired and garrisoned - by the Covenanters, under Sir James Fraser of Brae, who surrounded the town with a ditch, cut down a number of beautiful trees in the Grey Friars' and Chapel Yards, and erected a strong gate at the top of Castle Street. In 1645 it was besieged by Montrose, when he set fire to the outskirts of the town, but he failed to take it, being compelled to raise the siege and withdraw on the arrival of General Middleton at the head of the Covenanters. In 1650 it was taken by Mackenzie of Pluscardine and Urquhart of Cromarty, who destroyed a portion of it which was not restored until 1718.

In 1652 Oliver Cromwell took possession of the town in name of the Commonwealth, and in the same year commenced to build a fort, still called after him, on the east side of the river, below the present harbour.

In 1664, on the 28th of September, the old wooden bridge across the Ness, built in 1624, was carried away while in the course of being repaired. The incident is described by a contemporary writer in the following terms :—

"The great old wooden bridge of Inverness was repairing, and by the inadvertency of a carpenter cutting a beam that lay betwixt two couples, the bridge tending that way, ten of the old couples fell flat on the river, with about two hundred persons—men, women, and children—on it. Four of the townsmen broke legs and thighs; some sixteen had their heads, arms, and thighs bruised; all the children safe without a scart—a signal providence and a dreadful sight, at 10 forenoon."

In 1685, a fine stone bridge was erected in its place. It consisted of seven arches, and was built, partly at the expense of the town, and partly by subscription. Macleod of Macleod, Lord Lovat, and other lairds contributed handsomely, and on that account their clans were afterwards allowed to pass over the bridge without paying toll. Some years after, however, Lord Lovat gave up his privilege to the town for a consideration, and the Frasers had afterwards to pay like other people. Macleod of Macleod's coat-of-arms was placed over the gateway of the bridge in special acknowledgment of his subscription towards the cost of its erection.

The subscriptions were demanded, by the highest authority —the Privy Council—from all parts of Scotland, as will be

From   Inverness in 1662.   [Slezer.

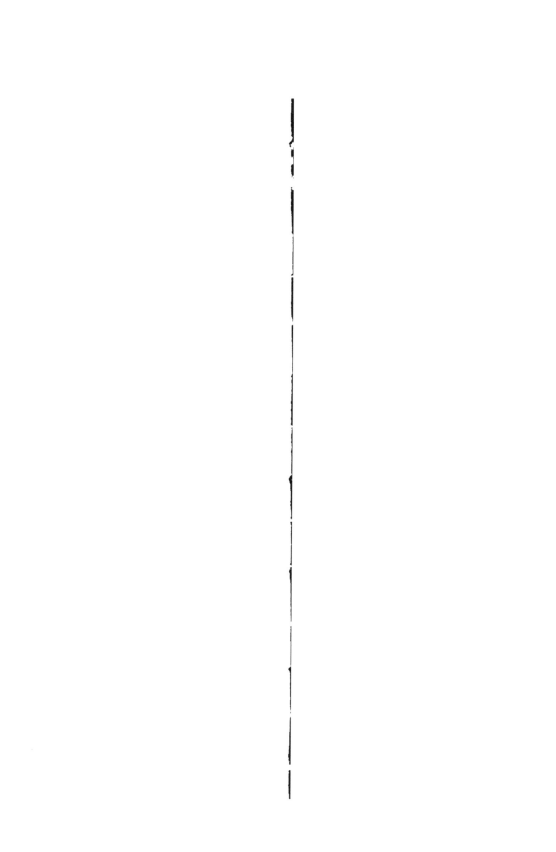

seen by the following extract from the Presbytery of Brechin records :—" 3rd March, 1680—Printed papers remitted by the Lords of His Majesty's Privy Council appointed a voluntary contribution to be collected in this kingdom for building a stone bridge across the great river Ness, near the famous city of Inverness, were dispersed this day through the Presbytery and through the ministers appointed to make intimation thereof in their respective bounds." And again two years later—" 29 March, 1682—the Moderator recommended the upgathering of the voluntary contribution for the bridge at Inverness to the ministers of the Presbytery, according to Council." What the result of this remit and upgathering was has not been ascertained, but it is curious that the appeal should have been made at such a distance and to a people who could have but little interest in Inverness and its surroundings. This bridge, built in 1685, stood until it was carried away by the great flood of 1849.

Some of the inhabitants of the town hit upon a novel expedient for getting relieved of the bridge toll. One Sunday, as the people were coming from church, they and their minister were shocked to see a number of people playing shinty on the green of Muirtown. On being remonstrated with, the Sabbath breakers alleged that they could not pay the toll, and were therefore unable to go to church, and that they had nothing else to do but to amuse themselves. The minister applied to the Magistrates, with the result that no toll was ever after exacted on Sundays.

After the Revolution of 1688, the inhabitants continued to be warmly attached to Episcopacy and to the Jacobite cause. In 1691, at the placing of the first Presbyterian minister, after the abolition of Episcopacy, the Magistrates stationed an armed force at the doors of the parish church to prevent his admission, and it was not until after a regiment arrived, sent by order of the Government, that the settlement was completed. From this period till after the battle of Culloden the town continued to decline.

2

The first regular service of letters between Edinburgh and Inverness was established in 1669, when letters were carried by foot-runners once a week, wind and weather permitting. But some years later an enterprising carrier advertised that his waggon would leave the Grassmarket for Inverness every Tuesday, God willing, and on Wednesday whether or no. Soon after this, the letters were carried on horseback, and then on single-seated cars. Since then the mail coach has come and gone to give place to the railway train. In 1675 the old quay at Portland Place was built, and the new one in 1738. Until far on in the last century, fishing boats sailed up on the east side of the Maggot to the foot of Chapel Street, thus making the place almost an island. In 1698 the Town Council decided to get "two able shoemakers to come from the south." The old Town Hall recently taken down to make room for the present beautiful Municipal Buildings was erected in 1709, on the site of Lord Lovat's town house in that year, when it was acquired by the Town Council in a ruinous condition.

In 1714 the Magistrates and Town Council, on the 14th of June, entered into a contract "for cleaning and keeping the streets and lanes or common vennels of the burgh free from muck, filth, dunghill, or other nastiness whatsoever, both on this and the other side of the river," and the contractor was taken bound to perform the "offices of a scavenger, as is usual and customary in other parts of this nation." These extracts from the Council records completely dispose of Burt and his remarks about the Magistrates and "the shower," as well as of the statement by Dr Carruthers that Inverness was swept at the public expense for the first time by order of the Duke of Cumberland in 1746.

The first carriage seen in the town or neighbourhood was one brought by the Earl of Seaforth in 1715, when "the country people, ignorant of the use and nature of such a vehicle, looked upon the driver as the most important personage connected with it, and accordingly made him low obeisances in passing."

On the 12th of September, the same year, the Magistrates secured admittance to the Castle for the adherents of the Chevalier, under the Earl of Mar, but they were shortly after expelled by a strong body of Royalists, led by Rose of Kilravock. In Captain Burt's time the Castle, which was built of unhewn stone, consisted of twelve apartments for officers' lodgings, offices, and a gallery. Describing the Town Hall of that day, the same author says, "there is one room in it where the Magistrates meet upon the town business, which would be tolerably handsome, but the walls are rough, not whitewashed or so much as plastered; and no furniture in it but a table, some bad chairs, and altogether immoderately dirty."

In 1726 Captain Burt was stationed in the Castle. For some time after this there were only five dress hats worn in the town, these being the property of the Sheriff, Provost, and the three ministers. Soon after, however, the members of the Town Council took to wearing hats on the days of the meetings. The first of these dignitaries who wore one was Deacon Young of the Weavers, and the people stared at him so much on the first occasion on which he appeared in it, that he exclaimed, "Well, after all, what am I but a mortal man like yourselves?"

In 1740 the Magistrates advertised for "a saddler to come and settle in the town," there being no such tradesman prior to that date.

In 1745-46, the Castle was for some time occupied by Sir John Cope and afterwards by Lord Loudon. The latter, however, on the 17th of February, 1746, retired into Ross-shire, whereupon, after a siege of two days, the followers of Prince Charles obtained possession of the Castle, which, on the 19th, they blew up before starting on their southward march. It is recorded that the engineer who applied the match to the train laid for the destruction of the stronghold, approached the second time to relight the fuse ; and as he came near it, the explosion took place, when he was thrown into the air, along with the materials of the building.   His mutilated body was landed 300 yards distant, on the Green on the west side of the river ; but though he was killed on the spot, a little dog which accompanied him is said to have completed the aerial journey, with the body of his master, quite unhurt.

The night before the battle of Culloden the Prince took up his quarters at a house belonging to Lady Drummuir, in Church Street, four doors below the Caledonian Hotel, No. 43, now occupied by Mr Alexander Mackenzie, wine and spirit merchant.   The night after the battle the Duke of Cumberland slept in the same room and in the same bed.   The house is said to have been the only one at that time in the town that contained a room without a bed in it.   The workmen, while pulling it down in 1843, came upon two ancient-looking muskets, which had been concealed in the north wall.   Buried under a large stone they found a jewelled ring, and in another part of the building a knife and fork with ivory handles.

In 1760 the first chaise for hire was kept in the town, and the first baker only made his appearance in 1763. The chaise was the property of a Mr Duncan Robertson, farmer, Beauly.

In 1765 a hemp factory was built at Cromwell's Fort, which in 1790 employed about a thousand people.   That it turned out a large amount of manufactured goods is proved from the fact that in 1770-71 the quantity of linen stamped for Inverness numbered 233,798 yards.   As late as 1846 it employed 300 hands.

The High Church was built in 1769-72, except the steeple, which is of much older date.   The spire is, however, of the same date as the Church and is not nearly so ornamental as the former one.   The first coal imported to Inverness was in 1770, and one cargo sufficed for the population for a year. The first bookseller's shop opened in the town was in 1775.

In 1779 a fire broke out in a house which stood on the site of the present Northern Meeting Rooms, during the Court of Justiciary week, when one of the Judges, Lord Gardenstone, who lodged in the house, narrowly escaped being burnt to death. He was rescued by the cook, who rushed into his room, rolled 'him up in the blankets and carried his Lordship through the flames and smoke into the street, at the risk of her life. All his clothes were burnt, and, being Saturday night, there was no help for it but to employ a tailor all Sunday to clothe him anew. His fair deliverer was afterwards rewarded with a life-pension.

In 1783 a thread factory was established in Inverness, which gave employment to more than a thousand men, women, and children. It was discontinued in 1813 when the building, in Albert Street, was converted into dwelling-houses.

The Northern Meeting was instituted in 1788. In 1791 the old Jail and town Steeple were built ; and in the following year the Royal Academy, which in 1895 was removed to the handsome and commodious buildings now occupied by it on the Hill, was opened. The old Gaelic Church was erected in 1792. It was re-roofed, re-seated, and completely renovated internally in 1886-87.

The Caledonian Canal was commenced in 1803 and opened for traffic in 1822, the passage from sea to sea having been made on the 23rd and 24th of October in that year. The total cost was £1,200,000.

The Northern Infirmary was opened for the admission of patients in 1804. In 1806 the first coach was established between Inverness and Perth.

The *Inverness Journal*, the first newspaper established in the town, was started in 1807. The wooden bridge was erected in 1808 at a cost of £4000. In 1811 the first mail coach, driven by two horses, was established between

Inverness and Aberdeen. In 1819 a coach was put on between Inverness and Thurso, driven, as far as Tain, four-in-hand.

In 1820 a steamer began to ply for the first time on the Caledonian Canal—between Inverness and Fort-Augustus.

In 1826 the town was' lighted with gas at a cost of £8757, and in 1859 the first waterworks were completed for a sum of £4872. In 1831 the streets were laid with common sewers, causewayed anew with granite blocks, and the foot pavements laid down with Caithness flags at a cost of £6000. More than £15,000 was expended on drainage and street pavement within the last ten years.

In 1834-5 the present Court-house was built on the site of the old Castle at a cost of some £10,000. The Catholic Chapel in Huntly Street was erected in 1836. In 1837 the Free North Church, for so many years occupied by the Rev. Dr George Mackay, was built. In 1839 St. John's Episcopal Chapel in Church Street was opened. In 1840 the West Parish Church was built. Bell's Institution, off Academy Street, was erected in 1841. In 1842-3, the Old Post-Office, now the Inland Revenue Office, was erected, and it was opened for business in the following year.

In 1844 the Crown Prince of Denmark and the King of Saxony visited the town. In 1845 the General Assembly of the Free Church was held in Inverness in a large pavilion specially erected in the playground of Bell's Institution. It was again held in Inverness in a similar building, capable of holding between 3000 and 4000 people, in 1888, on the site now occupied by the Palace Hotel.

In 1846-48 the new prison, adjoining the Court-House on the Castle Hill, was erected, the foundation stone having been laid in July, 1846.

The Suspension Bridge at the foot of Bridge Street, erected in place of the old Stone Bridge carried away by the great flood of 1849, was opened for traffic in 1855.

The Free High Church was opened in 1852 and the

From the]   Inverness in 1823.   [Godsman's Walk.

[From Photo. by]

Inverness in 1893.

[D. Whyte.

Cathedral in 1867. The new Free North Church was built in 1892-93.

In 1855 the Inverness and Nairn Railway was opened; and in 1858 it was continued to Keith, thus making it possible for the first time (*via* Aberdeen) to travel from north to south by rail. In 1863 the line from Forres to Perth, across Druimuachdar, was opened.

In 1862 the first line north of Inverness, extending from thence to Dingwall was completed. In 1863 it was continued to Invergordon, and in 1864 to Meikle Ferry, and thence to Bonar Bridge. In 1868 the Sutherland Railway from Bonar Bridge to Golspie was completed. In 1870 the Dingwall and Skye line was opened. The Duke of Sutherland's Railway was continued from Golspie to Helmsdale in 1871. In 1874 the Sutherland and Caithness Railway was extended to Wick and Thurso. In 1884 the Keith and Portessie branch was opened; and in the same year all these lines, together extending to 425¼ miles, were amalgamated into one great system under the designation of the Highland Railway. In 1885 the Dingwall and Strathpeffer branch was opened. In 1892 the first section of the new line from Aviemore to Inverness, *via* Slochd Muich and the Valley of the Findhorn, was completed and used for traffic as far as Carrbridge; and in 1899 it was opened to Aviemore, thus shortening the journey from Inverness to Perth by 28 miles (see page 177). The Hopeman extension —2 miles—was also finished in 1892. On the 1st of February, 1894, the new branch from Muir of Ord, through the Black Isle, to Fortrose was completed. In 1899 the branch from Gollanfield Junction to Fort-George was opened (see page 133).

The Workmen's Club, in Bridge Street, was opened in

1872. The Collegiate School, in Ardross Street was built in 1873.

The new Town Hall was erected in 1878-80 and formally opened by His Royal Highness the Duke of Edinburgh on the 19th of January, 1882. The Forbes Fountain on the Exchange was put up in 1880. The Theatre Royal in Bank Street was built in 1882. The Public Library and Museum Buildings, situated in the Castle Wynd, were opened in 1883. The new Barracks, forming the Depot of the 79th Queen's Own Cameron Highlanders, and erected at a cost of £60,000, were completed in 1886. The new High School was built in 1879-81 and opened in the latter year. The General Post-Office in Queen's Gate was opened in 1890.

The New Markets, originally erected in 1870, were burnt down in 1890, and re-built in 1890-91, at a cost, exclusive of the old site, of £7158 1s 2d.

The new Royal Academy Buildings on the Crown were built in 1894 and opened in 1895.

On the 22nd of June, 1897, the new Public Park, on the west side of the River, was declared open by Provost Macbean, on behalf of the Corporation.

SITUATION AND CLIMATE.

Some sing of Rome and some of Florence ; I
Will sound thy Highland praise, fair Inverness;
And, till some worthier bard thy thanks may buy
Hope for the greater, but don't spurn the less.
All things that make a city fair are thine.
The rightful queen and sovereign of this land
Of bens and glens and valiant men, who shine
Brightest in Britain's glory-roll, and stand
Best bulwark of her bounds—wide circling sweep
Of rich green slope and brown empurpled brae,
And flowery mead, and far in-winding bay,
Temple and tower are thine, and castled keep,
And ample stream that round fair gardened isles
Rolls its majestic current, wreathed in smiles.

So sang Professor John Stuart Blackie. But a greater
than he sounded the praises of Inverness centuries ago.
Referring to MacBeth's castle, which is supposed to have
stood on the Crown, Shakespeare makes King Duncan
speak of its fine situation and balmy climate in the following
immortal lines :—

King Duncan—This Castle hath a pleasant seat ; the air
    Nimbly and sweetly recommends itself
    Unto our gentle senses.

Banquo—   . . . I have observed the air
    Is delicate.

Inverness is beautifully situated on a peninsula through
which the rapid and sparkling River Ness finds its way to
the Moray Firth. In ancient times nearly the whole of the
town was on the right or east bank of the river, but it has

during this century extended to the left or west side, where there is now a large population, many handsome new streets, and villa residences. For richness, variety, and beauty, the surroundings of Inverness are unsurpassed in Scotland, and several strikingly picturesque views of it may be obtained without having far to go, particularly those from the Castle Hill, Tomnahurich, and Craig Phadruig.

Behind the town on the east side of the river a gravel terrace rises to a height of about 100 feet, beyond which is a long stretch of fertile table land, extending to Loch Ness on the one hand and the Spey on the other. The portion in the immediate vicinity of Inverness is to a large extent covered over with handsome villas, gentlemen's residences, and their beautifully laid out lawns and gardens, mostly within the extended Royalty or Municipal boundary.

A little further back the district is surrounded on either side of the river by a range of hills which shelters the town from the prevailing winds and draws away the rain clouds. Loch Ness never freezes, the lowest temperature which it was ever known to reach being eight degrees above freezing point, while the lowest temperature the river flowing from it ever attained was within four degrees—·36 Fahr.—as it entered the sea after running a course of six miles from its source. The winds which sweep along these warm waters of the Loch and River Ness for a distance of thirty miles, and an equal distance over Loch Oich and Loch Lochy farther west, lose much of their force before they reach Inverness. The average rain-fall during twelve months, reduced to a minimum by the influence of the surrounding hills, is only 30 inches. On half the days in the year on an average there is no rain at all, and during the other half it falls in small quantities. The average temperature is 46·8, a record only equalled in Scotland by certain favoured portions of the Lothians and the county of Moray.

Burt, in his famous *Letters from the Highlands* more than a century and a half ago, referring to the climate of the

district, says :—" The air of the Highlands is pure and consequently healthy ; insomuch that I have known such cures
done by it as might be thought next to miracles—I mean
in distempers of the lungs, as cough, consumptions, etc."

A careful writer who knew the Capital of the Highlands
well, describing it about fifty years ago, says that " Notwithstanding its high latitude, the climate of Inverness is
exceedingly mild, temperate, and healthy. Sheltered by
the hills which surround it at a little distance on every
side, the town is warm and comparatively dry, and its
temperature exceedingly moderate, even when the heights
in the neighbourhood are covered with snow. ' Lying
near the inland termination of the Moray Firth,' says a
late report on the sanitary condition of the town, ' and
well protected by surrounding hills, the cold north-east
winds which, especially in spring, blow from off the German
Ocean, are felt much less severely here than more to the
east and south ; while placed as the town is at the end
of the Great Glen or Caledonian Valley, which, with its
lateral mountains, acts as a mighty tunnel to carry along
and conduct across the island the softness of the west coast
breezes without their usual excess of rain ; and situated
between the Moray Firth and Loch Ness, the whole district
partakes of a free and mild atmosphere. Hence snow
seldom lies above a few days on the plain around Inverness, and the severity of the frost is less than is frequent
about Edinburgh, or even London. The constant flow of a
broad rapid river, which was never known to be frozen,
through the centre of the town, must also contribute very
essentially to keep up a due circulation of air, and to
promote the health of the inhabitants ; and the regular sea
breezes, which daily affects the lower parts, at least, of the
town, must add to its salubrity.' " Having so far drawn
upon this report the writer proceeds to say for himself—
" The scenery in the vicinity is so rich, so varied, and
viewed from the high ground, so extensive, that it is allowed

tn be almost unsurpassed in Scotland." Our author then
quotes the well-known Dr MacCulloch, who, comparing
Inverness with Edinburgh, in his *Letters on the Highlands*,
says—" When I have stood in Queen Street of Edinburgh, and
looking towards Fife, I have sometimes wondered whether
Scotland contained a finer view of its class. But I have
forgotten this on my arrival at Inverness. If a comparison
is to be made with Edinburgh, always excepting its own
romantic disposition, the Firth of Forth must yield altogether and Inverness must take the highest rank. Everything is done, too, for Inverness that can be effected by
wood and cultivation ; the characters of which here have
altogether a richness, a variety, and a freedom, which we
miss round Edinburgh. The mountain scenes are finer,
more various, and nearer. Each outlet is different from
the others, and each is beautiful, whether we proceed
towards Fort-George, or towards Moy, or enter the valley
of the Ness, or skirt the shores of the Beauly Firth ; while
a short and commodious ferry wafts us to the lovely country
opposite, rich with woods, and country seats, and cultivation.
It is the boast also of Inverness to unite two opposed qualities, and each in the greatest perfection—the characters of
a rich open lowland country with those of the wildest Alpine
scenery, both being close at hand, and in many places
intermixed, while, to all this is added a series of maritime
landscape not often equalled." Inverness has now many other
attractions and advantages which it had not when these
descriptions of it were originally written. It is the centre
of railway and steamboat communication with every part of
the kingdom, north and south, east and west. Its roads
and streets have been vastly improved, and it has been
most thoroughly drained into large intercepting sewers on
both sides of the river. It possesses many handsome public
buildings and the hotel accommodation so extensively provided for visitors is in every respect unequalled in any town
of its size in Great Britain.

PRINCIPAL BUILDINGS AND PLACES
OF INTEREST.

————:o:————

STARTING from THE EXCHANGE, in front of the Town
Hall, we shall accompany the reader through the town and
point out the principal places of interest within the burgh
and its more immediate neighbourhood.

THE FORBES FOUNTAIN, on the centre of The Exchange,
was in 1880 gifted to the town by the late Dr George
Fiddes Forbes of Millburn, who also bequeathed £6000 to
the Inverness Dispensary, and £4000 to the Royal Academy.
It was erected by Messrs D. & A. Davidson, sculptors,
Waterloo Place, and cost £520. Close to the Hall is now
erected, through the liberality of Sir R. B. Finlay, K.C.,
M.P. for the Inverness Burghs, and Attorney-General for
England, the Mercat Cross, from which public proclamations
are made. At the base of this is the

CLACH-NA-CUDAIN,

the palladium of Inverness. The Clach in more remote
times lay in front of the Exchange, in the neighbourhood of
an old apple tree which grew in the gutter between the
open space and the street. On this tree, after the battle of
Culloden, a Highlander was hanged by Cumberland's followers, on suspicion of conveying news regarding the king's
army to the followers of Prince Charles, and the tree is said
to have taken the matter so much to heart that it never
after showed any signs of life, and finally withered away.
The famous stone, a boulder of bluish colour, oval in shape,
is now ensconced in the base of the Mercat Cross. It
has always been looked upon with veneration by Inver-

nessians at home and abroad. Its history is lost in remote antiquity, but it is said that in olden times it had its seat in the west, and that standing upon it ages gone by were crowned many of the earlier Lords of the Isles. How it found its way to the Highland Capital is a mystery, but it soon became an object of the greatest interest to the natives. It acquired its modern name of " Clach-na-cudain," or Stone of the Tub, from the following circumstances :— The servants and lasses who were accustomed to carry tubs or stoups of water from the river, before the days of water works, by means of a pole across their shoulders invariably made the Clach a resting place. " Hither the lads were also wont to resort, and, in those times, when the press had not penetrated so far north, the neighbourhood of the Clach was the grand rendezvous for telling and hearing, not only 'the news of the parish,' but the contents of many a private letter, from outlandish parts, conveying intelligence of sights and deeds which could not fail to astonish the natives. In addition to being the headquarters for gossip, the locality was notorious for courting, and many a fair lassie there effectually won the affections of amorous swains, and there many a match was made."*

The Clach has been designated by Sir Walter Scott, the Charter Stone of the burgh, and the term " Clachnacudain boy " is a sufficient passport to a meeting of Invernessians in any part of the world.

THE TOWN HALL,

which we shall now enter, is in the early decorated Gothic style, and covers an area of 700 square yards. The foundation stone was laid on the 14th of August, 1878, and it was formally opened by His Royal Highness the Duke of Edinburgh on the 19th of January, 1882. The contract price was close upon £10,000, to which falls to be added £2500 paid for a building at the back of the old Hall,

* Recollections of a Nonagenarian: Inverness, 1842.

From Photo. by]   **Inverness Town Hall.**   [D. Whyte.

purchased and removed to admit of the widening of the Exchange, about £1000 for furnishings, and £500 for enlarging and partly re-furnishing the Council Chamber in 1894, making the total cost of the present handsome building somewhere about £14,000. Of this amount £5000 was bequeathed by the late Duncan Grant of. Bught, for many years Convener of the County, and son of James Grant, an old Provost of the burgh, to be laid out upon the public hall proper. The building is erected of a fine light-coloured and very hard sandstone from the Overwood Quarries, in the vicinity of Glasgow, from designs by Matthews & Lawrie, architects, Inverness. On a large pane over the centre window, in a gable with round towers corbelled out on the angles, facing the Exchange, the Town Arms are sculptured. A feature of the structure is the entrance hall, which is continued by a groined vestibule leading to the principal staircase, the stained glass windows of which are blazoned with the Royal, Scottish, and Burgh Arms. On either side of the main entrance there are splendid suites of Municipal offices ; those to the right being occupied by the Town Clerk, and those on the left by the Town Chamberlain and Treasurer and Collector of the Police Commissioners. Behind the Town Clerk's principal offices are two fire-proof strong rooms containing the town charters and other burgh records. Proceeding up the staircase we come upon the Public Hall, extending the full length of the building from Castle Street to the Castle Wynd, 66 feet long, 35 feet broad, and 33 feet from floor to ceiling.

The centre window, presented by Mrs Warrand of Bught, contains figures of Ossian and of Sir Walter Scott, appropriately representing ancient and modern literature, while the smaller figures represent Justice and Religion.

In the recess of this window stands a life-like bust in marble of the late Robert Carruthers, LL.D., for many years proprietor and editor of the *Inverness Courier*, by his distinguished son-in-law, the late Alexander Munro, a native of Inverness. In the corner on the left of the platform stands an excellently executed bust, true to life, of the late Rev. Dr Donald Macdonald, for 47 years minister of the High Church, by Andrew Davidson, sculptor, Inverness.

The windows in front of the Hall are filled in with stained glass, and with the arms of the leading Highland clans in the following order from right to left, beginning with the top panel in each window :—

1st. Lord of the Isles, Macdonald of Glengarry, and Macdonald of Clanranald.

2nd. Mackintosh, Macpherson, and Cameron.

3rd. Munro, Maclean, and Robertson.

4th. Ross, Mackenzie, and Matheson.

5th. Macgregor, Grant of Grant, and Grant of Glenmoriston ; and

6th. Macleod, Campbell, and Mackay.

In the upper portions of the eastern window, facing Castle Street, are the Royal, Scottish, and Town Arms, while opposite, in the Castle Wynd end are shown the arms of the Frasers, Forbeses, and Chisholms, three clans not of Celtic origin. The other subjects in either gable represent Art, Science, Law, Agriculture, Education, Literature, and the Incorporated Trades of the Burgh. The ceiling, which is arched, is tastefully panelled with shields, intended, at some remote period we fear, to be decorated with the arms of the Provosts and other prominent citizens of the town.

The portraits hung up in the Hall, commencing with those on the Castle Street gable are on the left when looking towards the platform, in the corner next High Street,

Provost William Inglis, of Kingsmills, who occupied the position of Chief Magistrate from 1797 to 1800. In the right-hand corner, when looking towards the platform, is

Duncan Forbes of Culloden, Lord President of the Court of Session, so justly famed in connection with the Rising of 1745. This painting is a copy by Grigor Urquhart, an

Inverness artist, from the original in Culloden House. Next comes

A full length portrait of Queen Anne, taken soon after the Peace of Utrecht, presented by Sir William Augustus Fraser of Ledclune, Baronet. Next comes a life-like portrait of

Sir Henry Cockburn Macandrew, Provost of Inverness from 1883 to 1889. He was knighted by the Queen in 1887, on the occasion of Her Majesty's Jubilee, and this portrait, painted by Sir George Reid, President of the Royal Scottish Academy, was subscribed for by Sir Henry's fellow citizens and other admirers, and presented in their name by Mr Æneas Mackintosh of Raigmore, to Provost Alexander Ross, as representing the community, on Friday, 31st October, 1892. The next picture is

Flora Macdonald, the ever-memorable heroine of the 'Forty-five—a copy by Grigor Urquhart of Allan Ramsay's famous original, in the Bodleian Library, Oxford.

Duncan Forbes of Culloden, Provost of Inverness in 1626, and founder of the Culloden family, in a suit of armour, is in the next panel to the right.

Dr John Inglis Nicol, Provost of Inverness from 1840 to 1845, comes next, while on the other side of the doorway is

The Holy Family, long supposed to have been an original painting by Sasso Ferreato, an Italian, representing John the Baptist worshipping the child Jesus, while Joseph and Mary with anxious expression bend over them. Mr Fraser-Mackintosh informs us that the picture was presented to the Directors of the Royal Academy in 1799 by Mr James Clark, a native of Inverness, who, "was long settled in Naples as a painter." Along with this painting he bequeathed £725 to the funds of the institution and £150 to the poor of the town. Mr Fraser-Mackintosh adds that the picture "is of comparatively little value." "As Mr Clark must have been a thorough judge, it is clear he would not think of bequeathing an inferior painting to be placed in a prominent place in the town of his birth, and the great probability is that those entrusted with the transmission of the picture from Naples substituted the present inferior picture, defeating the wishes of the testator, and doing his best to cast a slur on his knowledge and taste. Such paintings do not disappear, and it would be interesting to know where Mr Clark's real picture is."* It is described in the will as "The Holy Family—Jesus Christ, the Virgin Mary, Joseph, and St. John—by Sassoferreatto "—one word.

General Sir Hector Munro, C.B., who represented the Inverness Burghs in Parliament from 1768 to 1780, and again from 1784 to 1802—in all five sessions—is represented by the first portrait on the Castle Wynd gable of the Hall, while in the other corner we have one of

Major James Fraser of Castle Leathers, dressed in a unique Highland costume, a brother of Alexander Fraser of Culduthel. This is also a copy by Grigor Urquhart of the original (artist unknown), which was in possession of the late Sir James Fraser, Commissioner of the City of London Police, who died in 1892, and is now the property of his only brother, General Robert Macleod Fraser, London.

William Simpson, Provost of Inverness from 1847 to 1852, has his portrait on the left side of the centre front window, while on the right is a portrait of

Phineas Mackintosh of Drummond, who occupied the civic chair from 1770 to 1773; 1776 to 1779; 1782 to 1785; and from 1788 to 1791. It is a copy by Park, grandson of Dr Robert Carruthers, of the original at Holme, presented by Mr Charles Fraser-Mackintosh, the Provost's great grand-nephew, M.P. for the Inverness Burghs from 1874 to 1885 and for the County from 1885 to 1892.

THE PROVOST'S ROOM.

Leaving the Hall by the eastern door, the Provost's Room, generally used as a Waiting Room, may be entered on

* *Letters of Two Centuries.* A. & W. Mackenzie, Inverness, 1890.

the left.   Several engravings of Old Inverness exhibited on the walls, two of which are reproduced in this Guide, will be found interesting by those of an antiquarian turn of mind who like to compare the present with the past.

THE COUNCIL CHAMBER.

Proceeding to the opposite end of the landing we find our way to the Council Chamber, a neatly furnished and compact apartment, considerably enlarged and a press gallery provided in 1894, with a richly panelled ceiling. On the left wall as you enter is a portrait by Syme of James Robertson, Altanaskiach, Provost from 1816 to 1818 ; 1822 to 1823 ; 1824 to 1827 ; and from 1829 to 1831 ; and over the mantlepiece, one of the late Prince Consort, in full Highland dress—a copy of one painted more than twenty years ago for the Corporation of Aberdeen by Sir George Reid, now President of the Royal Scottish Academy.   His Royal Highness was presented with the freedom of the burgh in 1846, when he was received by the inhabitants with unbounded enthusiasm. Next, in the Castle Wynd corner, is a portrait of one of the Cuthberts, at one time Chief Magistrate.   Facing the fireplace is a painting of Sir John Barnard, a London Alderman, Lord Mayor, and M.P., who some time last century took charge of a bill regulating the Ale Tax for the Inverness Corporation, and afterwards, as a memento, presented them with this picture of himself.

OLD BURGH AND OTHER ARMS.

Two panels bearing the Royal, National, and Town arms, painted during the reign of Charles I., will be seen in the staircase. A few years ago they were discovered in a dark cellar below the burgh court-house, along with several other local curiosities of antiquarian interest, but no one knows what they were intended for.   In the Castle Wynd gable of the Town Hall is built in the arms of the burgh in the year 1686, which originally occupied a panel in the old stone bridge, carried away in 1849, and in the Castle Street gable there is a well-cut coat of the Royal Arms of the reign of Charles II., also from the bridge.

THE TOWN STEEPLE.

Opposite the Exchange, forming the junction of Bridge and Church Streets, showing its fine and graceful proportions, stands the Town Steeple, crowned by an elegant spire, built in 1789-1791, at a cost of £1600. The foundation stone was laid with masonic honours on the 28th of August, 1789, and it was completed in 1791. It is 155 feet high; and it is very doubtful if a better example exists of a spire and tower combined, with distinct Gothic features brought within the lines and limits of a classic mould. The total cost of the old jail and court-house which adjoined it, built on the site of an older jail, and of the Steeple itself, was £3350. Of this sum the Town Council paid £1250, the Government, £1000, private subscriptions, £600, and the Northern Counties, £500. Of the private subscriptions, General Sir Hector Munro, C.B., then M.P. for Inverness, subscribed £200, and in addition presented the town with the clock in the Steeple. Early in the century the spire was struck by lightning and very badly twisted. It was, with much difficulty, restored to its present position, the late James Fraser, painter, a local character, better known as "Jamie Lazy," taking a prominent part in the work. The bells, which were cracked on the occasion of some special rejoicings, were afterwards contemptuously termed "The Skellats" from the thin tin-pot sounds they subsequently gave forth.

Turning to the west end of the Exchange we now proceed up the Castle Wynd, passing on the right a substantial, central, but otherwise badly-situated building, erected for a

PUBLIC LIBRARY, MUSEUM, AND SCHOOL OF ART.

The Library was opened in 1883. It contains about seven thousand volumes   Mr Andrew Carnegie of Pittsburg gave the very handsome donation of £1750, a few years ago to pay off the Library debt, and the Town Council thereafter conferred upon him the Freedom of the Burgh. The Museum, though containing many relics of local interest, is only in course of formation, and falls far short of what such an institution in the Capital of the Highlands ought to be. The School of Science and Art since 1892 is under the charge of the Public Library Committee, under whose management it has received a decided and much required impetus. The next building, on the same side of the Wynd, contains the Police Office and Burgh Court-House where the local magistrates preside in turn, month by month. Passing up the brae we leave the new prison, built in 1846-48, on the right, after which we pass round to the front of the County Buildings and Court-house, which occupy the site of the old Castle of Inverness. In front of the building there stands, erected in 1898, a monument in memory of Flora Macdonald, the heroine of the '45 rebellion, the gift of Captain J. Henderson Macdonald of Caskuben, Aberdeenshire, and 78th Highlanders ; and executed by Mr Andrew Davidson, sculptor, Rome, a native of Inverness.

Here a view presents itself which for variety and beauty is unsurpassed in any part of the world. Immediately below flows the river Ness. Further away to the north-west, on the lower level of the valley, the Caledonian Canal sweeps along between Tomnahurich and Tor-a-Vean, while to the north the Moray and Beauly Firths stretch along for miles. Further north still rise against the horizon, the Ross-shire hills, prominent among them the huge Ben Wyvis and Sgur-a-Vullin, further west, in the direction of Achnasheen, 3429 and 2750 feet respectively above the level of the sea. Immediately opposite, across the river, is Saint Andrew's Cathedral. Beyond, about a mile distant, is Tomnahurich, and further away still, slightly to the north beyond the Canal, stands prominently Craig Phadruig–Larach-an-Tigh Mhoir–with its prehistoric vitrified fort on the summit. The large building in the distance, across the Caledonian Canal, situated under the shelter of Creag Dunain, in a line from where we stand, slightly to the right of Tomnahurich, is the Inverness District Lunatic Asylum, which usually contains from four hundred to five hundred inmates.   Away to the south is a glorious view of the great Caledonian valley reaching almost to the end of Loch Ness, while far beyond Mealfourvonie towers majestically above its peers.   To the south-east of the Castle, on an elevated plateau, numerous modern villas and residences are thickly studded, forming almost a second Inverness, most of them within the municipal boundary.   Beyond is the district of Leys ; the whole surroundings as far as the eye can reach forming one of the most charming and magnificent landscapes in the kingdom.   Those wishing to enter

THE CASTLE OR COUNTY BUILDINGS

may do so.   Here they will find a commodious Court-Room, where the Sheriff presides almost daily, where the Lords of Justiciary hold courts for the whole of the Northern Counties, twice a year, and where the County Council has its meetings.   In the building will also be found the principal County offices.

The County portion of the Castle, which is only two storeyed but massive, and lofty, was erected in 1834-35, the foundation stone having been laid with masonic honours on the 2nd of May in the first-named year.   It was built by Mr Cousin, contractor, Edinburgh, from an elegant design by Mr Burn, architect of that city, and afterwards of London.   It is in the English castellated style of the Tudor period, and was originally intended to be turreted. It cost close upon £10,000, defrayed by a voluntary assessment spread over twenty years.   In the Court-Room is a portrait by Raeburn, subscribed for by the county, of the Right Hon. Charles Grant (father of Lord Glenelg) for several years M.P. for Inverness-shire.   In a niche in the main stair is a bust, by Park, of William Fraser-Tytler, for many years Principal Sheriff and County Convener. The portion of the building occupied as a prison was built

From Photo. by] **Flora Macdonald's Statue.** [Watson & Senior.

[From Photo. by] **High Street, Inverness.** [J. Valentine & Sons.

in 1846-48 in the same style of architecture but with a more dignified and pleasing effect, much enhancing the strikingly picturesque appearance of the whole structure. The foundation stone of this part of the building was also laid with masonic honours, in July, 1846.

HIGH STREET.

We shall now return by the Castle Wynd, or by the gate at the western extremity of the Castle grounds, and turn to the left into Castle Street (formerly called Domesdale Street, and cut out of the Barn Hills to form on that side a better defence of the Castle), one of the oldest in the Burgh. By either route we shall soon find ourselves back at the Exchange. In the corner of Church and High Streets is the far-famed establishment of Mr P. G. Wilson, jeweller to Her Majesty the Queen and other members of the Royal family.

A few doors eastward, in High Street, is the head office of the Caledonian Bank, opened on the 10th of February, 1838, in which year the company was formed. It is one of the most ornate building in Inverness. Immediately opposite, at the junction of Castle Street with High Street, is the Young Men's Christian Association Buildings, a classical structure of the Corinthian order, erected by public subscription from designs by the late John Rhind, architect, Inverness. It has a striking sculptured group above the entablature representing the three Graces, Faith, Hope, and Charity. The ground floor is occupied by Messrs Johnstone and Edgar's (late Mr William Mackay's) clan tartan, tweed, and general drapery warehouse. Proceeding in the same direction, the Royal Tartan Warehouse, popularly known as " Macdougall's." strikes the visitor as one of the handsomest buildings in the burgh. Those who take an interest in our Highland products should most certainly pay " Macdougall's " a visit. The London branch is situated at 42 Sackville Street, Piccadilly, W., and if a visitor has not sufficient time to spare at Inverness, the order given may be finished at London. The two houses have just recently passed under complete new management.   Macdougall's are under the special patronage of the King and Royal family, and almost every Court in Europe.

A little further on, on the same side, is the Highland Club, a substantial and commodious structure erected for an hotel in 1839 by the late Thomas Alexander Fraser, twelfth Lord Lovat, the Grants of Glenmoriston and Ballin-dalloch, Mackenzie of Kilcoy, and others, in opposition to the Caledonian Hotel.   The prominent building next door past the Club is occupied by the British Linen Banking Company.

The last building on the right, in High Street, where the extensive business of the Inverness General Post Office was carried on from 1844 to 1890, is now occupied, on the ground floor by the Inland Revenue Office, and on the second floor by the Government and County assessors for Inverness-shire, and for Ross and Cromarty; also by the Government assessor for Sutherlandshire.

Connecting High Street with Union Street is Lombard Street, a busy little thoroughfare.

Eastgate (Petty Street) is a continuation eastward of High Street, but there is nothing in that direction of special inter-est to the tourist, unless he desires to visit the Cameron Barracks, to which attention will be directed in our Excur-sions to Culloden, Cawdor Castle, and to Nairn, by road or rail.   We shall in the meantime accompany the reader along Inglis, Academy, Chapel, and Shore Streets to Cromwell's Fort and the Longman.   Crossing to

INGLIS STREET,

we pass the Inverness office of the Town and County Bank in the right-hand corner, in Hamilton Place, directly opposite.   The Wesleyan Chapel, a neat building, forms the north corner at the other end of the Street.

ACADEMY STREET.

The Inverness office of the Royal Bank, in the open space at the top of Academy Street, is next passed on the same side.   Immediately opposite is the Imperial Hotel, in the angle formed by Academy Street and Baron Taylor's Lane.   Almost directly facing the latter, on the right hand side of the street, stands the Station Hotel, forming one side of the Railway Station Square, two of the other sides consisting of handsome blocks in the Italian style, with a good deal of ornament.   One of these forms the front elevation of the Station and the other contains the principal offices of the Company.   In 1875 £12,000 and in 1881 £8000 were spent on extending and improving the original building, which was found quite inadequate for the growing requirements of the steadily and fast increasing traffic of the last twenty years.   The fourth side of the square is formed by Academy Street and the Royal Hotel, the latter directly facing the principal entrance to the Station.   The local office of the North of Scotland Bank is in the corner of the Hotel buildings.

In 1893 the handsome monument commemorating the officers and men of the 79th Queen's Own Cameron Highlanders who fell in the Egyptian campaign was erected in the square in line with the Academy Street foot pavement. It is of white Portland stone, designed and executed by Mr George Wade, sculptor, London, and subscribed for by the officers and men of the regiment.   It was unveiled by Lochiel, Chief of the Camerons, on the 14th of July, 1893, in presence of a great crowd.

UNION STREET.

Opposite the Station Hotel, Union Street, formed of four handsome blocks of classic dignity, strikes to the left in a line parallel with High Street, and uniting Academy Street

with Church Street. This beautiful thoroughfare was erected
in 1861-64 on the site of a number of narrow lanes, closes,
and insanitary hovels, by four enterprising citizens—Mr
Charles Fraser-Mackintosh, afterwards for eleven years M.P.
for the Inverness burghs, Mr Donald Davidson, presently
Sheriff of Fort-William, the late Mr George G. Mackay,
and the late Mr Hugh Rose, solicitor.

The principal buildings in Union Street are the United
Presbyterian Church and the Waverley Hotel on the left or
south side, in either corner formed by its junction with
Drummond Street ; and on the right or north side, directly
opposite the last-named street—about the centre and immediately beyond the Union Street entry to the New
Markets—the Music Hall, with shops underneath, and seated
to accommodate about 1300 persons. The Bank of Scotland,
a strikingly fine and substantial building, is in the angle
formed by the junction on that side of Union and Church
Streets. Continuing his course along

ACADEMY STREET

the reader, immediately after passing the Royal Hotel, finds
himself at the main entrance to

THE NEW MARKETS,

first erected by the Town Council in 1870 at a cost,
including the site, of £3860. That building was, however,
burnt down in 1889, and re-erected in 1890-91—much
extended by the addition of a large hall capable of holding
from 3000 to 4000 people, and a new fish market—at an
expenditure, excluding the value of the old site, of £7158.

THE OLD ROYAL ACADEMY SITE.

Here on the right stood, until in 1895 the Royal Academy
was removed to the new premises on the Hill, a plain but
imposing building. It was the old Academy, originally
built by public subscription, and incorporated by Royal
Charter in 1792. Until, in May, 1887, it was re-constituted

under the Educational Endowments (Scotland) Act 1882, the directors continued to be the Provost of Inverness, the four Bailies, and Dean of Guild ; the Sheriff of the county, the Moderator of the Presbytery of Inverness, five Commissioners of Supply, elected annually by their own body, subscribers of £50, and the heirs and successors of original subscribers of £100 each. Since the new Inverness Academy and Educational Trust Scheme under the above-named Act came into operation, the governing body has been composed of three representatives each from the Town Council, from the Inverness-shire County Council, and from the Burgh School Board.

The old building is now transformed into a handsome block of shops and offices, while the play-ground at the back has been occupied by the great Posting Establishment of Messrs Macrae & Dick, the well known horse-hirers, since 1895.

Almost directly opposite, Queensgate, a new street, strikes westward, connecting Academy Street with Church Street in a parallel line with and a hundred yards north of Union Street. The right hand corner, abutting on Academy Street, of a very handsome block erected in 1896 is occupied as the Inverness Office of the Lancashire Insurance Company, while the western or corresponding corner of the same block is occupied by the well-known firm of Morel Bros., Cobbett & Son, Limited, wine merchants, of Inverness and London. The principal building—the fine central block—on the north side is the

NEW GENERAL POST-OFFICE,

erected by the Government in 1889-90, at a cost of £14,000. This handsome, imposing, and commodious structure is in the Renaissance style, freely and ably treated. It has a recessed centre, flanked with slightly projecting wings, and is three storeys high, terminating in a fine rich cornice and balustrade, the whole embellished with classic features and finished in the very best polished ashlar work. It has ample accommodation not only for the ordinary Post-Office

work but also for the growing telegraphic requirements of
Inverness, which, next to those of Edinburgh and Glasgow,
are the most extensive in Scotland.   Retracing our steps to

ACADEMY STREET

we pass the United Free East Church on the right, and
looking along Margaret Street observe the Artillery Drill
Hall on the left, while in front is

DR BELL'S SCHOOL,

surrounded by an extensive playground, a very chaste building, Grecian in style, with a strikingly handsome and beautifully proportioned portico of six Doric pillars.   It was erected
in 1841.   Until the Inverness Academy and Educational
Trust Scheme came into force in 1887 this institution was
managed by the Provost, Magistrates, and Town Council,
to whom Dr Andrew Bell, of Westminster, author of the
Madras system of Education, left £10,000 three per cent.
consols, to conduct the school on that system, which, however, had not been done for many years., In 1890 it was
taken over by the Burgh School Board, under whose management it is now conducted as one of their ordinary
elementary schools.

Proceeding along Academy Street and continuing our
course shorewards we pass along Rose Street, where the extensive workshops of the Rose Street Foundry and Engine-
ering Co., Ltd., with its warerooms and offices facing Academy
Street, are situated, the only industry of any extent in the
town, with the single exception of the Highland Railway
Company's works.   On the right is the commodious Drill
Hall of the First Volunteer Battalion Cameron Highlanders.
Continuing on we cross the bridge over the railway going
north and get on to the road leading to the Longman, a long
stretch of common way extending from the shore at mouth
of river Ness to Millburn Road.

Entering Chapel Street we come upon

THE CHAPEL YARD,

said to have been presented to the town by the Cuthberts of Castle Hill, but really included in Queen Mary's charter to the burgh in 1557. It contained an ancient place of worship, known as St. Mary's Chapel, and the Cemetery of St. Mary is referred to in authentic records as early as 1361. The Chapel was destroyed by Cromwell, the materials being used to build his fort, described below. There are still many ancient and curious tombs and gravestones in the Chapel Yard, although several, beautifully sculptured and of great interest, were destroyed by the followers of Prince Charles in 1746, after they blew up the Castle, because the owners refused to join and follow them to Drummosie Moor. After the battle of Culloden this God's Acre was used by Cumberland as a fold for cattle taken in from Lord Lovat's estates, which were forfeited on account of his lordship's support of Prince Charles. Among other families buried in it are those of Holme, Culloden, Drummond, Fairfield, and Kingsmills.

Leaving the Chapel Yard the visitor keeps to the right, passes under the handsome and substantial railway stone viaduct which crosses the Ness below the Waterloo Bridge, leaves the Harbour and Docks on the left, and soon finds himself treading across a soft green sward, which once formed the area of

CROMWELL'S FORT.

In 1652 Oliver Cromwell took possession of Inverness, and in 1653 began to erect the fort named after him. It was five years in building, and cost £80,000 sterling. It was a regular pentagon, with ramparts, bastions, and wet ditch. Its west side was washed by the river ; and the ditch, which was supplied from the river, contained, at full tide, sufficient depth and breadth of water to float a small bark. The breast-work was three storeys high, constructed of hewn stone and lined on the inside with brick. The sally-port lay towards the town, and the principal gateway faced the north. The latter was approached by a strong draw-bridge of oak, over which was a stately structure, bearing the motto " *Togam tuentur arma.*" From the bridge the passage to the citadel lay through a vaulted passage, 70 feet long, having seats on each side. In the centre of the area stood a large square edifice, three storeys high, the first and second of which contained the powder magazine, granary and provision store, while the highest was fitted up as a church. The building was covered with a pavilion roof, surmounted with a neat steeple containing a clock and four bells. At opposite sides of the area, within the ramparts, stood two large buildings, each four storeys high—one called the English building, having been built by English masons—the other the Scotch building, having been the work of Scotsmen. The fort altogether had accommodation for about 1000 men. Cromwell was at no loss for the materials required in the erection of it, nor was he scrupulous as to the means employed to procure them. The Greyfriar's Church and St. Mary's Chapel in Inverness, the monasteries of Beauly and Kinloss, and the Episcopal castle of Chanonry were all demolished to furnish the stonework, while the fir woods of Strathglass contributed their share towards the erection of the wooden part of it—the oak used having been brought from England. This fort so annoyed the Highland chiefs, who had writhed under the iron will of Cromwell, that at their request, and in acknowledgment of their loyalty, it was demolished in 1662, after the Restoration of Charles II. The stone bridge, the old Academy, and most of the oldest existing houses in the town were built of its materials. The outline of the fort is still quite distinct, and the ramparts along one of the sides remain to this day almost entire ; while in some places part of the outer wall may still be seen. The southern

entry to the ditch has been widened into a commodious
wet-dock, which forms part of the harbour.   From this
point a good view can be obtained of Fortrose and Fort-
George, on either side of the Moray Firth, about twelve
miles distant, as well as of the whole surrounding country
in all directions.

We now retrace our steps, and, passing under the Railway
Viaduct, turn to the right and take a look at the new Waterloo
steel girder Bridge, built at a cost of between £8000 and £9000
and declared open by Mrs Provost William Macbean on 26th
February, 1896.   Turning at this point to the left we proceed
by Waterloo Place, and leaving the Maggot Green on the
right, again pass the Chapel Yard.   Arriving at the angle
of Academy and Church Streets we keep to the right, and
continue our course along the latter until we reach and turn
first, on the right, into

FRIARS LANE, and then into FRIARS STREET.   Passing
a few doors in the latter, also on the right, we come upon
the entrance gate of

THE GREYFRIARS CHURCH YARD

which is usually kept locked, but the key can be obtained
from the sexton, whose office is inside the Chapel Yard
gateway.   On entering, the first object that strikes the
visitor is the only remains of the old monastery—the shaft
of a red granite column in good preservation.   It appears
from the Town records that the stones of the monastery
were used by Colonel Lilburn, commanding the Protector's
troops, in 1653 for building Cromwell's Fort.   A little further
on will be observed built in the south wall a figure in
armour with the head and arms broken off, supposed to be
a portion of the monumental tomb erected to the memory of
John Stuart, Prior of Coldingham, natural brother of the
Earl of Moray, who died at Inverness in 1563.   In its
original position the effigy represented the prior "lying on
a couch with his head resting on a Bible."   More recently

it has been suggested that the effigy may have been that
of Alexander Stuart, Earl of Mar, who commanded the
Lowland army at the battle of Harlaw in 1411. His lordship
was Justiciar for the north and he died at Inverness in
1435, all of which lends plausibility to the suggestion. Many
men of note are interred in the Greyfriar's Churchyard,
including the Chiefs of Mackintosh down to 1606. The
principal families buried in it are the Baillies of Dunain,
Macleans of Dochgarroch, and Mackintoshes of Borlum,
and there are monuments to the memory of Dr William
Chisholm of Buntait, Provost of Inverness from 1773 to
1776 and from 1779 to 1782 ; of Colin Munro of Granada,
his son-in-law ; and of several other well-known Highland
names. Cameron in his *History of Inverness* says—" This
Monastery of Greyfriars was presented by Alexander II. in
1233, and was occupied by an importation of Greyfriars from
St. Johnston or Perth. The buildings, which are said to
have been spacious and elegant, were destroyed by Alexander of the Isles when he burnt the town in 1428. After
this they were rebuilt, but not so well as before. The
second suite of buildings were thrown into ruins at the
Reformation, and their destruction completed by Oliver
Cromwell to aid the building of the fort." According to
" Nonagenarian " a passage from the Monastery communi-
cated with the Church which originally stood on the hill
now occupied by the High Church, evidences of which, he
says, in the shape of arched walls, were found in his own
time. Returning to

CHURCH STREET

we continue our course for a short distance until we come to

THE GAELIC CHURCH,

which is reached a few yards before our arrival at the
entrance to the High Church and Church Yard. There
is nothing striking about the Gaelic Church, but within it
is an elegant oak pulpit. It was at first called the " Little

Desk" and it came, not from Culloden, as alleged by
"Nonagenarian" and others, but from Holland, being
originally used there as an auctioneer's rostrum.   In some
way it became the property of Janet Sinclair of Rattar,
mother of William Robertson of Inshes ; and according to
the Session records, under date of 1st August, 1676, that
gentleman made a gift of it to the Church in return for
two pews in heritage forever :—" for which two pews the
said William did give the little desk belonging some time
to his mother."   It was the same lady—the owner of this
curious pulpit—who erected the very handsome family
burying place of the Robertsons of Inshes, still in fair
preservation, inside the Church Yard gate.* · The Gaelic
Church was erected in 1792 on the site of an older one
built in 1649, and which, after the battle of Culloden, was
used as an hospital and prison for the followers of Prince
Charles.   Among them were Provost Hossack, and ex-Pro-
vost Fraser of the family of Achnagairn, both of whom
" were supposed from their lukewarmness to the House of
Brunswick to have been secret supporters of the Stuarts."
These two magnates were, however, released on the following day, through the mediation of the minister.   The Church
was completely gutted out, re-roofed, floored, seated, and
internally renovated in 1886 and re-opened for public worship
in January 1887.   A platform and desk has now taken the
place of the old carved pulpit, which has, however, been
placed on the right of its less interesting substitute and is
still used on special occasions.

Immediately entering the Church Yard, we come upon

THE HIGH CHURCH,

erected in 1769-72, and seated for 1860 people, at a cost of
£1000 sterling, excluding the square tower attached to it,
which belonged to the ancient Church.   One of the bells
which it contains was, according to tradition, brought by

* *Invernessiana*, p. 115.

Cromwell from the old Cathedral of Fortrose, destroyed by him to procure material for his fort, already referred to. This Church was re-seated and otherwise internally improved in 1891. There are several handsome monumental tablets erected to eminent persons connected with the town and neighbourhood inside the building, while outside in the Church Yard there are a few ancient vaults and tombstones. Several of Prince Charlie's followers were shot here by Cumberland's orders the day after Culloden, and a headstone on which the executioners rested their muskets while taking aim at the unfortunate victims is still pointed out.

Leaving the Church Yard we immediately come upon an ancient-looking building, directly opposite, popularly known as

THE OLD ACADEMY,

It was built with materials from Cromwell's Fort. In 1668 it was bequeathed to the town by Provost Alexander Dunbar, as an Hospital, and it was afterwards, until the opening of the Royal Academy in 1792, used as the Burgh Grammar School, when its funds, amounting to £70 per annum, were made over, and are still paid by the Town Council to that institution. The building was subsequently used for various purposes, such as parish library, female school, female work society rooms, and for the fire engines of the burgh. When the cholera raged in the town it was again used as an hospital, then as a poor house; and more recently it has been at the same time used for the sale of beer and the head-quarters of a lodge of Good Templars.

In Church Lane, which, directly opposite, leads to the Greig Street Suspension Bridge, will be noticed, in the farthest left-hand corner, the fine church, with its massive tower and lofty spire, erected in 1892 by the Free North Congregation at a cost of £9500. It is seated for 1450. The whole of the south side of the Lane is occupied by this handsome building, the schools and offices attached, and the old manse, while the opposite side is lined by the Church Yard wall.

Proceeding along Church Street, and crossing to its west side we enter the court numbered 71, to look at the only remaining example in the town of the ancient turnpike stair, since the one in the Castle Wynd was removed when the old Commercial Hotel was pulled down to make room for the new Town Hall.   These stairs were at one time very common in Inverness, the second storey in almost every house in the principal streets being, until a comparatively recent date, entered by them from the outside.

The Commercial Bank of Scotland, in the angle formed at this point by Fraser Street is next passed on the same side.   At the other end of Fraser Street on the left will be observed the Free High Church, with its graceful and elegant spire, and, on the right, the Fraser Street Hall, built in 1826 for an Independent Chapel at a cost of £800, with seating accommodation for 650 persons, and until a few years ago occupied as such.   Immediately opposite the Commercial Bank is Queensgate (which at this point connects Church and Academy Streets) and the new Post Office buildings described at page 39.

Higher up on the opposite side we observe past No. 34 the Church Street entrance to the New Markets, and immediately afterwards St. John's Episcopal Church, built in 1839.   Then comes the Bank of Scotland, forming the corner of Union Street.   Almost directly opposite is the site of

LADY DRUMMUIR'S HOUSE

where Prince Charles Edward Stuart lodged the night before and the Duke of Cumberland the night after the battle of Culloden, referred to at page 16.   The spot on which this old and historic building stood is now occupied by the business premises of Mr Alexander Mackenzie, wine and spirit merchant, at No. 43.   Four doors further on we pass on the same side the Caledonian Hotel, facing Union Street, and in the opposite corner, the well-known Highland ornament establishment of Messrs Ferguson & Macbean, jewellers to His Royal Highness the Prince of Wales and other members of the Royal family.

Leaving Bank Lane on the right we next pass the Inverness office of the National Bank of Scotland on the same side, and the Northern Meeting Rooms, a plain but commodious building, directly facing it, on the left. It was built by subscription in 1789, the Meeting itself having been instituted the previous year. The building was originally three storeys high, but having been injured by an explosion of powder which took place in its neighbourhood in 1801 it was re-erected in its present form. It has since then, however, been almost altogether internally reconstructed. A few steps more will take us to the Steeple Corner forming the junction of Church Street with

BRIDGE STREET

at the Exchange and in front of the Town Hall, from which we started at page 25. The first place of interest in this street, which is a continuation westward of High Street, next to the steeple already described, is

THE WORKMEN'S CLUB,

established in 1872 by the late Mr Donald Macdougall, the original founder of the business carried on so long and so successfully at the Royal Clan Tartan Warehouse. It is situated about half-way along the street on the left hand side. It contains a good library and reading room and is open to visitors on payment of one penny. The last building on the right hand side of the street has been known for centuries as

QUEEN MARY'S HOUSE,

so called from the fact that the beautiful but unfortunate Mary of Scots, who came north as far as Inverness in 1562, to put down an insurrection in that year by the Earl of Huntly, had been refused entrance to the Castle by the Governor, whereupon she occupied this house, and held

Court within it for several days, until the Frasers, Mackenzies, Rosses, and Munros, in answer to a proclamation, joined her standard, reduced the stronghold, gained admittance, and by Her Majesty's orders hanged the Governor, Alexander Gordon, who at the time held it for the Earl of Huntly, in front of the building. The outside of the house has since undergone considerable alterations.

Having now arrived at the principal Suspension Bridge, erected by Government in 1850-55 at a cost of £26,000, the reader may turn to the right and proceed along Bank Street on the east side of the river if he wishes to obtain a nearer view of the Free High and Free North Churches whose front elevations abut on the street and face the river, and of the Theatre Royal, a neat, comfortable, and well-arranged play-house sandwiched half-way between them He may then cross the Greig Street Foot Bridge and return along the left bank of the river by Huntly Street, leaving the new "Queen Street" Free Church, and the West Parish Church, originally built at a cost of £2000, on the right. It had seating accommodation for 1800 persons, and was opened for public worship in 1840. The small spire by which it is surmounted contains a couple of bells. A few years ago the Church was entirely re-seated and otherwise internally renovated. A large hall has been erected in connection with it, and when required it is let for public purposes, very much adding to the comfort and convenience at elections and on other important occasions of those who reside on the west side of the river. A short distance farther up the street, the Catholic Chapel, an elegant building, erected in 1836 at a cost of £2000, and seated for 450 persons, is passed, soon after which the pedestrian continuing in the same direction will find himself at the western end of

THE TRAFFIC SUSPENSION BRIDGE

which connects Bridge Street and the principal thoroughfares on the east of the river with those on the west side of

it. The visitor may, if so disposed, forego the whole detour
just described without losing anything of much consequence;
for nearly all the places referred to on either bank of the
Ness can be seen to excellent advantage from the Suspension Bridge.   The view from the Bridge itself is also
very fine, particularly up the river and right and left of
it to and far beyond the Islands.

Young and Tomnahurich Streets are a continuation of
Bridge Street and High Street across the bridge, and it is
slightly the shortest but by no means the most pleasant route
to Tomnahurich Cemetery.   The visitor should proceed by

NESS WALK

along the river bank.   He will first pass the Victoria Hotel
on the right, and then, next door, the recently erected
Palace Hotel.   From this point is got perhaps the best
view obtainable of the Castle and Castle Hill anywhere
in Inverness.   Passing along Ardross Terrace, which forms
the angle between Ness Walk and Ardross Street, those
wishing to visit Tomnahurich Cemetery without first seeing
the Islands will turn to the right and proceed along the
latter street, leaving on the left, first, Saint Andrew's
Cathedral, next the Northern Meeting Park and Stands,
and, at its western terminus, the Collegiate School, these
four buildings with their grounds forming the entire length
of the south side of Ardross Street.   The continuation of
this thoroughfare is the more direct route to Tomnahurich
Cemetery, but instead of proceeding in this direction we
would ask the reader to accompany us along the river bank
from Ness Walk to the Ness Islands, thence round by the
Bught to Tomnahurich Cemetery, and back to Inverness
by the Cemetery Road, Ardross Street, and Ness Walk.

Following the left bank of the river, immediately after
passing the angle of Ardross Terrace, we come upon

SAINT ANDREW'S CATHEDRAL,

standing in the right-hand corner, with Eden Court, the

From Photo. by]   **Castle and Cathedral.**   [D. Whyte.

From Photo. by]

The Ness Islands.

[D. Whyte.

seat of the Bishop of Moray, Ross, and Caithness, ensconced among the trees a short distance behind it.   The foundation stone of the Cathedral was laid in 1866, and that of Eden Court in 1876.   The former was completed and opened in 1869 ; and the latter finished and occupied in 1878.   The Cathedral cost some £20,000 to build, and the Bishop's residence £8000.   Both were erected from designs by Mr Alexander Ross, architect, Inverness.   The Cathedral is in the English Middle Pointed Gothic style and is 166 feet long, 72 feet broad, and 88 feet high to the ridge of the roof.   The original intention of the architect was to carry the towers up to a height of 200 feet, but the funds available at the time did not admit of the complete design being carried out. The Font in the Cathedral is of great interest, and worthy of inspection. It was copied from one made by Thorwalsden, which is in Copenhagen. The sculptor of the Inverness one was Redfern, who is now dead.   Mr Andrew Davidson, an Inverness sculptor now in Rome, has made several copies from the Inverness Font for American and other churches. The donor of the Inverness Font was Colonel Learmonth, and it cost about £300.   It is carved out of a solid block of white marble.   In the centre of the arch of the Baptistry is a head of Christ crowned with thorns, also in white marble, the gift of Mr Munro, a sculptor, and carved by the donor.   A little further on is

THE NORTHERN INFIRMARY,

opened for patients in 1804, the foundation stone having been laid with full Masonic honours on the 6th of May, 1799, when there was a great procession and general turnout of the brethren and of the public.   It was originally built by public subscriptions and donations, and has ever since been maintained by similar means.   The pedestrian may from this point continue along the west bank of the river to the upper bridge leading to   THE NESS ISLANDS ;
but we recommend him to cross to the east or right bank by the Haugh Suspension Bridge, and on the other side proceed by the Lady's Walk, formed on the narrow embankment between Eileanach House and grounds and the river, until, at the end of the high wall on his left, he arrives at the small wooden bridge which crosses an offshoot of the Ness and leads him into the first of this beautiful and unique group of Islands, which, with the exception of the walks and the series of elegant chain and neatly constructed wooden bridges by which they are united, are in their natural state, covered with wood, shrubbery, dense foliage, and wild

flowers, altogether forming one of the loveliest sylvan retreats that any community in the kingdom can boast of, and which no visitor to the Capital of the Highlands should fail to see.   The farthest away of the islands is exactly a mile from the Exchange.

During the last century it was the custom of the Provost, Magistrates, and Town Council to entertain the Lords of Justiciary when on Circuit to a sumptuous banquet on the largest of these islands, at which salmon, caught in the river before the eyes of their Lordships, formed the most interesting if not the principal dish, " while claret, brandy, and Hollands—which in those days were sold, even here, at prices which, at the present day, one can hardly credit— flowed in great abundance."   Having roamed through these shaded and lovely groves we cross to the west side of the river by the elegant bridge shown in our illustration, and, turning to the left, leave the General's Well in the im- mediate neighbourhood on the same side.   We then proceed, passing the Bught Mill on the left—Tor-a-Vean, across the Canal, towering behind it—with Bught House and grounds on the right, to

TOMNAHURICH CEMETERY,

rising abruptly out of the plain which we are now traversing, to a height of 222 feet above the level of the sea.   Looked at from the east or west, Tomnahurich Hill appears exactly like a boat or ship turned upside down, and the top, which is thickly studded with handsome and costly monuments, has been laid out in the form of a ship's deck.   The well-gravelled circular hollow below the general level, in which the carriage road terminates, represents the hold.   The southern portion, considerably higher than the other end, shows the quarter deck, while the remainder is laid out like the ordinary deck of a large vessel, and gradually narrows at the northern extremity to the form of a ship's prow.

The visitor adopting the Islands and Bught route will enter the Cemetery by the southern gate and, if in good

From Photo. by]   Tomnahurich Cemetery.   [J. Valentine & Sons.

5

heart, can climb to the top by a zig-zag foot-path in the face of the hill. He will, however, find it much more pleasant to follow the carriage drive round and up the west side to the top, from which he will see the most extensive, most diversified, and most beautiful panorama imaginable. The view of Inverness and its surroundings—the Moray Firth, with Chanonry Point and Fort-George in the distance, the Soutars of Cromarty, with the Sutherland hills far beyond to the north, and the fertile plains on the opposite side of the Firth to Morayshire in the east—is, except that from Craig' Phadruig, far and away the best that can be obtained in the neighbourhood of the town, and perhaps any-' where. Looking to the west and north the mountains of Strathglass and Ross form a splendid background, while the magnificent view to the south along the great Caledonian Valley—the River Ness rushing along in front, the Caledonian Canal sweeping around the base of Tor-a-Vean, the handsome villas forming new Inverness on the hundred feet terrace on the opposite side of the river, and the back setting of hill and dale, mountain and valley, culminating on a clear day in a glimpse of Loch Ness at the foot of the towering and majestic Mealfourvonie and its giant companions must be seen, not described.

The reader, if fond of walking, can now proceed by the Caledonian Canal right bank to the steamboat wharf, cross at the upper Muirtown lock, and walk by Balnafettack farm house to the top of Craig Phadruig, distant about a mile from Tomnahurich Cemetery. But the average tourist will make that a separate and more comfortable visit from Inverness, and in the meantime return by the northern gate at the superintendent's lodge, along Cemetery Road, passing

THE COLLEGIATE SCHOOL

already mentioned on page 50, in the right hand corner as he enters Ardross Street. This institution was built from designs by Mr Alexander Ross, Inverness, and opened

in 1873. It is conducted on the same system as the great
English public schools, its pupils being prepared for admission
sion direct to the Universities, to Sandhurst and Woolwich,
where many of them have been very successful and reflected
credit on the school. Passing the Northern Meeting Park,
its two grand stands, and the Cathedral, the visitor in a
few minutes will find himself back at his hotel, having now
seen, if he has followed our guidance, all the places of
interest in Inverness and its vicinity, except

CRAIG PHADRUIG,

a wood-capped rock about a mile and a half directly west
from the town, on the summit of which, 555 feet above
sea level, he will discover one of the best specimens of the
pre-historic vitrified forts in the Kingdom. These ancient
remains are known among the Gaelic-speaking natives as
" Larach an Tigh Mhoir," or the Site of the Big House,
and the place is supposed to have been the residence of
King Brude, where he was called upon in the sixth century
tury by Saint Columba during his visit to Inverness. But
this is by no means certain. The vitrified matter forms a
rampart 270 feet long by 103 broad, and some very good
specimens of vitrification—stones melted and welded together
by some firing process now unknown—can yet be seen in
great quantity. So many theories have been broached by
learned antiquarians regarding the origin of this and similar
vitrified remains that it would take a very bold man to
express any decided opinion on the subject.

Craig Phadruig may be reached on foot by Huntly Street,
Greig Street, and Fairfield Road, crossing the canal by the
upper lock at the steamboat wharf and proceeding up the
ascent past the farm house of Balnafettack to the top ; or
in a cab, by Telford Road and Muirtown Bridge, along the
west bank of the canal to Balnafettack. From this point
the remaining short distance must be completed on foot.
The view from the summit is one of the most magnifi-

cent, extensive, and varied in the Highlands, and no possible description can do it justice.   After enjoying it to his heart's content the reader can return to Inverness by either of the routes already described.

Within 15 minutes' walk of the town, at Culcabock, there is a pretty nine-hole Golf Course.   The air is bracing, and the situation commands a pleasant view.   The Course has been recently extended, and in addition to the whin and other hazards, new bunkers are being formed, which should make the Course more varied and attractive.   There is a comfortable and commodious Club House.   Comfortable apartments can be had in the town. Entrance fee, 6/-. Annual subscription—Gentlemen, 15/-; Ladies, 7/6.   Visitors' weekly ticket, 2/6.   Monthly tickets, 5/-.   No charge is made for visitors playing over the Course for a day.   The secretary is Mr David Ross, solicitor, Church Street, Inverness.

GUIDE TO THE HIGHLANDS.

I. INVERNESS TO BEAULY, MUIR OF ORD, AND FORTROSE IN THE BLACK ISLE.

STARTING from Inverness, the tourist, almost immediately after leaving the Railway Station, crosses the River Ness by a massive stone viaduct of nine arches, five of which, 73 feet span each, cross the bed of the river, with two of 20 feet span on land, across the streets which run at either end of the bridge. From this point, for about half a mile, a very fine view is obtained on the left of the Ness Valley and the Great Caledonian Glen. Tomnahurich on the east bank of the Canal, rises abruptly from the level plain on which it stands, while further to the north-west, on the opposite side, Craig Phadruig, with its pre-historic vitrified fort, meets the eye. Kessock Ferry, by which the Moray Firth is crossed into Ross-shire, is passed on the right, at the point where the Beauly Firth begins, and on the farther shore rises gently the fertile lands of the Black Isle, while the massive Ben Wyvis and other towering Ross-shire hills in its neighbourhood rear their summits in the distance beyond. An object of interest noticed in the Canal Basin is the training ship *Briton*, formerly the *Brilliant*.

Crossing the Caledonian Canal by a swing bridge, the train pulls up at the old-fashioned fishing village of Clachnaharry. On the rocky heights above, a few yards past the Station, and opposite the bridge by which the high road crosses the railway, a desperate Clan battle was fought in 1454 between the Munros of Fowlis, who were returning home with the fruits of a raid in the south, and a band of Mackintoshes, who pursued them. This engagement has been commemorated by a tall obelisk erected in 1821 on the highest point of the rock, by the late Major H. Robert Duff of Muirtown. On the side facing Ross-shire, the country of the Munros, it bears the word "Monro," and on the south side the words "Clan Chattan," with the legend "Has inter rupes ossa conduntur." The Tutor of Fowlis, who led the Munros, was severely wounded. He lost an arm and was left for dead on the field, but afterwards recovered. Malcolm Og, grandson of Mackintosh of Mackintosh, who "led" the other side, was not present, the battle being over before he arrived on the scene.

Closely skirting the Beauly Firth, the train next pulls up at Bunchrew station, near which, surrounded by a clump of tall trees, close to the seashore, stands Bunchrew House in which the famous President Forbes of the 'Forty-five was born. The extensive manure manufactory belonging to Messrs Cran & Co. is at the railway platform. As the traveller proceeds westward, the valley begins to open up to the left, until, at Lentran station, it extends to a wide expanse of level country, while away in the distance, straight ahead, stand out prominently the great mountain sentinels of Strathglass, Glenstrathfarrar, and Strathconon, some of which rise to an altitude of 3400 feet. Across the Firth, to the north, Red Castle, the oldest inhabited residence in the Highlands, having been originally built by William the Lion in 1179, nestles among the surrounding woods.

At this point the coach road, which hitherto ran close to the line, takes a detour to the left.

Following the railway, the next station is Clunes. A few minutes after leaving it the train passes through the lands

of Easter and Wester Lovat. Here was situated the ancient
residence of the Frasers, and it is from this particular spot
that they take their title. Leaving these two fine farms on the
right, the river Beauly is crossed by an iron girder bridge
from which, and as the train glides towards the Beauly railway station, the imposing modern residence of Lord Lovat,
erected in 1885, may be seen on the left, rearing its turrets
above the wooded eminences which adorn the extensive
policies by which it is surrounded. The new mansion house
is built on the site of Castle Dounie, described by Sir
Walter Scott in his "Tales of a Grandfather," and destroyed
by Cumberland's troops after the battle of Culloden. This
splendid modern mansion is in the Scottish baronial style,
with heavy masonry—built of old red sandstone from the
Redburn quarry, about two miles from Beauly, on his Lordship's own estate—with mullioned windows, bill-roofed turrets,
and crow-stepped gables. It is 300 feet in length with an
average width of 80 feet. The main building, which contains
86 different rooms, including the family Chapel, consists of
a western tower, a central block of private apartments, and
an entrance tower, flanked by a central tower 100 feet high.
It is altogether a picturesque and imposing pile, distinctly
seen from either road or rail, a prominent and striking
object in the beautiful and varied landscape by which it is
on every side surrounded.

BEAULY.

The venerable ruin of the Priory, close to the village of
Beauly, is well worth a visit. It was founded in 1230 by
John Bisset, then proprietor of the district, but several additions were subsequently made to it by successive Lords Lovat.
It is a noble and graceful building, though for many years
a roofless ruin, and now only used as the burying-place,
principally of the leading families of the Frasers, the Chisholms, and the Mackenzies of Gairloch. Among other
monuments of note, it contains a recumbent effigy, in full
armour, of the famous Kenneth-a-Bhlair, seventh Baron of

From Photo. by]   **Beaufort Castle.**   [J. Valentine & Sons.

From Photo. by]

Fortrose Cathedral.

[]. Valentine & Sons.

Kintail, who, according to the inscription, died in 1493. A little further north are the restored ruins of the ancient church of Cilliechriost, where a shocking tragedy is said to have taken place in 1603, when the Macdonalds of Glengarry, under Allan of Lundie, set fire to the sacred edifice, a thatched building, while the Sunday service was proceeding. The church was crowded with a congregation of the Mackenzies of the district, and not a soul—man, woman, or child—was allowed to escape. But the horrid deed was soon after amply revenged by the friends of the victims, who pursued the Macdonalds and put almost every one of them, in the most merciless manner, to the sword. The Lovat Arms Hotel, the principal one in the village, is first class.

The next station, after leaving Beauly, is MUIR OF ORD JUNCTION, where the Black Isle branch,

FOR FORTROSE AND ROSEMARKIE,

joins the main line. Here all passengers for all parts of the Black Isle change carriages and enter the Fortrose train at the platform on the left.

The Black Isle Railway, which was opened for traffic on the 1st of February, 1894, opens up a new and attractive route for tourists, and brings the Royal Burghs of Fortrose and Rosemarkie, which in recent years have been getting so popular as seaside resorts for those in search of health and pleasure, within an hour's journey of Inverness. The train almost immediately crosses the main line and proceeds slowly along a curve of 11 chains for 460 yards through a comparatively uninteresting country. The slope of the Mulbuie, covered by crofts and crofters' houses for six miles, is skirted on the left. After passing through several plantations, and having to the right obtained several peeps of the Aird slope and hills on the opposite side of the Beauly Firth, of which a particularly striking view as well as of the Inverness-shire hills—which extend along its southern slopes for miles—is got at this point, on the

same side a few yards distant, and just before pulling up
at Redcastle Station,

KILCOY CASTLE,

restored in 1890 by its owner, Colonel John Edward Burton-
Mackenzie, towers prominently on the left. This castle, now
inhabited, is as it stands a particularly good specimen of
the more modern castle, which came into vogue during the
fifteenth and sixteenth centuries—half stronghold and half
family residence—combining considerable strength, elegance,
and comfort. Tradition says that it was a hunting-box of
the Kings of Scotland, and the Stewart arms, supported
by a crown, are carved on a gablet of the large round
west tower. Mr Alexander Ross, architect, Inverness, who
restored the castle, says of it that it was a simple
quadrangular structure, with overhanging turrets at the
angles, and round towers at the diagonal corners, by which
the side walls were effectually flanked and protected, while
the small entrance door, situated in an angle of the tower,
was covered by the adjoining doven. The lower part of
the building was covered by a hall and circular vault, all
roofed in stone. A circular stair in the south-east tower
led to the upper flats. The dining hall occupied the first
flat above the kitchen, and on the lintel over the fireplace,
which bears the date of 1679, were three elegantly carved
coats-of-arms, one being that of the founder of the family,
Alexander, third son of Colin Cam Mackenzie, XI. Baron of
Kintail, and his wife, Jean, daughter of Thomas Fraser
of Strichen, to whom he was married in 1611. Alexander
Mackenzie, the first of the family represented by the present
owner, has a charter of the lands of Kilcoy, Drumnamarg,
and Muirton, in 1616, and a Crown charter of the Barony
of Kilcoy in 1618. The last of the family who lived in the
castle, until its restoration, was Charles Mackenzie, VII.
of Kilcoy, who was born in 1756, married in 1781, and
died in 1813. The old roof remained intact until about 1860.
A little to the right of the Railway Station is Killearnan

Free Church, a plain and common-place building, and immediately below the Church, but not seen from the train, is the ancient and historic stronghold of Redcastle, sheltered by thickly-wooded hills—the western one of which is the old Gallows Hill—to the north and east of it, which form a striking feature in the landscape on the right as seen from the carriage windows. Leaving Redcastle Station the train proceeds through a gently-sloping valley, passing the Free Church Manse and a continuation of the Mulbuie crofts on the left slope, with the farmhouse of Linnie on the right. It then enters another hollow, with broken plantations on either side, in course of which nothing of interest is seen from the train until Allangrange is reached and left behind. Immediately on leaving this Station the line passes under a bridge over which the county road from Kessock Ferry to Conon Bridge and Dingwall is carried, and skirts a young plantation on the right, after which the first sight of the Ord Hill, 633 feet above sea level, also on the right, is obtained, the hills and mountains of Inverness-shire, still further off across the Firth extending for miles east and west. Here also, away to the north on the left, a passing glimpse is got of the massive Ben Wyvis, rising to an altitude of 3429 feet above the level of the sea. From this point the train passes through low-lying country covered over more or less with plantations all the way to

MUNLOCHY STATION

where it pulls up a few yards distant from the pretty village of that name, snugly ensconced and completely sheltered in from the north, east, and west, in the valley below. Munlochy has an inn, a Free Church, a bank, doctor, public school, post, telegraph, and postal order offices, a large hall, a fine company of Rifle Volunteers and all the other accompaniments of modern civilization. Just before entering the Station the Munlochy Burn and valley is crossed over an embankment 53 feet deep and a large culvert for the stream. From this point a fine view is obtained of Munlochy Bay, with the famous Craigiehow of Fingalian and fairy romance towering, and as if guarding its entrance, on the right bank, in the angle formed by the junction of the bay with the Moray Firth, of which a considerable stretch here comes into view, the Inverness-shire coast forming a magnificent and far extending setting on the opposite side. Immediately opposite Munlochy, on the slope between the village and Ord Hill, the summit of which is crowned by the remains of a vitrified hill fort, is

DRUMDERFIT, OR THE RIDGE OF TEARS,

on which was fought a most sanguinary clan conflict. In 1372 a body of Maclennans from the west invaded the eastern portion of Ross and pillaged Tain and Chanonry. Returning westward they encamped for the night on this ridge. Hugh Fraser of Lovat, at the time King's Lieutenant in the North, having heard of their depredations resolved to punish them. Collecting his men, he marched to their encampment, and by the aid of the Provost and citizens of Inverness who, in terms of a preconcerted plan, there met him, he put every man of them to the sword, except one individual who concealed himself unobserved under a "Lopan," a primitive kind of cart, from which, according to tradition, his descendants, who afterwards occupied the farm of Druim-a-deur, or Drumderfit, for four hundred years, derived the name of Loban, modernised into Logan.

The Frasers and Macraes who then resided at Clunes in the Aird, as vassals of the Frasers of Lovat, secured the assistance of the citizens of Inverness under the following circumstances. The Maclennans had sent word to the Provost from their encampment that unless Inverness paid a heavy ransom the invaders would cross the Firth, set fire to the town, and put the inhabitants to the sword. Provost Junor made a pretence of agreeing to their proposal, and as an earnest of his intention and good faith, despatched a large quantity of strong liquor to the camp. The Mac-lennans being greatly fatigued and without provisions, eagerly partook of the intoxicating fluid, and then fell into a pro-found slumber. In the meantime the wily Provost collected the stoutest and most warlike of the citizens, ferried them across Kessock during the night, and meeting the Frasers and Macraes, who had just arrived as previously agreed upon, joined them and at once attacked and slaughtered every soul in the camp, except the one man already named. The ridge is still thickly strewn over with cairns to commemorate the dead, and it is to this day known as "Druim-a-deur," anglicised Drumderfit, or the Ridge of Tears.

From Munlochy to Fortrose the country is very pretty and the remainder of the journey becomes most interesting. On leaving the Station the train for a short distance runs through a gently-sloping valley, skirting a thickly-wooded hill on the right. In a few minutes Rosehaugh Gate Lodge is passed on the left, and immediately afterwards Rosehaugh House, the beautiful Highland residence of Mr James Douglas Fletcher, owner of the lovely estate of that name, is observed picturesquely situated on a slight eminence on the left, surrounded by its fine wooded policies, gardens, hot-houses, and all the other accompaniments of a modern millionaire's mansion. Proceeding through a cutting the train in a few minutes passes under a bridge by which the county road from Dingwall and Kessock Ferry to Avoch and Fortrose crosses from the north to the south side of the line. The Rosehaugh valley, through which the Avoch Burn runs on the left, is extremely beautiful, and a striking object on its northern slope is the ruin of old Avoch House, burnt down some years ago, but still surrounded by its grand old trees and well-kept gardens. A little above it, on a terrace, stands Ardendeith Tower. Away to the south on the pro-montory between Munlochy and Avoch Bay is the prettily wooded hill on which once stood the ancient Castle of Avoch, but it is not seen from the Railway until Avoch is reached.

This fishing village had, in 1891, a population of 1817, several churches, a branch of the Caledonian Bank, a public school, and a tweed factory. The view here from the railway, extending far out into the Moray Firth, along its southern coast and for miles inland—the landscape, comprising a large portion of Inverness, Nairn, and Moray shires—is varied and beautiful beyond description. At Avoch, those desiring to visit the interesting site of

THE ANCIENT CASTLE OF AVOCH

must leave the train, turn to the right, and walk or drive along a pretty private road made by the late Mr James Fletcher of Rosehaugh several years ago, almost to the summit of the Hill, distant a mile and a quarter and 390 feet above sea level. The Castle, of which only the foundations can now be traced, stood on the summit of Ormond Hill, now called Lady Hill, probably from its chapel having been dedicated to the Virgin Mary. Its situation is described by a writer of the seventeenth century as " Castletown with the ruins of a castle called the Castle of Ormond, which hath given styles to sundry Earls, and last to the Princes of Scotland." It held a commanding position both as regards land and sea, and no enemy could approach it from either without being observed by the occupants of the castle long before they could get near it. The earliest existing accounts in which there is any mention of it describes it as being in possession of the Regent, Sir Andrew Moray of Bothwell, a "lord of great bounty, of sober and chaste life, wise and upright in council, liberal and generous, devout and charitable, stout, hardy, and of great courage," who retired to it from the fatigues of a warlike career, died in it in 1338, and was buried in the " Cathedral Kirk of Rosmarkyn." The castle subsequently passed into the hands of the Earls of Ross, but on their forfeiture in 1476 it was annexed to the Crown, and in 1487 James III. created his own second son, James

Stewart, "Duke of Ross, Marquis of Ormond, and Earl of Edirdal, otherwise called Ardmanach." On the 13th of May, 1503, having received the richly-endowed Abbey of Dunfermline, the Prince resigned the dukedom into his Majesty's hands, but during his life he reserved the Hill of Dingwall for the ducal title, the Hill of Ormond for the style of Marquis, and the Redcastle of Ardmanach for that of Earl. Thus we had, in the remote district of the Black Isle, one of the regular appanages of the Royal family of Scotland ; and it is interesting to find that these titular designations still survive in the place names of the locality.

A MAGNIFICENT VIEW.

Leaving Avoch Station the train proceeds along the top of the Craigwood, 150 feet above the level of the sea, whose musical ripple may occasionally, on a calm day, be heard immediately below. The view from this summit simply baffles description. The Moray Firth stretches out into the German Ocean. The counties of Inverness, Nairn, Moray, and Banff, are fully in view for scores of miles along its southern shores, inland as far as the Cairngorm Hills and Grampian range, to the south and east. To the west a fine view is obtained of the town of Inverness and the great Caledonian Glen, with its towering mountains on either side, the summit of Ben Nevis, some 70 miles distant, being seen on a clear day. Immediately below and in front you have the ancient and picturesque

ROYAL BURGH OF FORTROSE,

the terminus of the line, where in another minute the train stops. Further away about a mile and a half is Chanonry Point, with its pretty light-house, and Fort-George on the opposite promontory across the Firth. Directly below is the Fortrose Pier, and a little to the east of it what remains of

FORTROSE CATHEDRAL.

The accompanying illustration shows all now standing of this historic building. The vandal hand of Cromwell destroyed the sacred edifice and carried away the stones of which it was constructed to build his fort at Inverness. The portion of the walls which are still standing consists of the south aisle to the chancel and nave, and of the chapter-house, some distance from the principal ruin, now used as the Burgh Town Hall and Council Chamber. In its complete state the Cathedral consisted of choir and nave, with aisles, eastern Lady-chapel, western tower, and chapter-house at the north-east end.

There is no authentic record of its erection, but it is supposed to have been built by the Countess of Ross, whose tomb is in the first or second existing aisle, towards the end of the thirteenth or early in the fourteenth century. It is described in Neale's *Ecclesiological Notes* as the "once glorious Cathedral," and "the style is the purest and most elaborate middle-pointed;" while, according to the same high authority, "the whole church, though probably not 120 feet long from east to west, must have been an architectural gem of the very first description. The exquisite beauty of the mouldings, after so many years of exposure to the air, is wonderful and shows that, in whatever other respects these remote parts of Scotland were barbarous, in ecclesiology, at least, they were on a par with any other branch of the mediæval Church." The piscina remained in 1848, when Neale wrote his Notes, and the mouldings, he says, were "truly the works of a master." The south aisle was separated from the chancel by two middle-pointed arches, now walled up, but not so much injured as to destroy their extreme loveliness. In the first of these arches is a canopied tomb for the Countess of Ross, who founded the church. This, Neale says, "must have been one of the most beautiful monuments I ever saw." The chancel arch is modern. The nave consists of four bays, much resembling the chancel in its details. The fourth bay is blocked up, and is used as the burying-place of the Mackenzies of Seaforth, several of whom are interred in it, as may be seen from the inscriptions on the wall. The rood turret still exists, and "is a very elegant though singular composition. It stands at the junction of the south aisle of nave and chancel, and acts as a buttress. Square at the base, it is bevelled into a semi-octagonal superstructure, and has elegant two-light windows on alternate sides. The top is modern." The large bell now hung in the spire bears the name of Thomas Tulloch, Bishop of Ross in 1460, and from the inscr.,tion it appears that the bell was dedicated to the Virgin Mary and Saint Boniface. The tomb of John Fraser, bishop 1485-1507, is still pointed out. When the workmen were engaged in 1854 cleaning out and repairing the Cathedral, they found, built in the wall, near the high altar, a stone sarcophagus, divided horizontally into two compartments, containing the skeleton of a tall man, supposed to be a bishop, with vestments almost entire, and at his left side was a piece of wood which looked like the remains of a crozier. The Cathedral was dedicated to Saints Peter and Boniface, and the seal of the Chapter, bearing the figures of these two saints, is still extant and used as the seal of the burgh. It has upon it the following inscription :—" SIGILLVM SANCTORVM PETRIE ET BONIFACCI DE ROSMARKIN," or the seal of Saints Peter and Boniface of Rosemarkie.

THE CASTLE.

There was a Castle of Fortrose, and a Bishop's Palace, of which not a vestige now remains. The palace stood near the Cathedral and was a residence of "great magnitude and grandeur." The castle, the site of which is pointed out at the west end of the burgh, was "greatly added to" by Colin, first Earl of Seaforth, who "lived most of his time at Chanonry in great state and very magnificently," where he died in the 36th year of his age, on the 15th of April, 1633, and, like his father before him, who also died and was buried "with great triumph" at Chanonry, was interred in the Cathedral "with great pomp and solemnity," in a spot chosen by himself, on the 18th of May following, the king having sent a gentleman all the way from Edinburgh to represent him at the funeral of the Mackenzie chief.*

After the battle of Auldearn General Middleton advanced to Fortrose and surrounded the castle, which was at the time held by Lady Seaforth. After a siege of four days her ladyship surrendered, but having secured the stores and ammunition, sent sometime previously by Queen Henrietta for the use of Montrose on his expected arrival there, Middleton gave Lady Seaforth, whom he treated " with the greatest civility and respect," possession of the castle. In 1649 General Leslie placed a garrison in it, but Seaforth soon after attacked and took it. Leslie subsequently came back, regained possession, placed another garrison in it, and returned south. The Highlanders again attacked and retook it, expelled the garrison, some of whom they hanged, demolished the walls, and razed the fortifications to the ground.†

THE ANCIENT CHANONRIE.

Fortrose was celebrated in its day not only on account of its Castle and Cathedral but for its position as a seat of learning. Its old name was Chanonrie, so called from its ecclesiastical position as the seat of the Bishop of Ross and the fact that within it was kept all official documents and writs connected with the Church and with the land of the county. In 1444, it was first and in 1455 finally united to Rosemarkie by a charter from James II., when the new Burgh, formed of the two old municipalities, was called Fort Ross, now softened down to Fortrose. This charter was confirmed by James VI. in 1592 and again in 1612, and it was further confirmed by Charles II. in 1661.

In 1622 Fortrose was "flourishing in the arts and sciences, being at that period the seat of divinity, law, and physic, in this corner of the kingdom." It is now but a poor shadow of

* Mackenzie's *History of the Mackenzies*, second edition, pp. 243-245.

† *Ibid.* pp. 258 and 268.

its former self. But increase and prosperity are yet in store for it. From the advent of the Black Isle Railway the ancient burgh has received a fresh impetus and a new life. It is beautifully situated on the north side of the Moray Firth, sheltered from the cold winds, and facing the sun. It has a salubrious and genial climate, and its vicinity abounds in places of historic, antiquarian, and scientific interest which cannot fail to have a special charm for the pleasure-seeker and the man of letters, especially the geologist and botanist. It also possesses one of the finest sea-bathing beaches in the north of Scotland.

There are several minor places of interest in and in the neighbourhood of Fortrose, among which may be specially mentioned the spot near Chanonry Point about three quarters of a mile from the Lighthouse and 160 yards east from the public road, marked by the stump of a stone cross, where "Coinneach Odhar," the far-famed Brahan Seer, was roasted to death in a burning barrel of tar about the middle of the seventeenth century. This spot, under the immediate eyes of the Church, is said to have been commonly used for burning witches, and the last who suffered for this supposed crime perished, according to tradition, on the same spot as the famous Brahan Seer.*

From Chanonry Point parties may cross by the ferry boat and visit Fort-George, the head-quarters of the Seaforth Highlanders, on the opposite promontory, completed about three years after Culloden at a cost of £160,000, with accommodation for 2180 men. There are several other places of interest to the antiquarian and geologist in the neighbourhood of Fort-George and Ardersier.

A very enjoyable excursion may be made from Fortrose to Avoch, a mile and a half distant, by road or rail, and from thence, on foot or drive, to Ormond Hill and Avoch Castle, a mile and a quarter farther. This excursion may be con-

* For a graphic description of the Seer's death see *The Prophecies of the Brahan Seer*, pp. 80-81.

tinued round and to the top of the hill, from which a magnificent view is obtained of Munlochy Bay and valley immediately on its western slope, as well as of Inverness, and the great Caledonian Valley, returning by rail from Munlochy, or, if driving the whole distance, past Bennet's Monument—as to the origin of which some very curious stories are told—Craigack Well, and the Sandstone Quarry which supplied the stones for the erection of Fort-George, making the return journey by Bennetsfield, and the beautiful "Vallis Rosarum" of Sir George Mackenzie, the whole extending to a walk or drive of between nine and ten miles, and altogether a most enjoyable day's outing.

Another may very profitably be made, especially by the botanist and geologist, to Mount Pleasant, a mile and a half, the Bog of Shannon, another mile, and along the road to Easter Auchterflow, to the Bishop's Well, the Petrifying Stream, and the old Burying-ground, 2¾ miles farther, making a total distance to be traversed both ways of about 9½ miles. Some extremely fine views are obtained in various directions in the course of this excursion. Curiously enough, in the district is found in great profusion the rare *Pingicula Alpina*, a plant which has not been met with elsewhere in Great Britain. Parties may return from this point by the Killen Burn and the Valley of Rosehaugh— taking the railway from Avoch—or by Raddery and the Hill of Fortrose.

THE BURGH OF ROSEMARKIE.

ROSEMARKIE, the church of which is exactly a mile from Fortrose Cathedral, is said to be much older than its neighbour, and to have been erected into a Royal Burgh by Alexander III. It flourished for a time, but about the middle of the seventeenth century it became "totally de- cayed." It was then almost entirely depopulated ; its houses and buildings being "altogether ruined and demolished." There was no trade or merchandise within its bounds. Its only residents were a few poor fishermen.   There were no Courts within it "for administration of justice and for punishing of delinquents, trespassers, and malefactors, nor yet any sure place, firmance, or tolbooth, wherein they may be secured and incarcerated till Justice have place and be duly executed upon them according to the degree of their guilt." This lamentable state of the affairs of the burgh, and much more, is detailed at length in the Act of 1661 confirming the union of the two burghs, from which these quotations are made.

Rosemarkie, like its sister burgh of Fortrose, has also a well-sheltered and very fine sea-bathing beach, which ought to make its fortune. Its principal antiquarian attraction is its beautifully executed runic cross or sculptured stone, originally found under the floor of its old church and now standing in the church-yard at the north-west corner of the substantial and stately modern edifice which occupies the site of its ancient predecessor. The cross is panelled and covered on both sides with very fine Celtic ornamentation. The stone is unfortunately broken into two parts, only kept together by supports and bandages, but is otherwise in a good state of preservation. It must, however, get destroyed in time from exposure to the elements, and some place should be found for such a valuable Celtic treasure inside the Church, or in Fortrose Cathedral.

It is said that Saint Maluag or Lagadius, abbot and bishop of Lismore, who died in 577, established a Columban monastery in Rosemarkie.   The old Church is said to have been founded by Saint Boniface, an Italian, surnamed Queretinus, who came to Scotland in the seventh or eighth century with the object of persuading the leaders of the Celtic Church of the period to conform to the Church of Rome.   He is said to have settled at Rosemarkie after having built churches in several other parts of the country, and to have erected one here, where he died and was buried.   The Church is referred to in 1510 in the "Aberdeen Breviary," as Saint

Maluag's burying-place.   But in Wynton's Chronicle it is mentioned as being founded and endowed in 716.

THE FAIRY GLEN.

Several specially interesting and instructive excursions can be made from Rosemarkie, particularly to the extraordinary valley and cliffs of boulder clay in the Rosemarkie Burn only half-a-mile distant, and almost seen from the burgh. Mr Angus Beaton in his first local "Guide to Fortrose and Vicinity," published in 1885, supplies the following graphic description :—

Immediately on leaving the town we observe the huge cliffs of boulder clay which recede from the shore far up the glen. The view looking northward from here is grand, for Rosemarkie Burn is one of the most charming scenes in the vicinity, with its red weather-worn cliffs of boulder clay, the denudation of many a winter's blast carving this huge mass into a thousand fantastic forms ; here towering for two hundred feet to a pinnacle capped by a solitary boulder ; there to perpendicular cliffs perforated with many a swallow's nestling abode like the cannon-shattered battlements of some ancient castle ; anon receding in deep-winding gullies, formed by the winter torrents of many ages ; while in the background, in summer, the varie-gated foliage forms a scene well worthy of its name, "The Fairy Glen."

Mr Beaton truly adds that apart from its scenic beauty the glen offers to the geologist a most interesting and puzzling problem—how such a vast accumulation of glacier debris could have been deposited in this particular locality, without any indication of the main flow of glaciers in its direction ? Hugh Miller, who did not himself venture any solution of this difficult problem, describes the scenery and the situation in powerful and characteristic style. From his description we abridge the following :—

Rosemarkie, with its long narrow valley and its abrupt red scaurs is chiefly interesting to the geologist for its vast beds of boulder clay. I am acquainted with no other locality in the kingdom where this deposit is hollowed into ravines so profound, or presents precipices so imposing and lofty.

It presents the appearance of a hill that had been cut sheer through the middle from top to base, and exhibits in its abrupt front a broad red perpendicular section of at least one hundred feet in height, barred transversely by thin layers of sand, and scored vertically by the slow action of the rains. Originally it must have stretched its vanished limb across the opening, like some huge snow-wreath accumulated athwart a frozen rivulet ; but only half the hill now remains. The clay presents here, more than in almost any other locality with which I am acquainted, the character of a stratified deposit. A little higher up the valley, on the western side, there occurs in the clay what may be termed a group of excavations of considerable depth and extent—hollows out of which the materials of pyramids might have been taken. The precipitous sides are fretted by jutting ridges and receding inflections that present in abundance their diversified alternations of light and shadow. Viewed by moonlight these excavations of the valley of Rosemarkie form scenes of strange and ghostly wildness ; the projecting buttress-like angles, the broken walls, the curved inflections, the pointed pinnacles—the turrets, with their masses of projecting coping—the utter lack of vegetation, save where the heath and furze rustle far above—all combine to form assemblages of dreary ruins, amid which, in the solitude of night, we almost expect to see spirits walk.

This excursion may be continued to St. Helena, a point on the height from which an exceedingly fine, varied, and extensive view of the surrounding country, including mountain, valley, and sea, is obtained in every direction. It is much resorted to by picnic parties. Other objects of interest are met with on the Invergordon and Cromarty Road, such as the massive " Carn Glas," about three and a half miles out, and along the high ground for some three miles westward from this point are several cairns and mounds said to mark an ancient battlefield where a severe contest was fought between the Scots and the Danes. Under one of these, called by the natives " Carn-a-chath," or the cairn of the contest, stone coffins and weapons of copper and other metals were discovered, which corroborate an old tradition still current that a great Danish chief was buried under it.

Another most interesting excursion is, either on foot or by boat, to the Burn of Eathie, seven miles eastward from Rosemarkie, along the shore of the Moray Firth. This burn is immortalised by Hugh Miller in his "Red Sandstone," and it would be difficult to find a spot where the geologist can spend a more profitable day's outing.

Excursionists from Inverness to Fortrose and Rosemarkie during the season may go by steamer from Thornbush Pier and return by railway, or reverse the journey, going by rail and returning by steamer.

The opening of the extended Course of the Fortrose and Rosemarkie Golf Club, on Chanonry Ness, adds greatly to the attractiveness of these Black Isle watering-places and to the popularity of a links which, in every respect except area, is an ideal home of golf. For more than a century, golf has been played on this ground, which stretches, in the shape of a narrowing peninsula, between the Moray Firth and the Inverness Firth, and commands magnificent views of their shores and of the mountains behind. The new first hole is 508 yards from the tee, and is named "Fort George," after the headquarters of the Seaforths, from which it is separated by about a mile of channel. The next three holes—"Chanonry," "Culloden," and "Rosehaugh"—also bear names of note specially applicable to the prospects they command. The links may be said indeed to be historic ground; there is a hole called after "Coinneach Odhar," the Brahan Seer, and one drives for the home hole from beside the stone cross where the unlucky possessor of Second Sight was burned to death for prophesying too truly. It may be of interest to those who care to combine botanising with golf to know that several plants, rare or found nowhere else in Scotland, grow on the course. A greater number will be pleased to learn that excellent hotel accommodation is to be had within a few minutes' walk of the links, at Hawkhill, Kincurdy, and Fortrose.

INVERNESS TO STRATHPEFFER, LOCH MAREE, AND GAIRLOCH, STROMEFERRY, SKYE, AND THE OUTER HEBRIDES.

MUIR OF ORD TO DINGWALL AND STRATHPEFFER.

RESUMING the journey north at Muir of Ord Junction, where we broke off for the Black Isle Railway, the train on leaving the station dashes across the neck of the Black Isle, and enters the valley of the Conon, on the opposite side of which, in the face of the hill, Brahan Castle, the ancient seat of the Mackenzies of Kintail and Seaforth, rears its head among the trees which adorn its time-honoured surroundings. Originally turreted, it was dismantled and completely modernised in outward appearance by Francis Humberston Mackenzie, who died in 1815, a performance which has been severely condemned as utterly devoid of the good taste and reverence for the past history of his race which might be expected of a man otherwise so high-souled and so eminent in intellect and in his country's annals as the "Last of the Seaforths" undoubtedly was. The fertile valley of Strathconon opens up to the left. Before pulling up at Conon Station, the train skirts for a considerable distance the extensive wooded policies in which, on the bank of the river, lie embosomed Conon House, the East Coast residence of Sir Kenneth Mackenzie of Gairloch. On leaving this station, the first glimpse is obtained of the Cromarty Firth, which forms the northern boundary of the Black Isle. The scenery on both sides, as seen from this point, is beautiful and diversified in the extreme. In a few minutes more, after crossing the River Conon by a stone viaduct of some 400 feet, passing the village of Conon on the right, and of Maryburgh on the left, the train pulls up at

DINGWALL,

the Capital of Ross-shire, an ancient Royal Burgh, having, according to the census of 1891, a population of 2290 souls. The principal points of interest here are the site of the Castle, on "St Colin's Isle," which, in the thirteenth, fourteenth, and fifteenth centuries belonged to the old Earls of Ross, and of which the foundations and fosse are still pointed out. There is also a very tall obelisk, erected to the memory of Sir Roderick Mor Mackenzie of Coigach, the famous "Tutor of Kintail," ancestor of the Earls of Cromartie, who is buried in its vicinity. The principal hotels in Dingwall are Robertson's National and Mackenzie's Caledonian.

STRATHPEFFER.

From Dingwall a short branch railway sets down the tourist in the attractive and ever-improving village of Strathpeffer, where ample accommodation of the very best can be procured at the Spa, the Ben Wyvis, the Strathpeffer, several private Hotels, and in the numerous and costly residences and lodging-houses which have been erected during recent years for the special entertainment of the thousands who, in search of pleasure, recreation, or health, annually throng this beautifully-situated and well-sheltered summer resort. Leaving the main line at Dingwall, the Strathpeffer train, after passing over a sharp curve, enters the beautiful and rich agricultural valley of the Peffrey, at the head of which, four and three quarters miles distant, is, protected by the surrounding hills and woods, the famous health-restoring Strathpeffer Spa.

On the left, about a mile on its way, the train skirts the base of Knockfarrel, the summit of which is crowned by a most perfect specimen of the pre-historic vitrified fort, of which so many remains are found in the Highlands—and

From Photo. by]   **Strathpeffer.**   [J. Valentine & Sons

The Spa Hotel, Strathpeffer.

A. WALLACE, *Manager.*

which every visitor to Strathpeffer should make a point of seeing. A most extensive and magnificent view is obtained from the summit.

A short distance above the Spa a great Clan battle, known as "Blar-na-Pairc," or the Battle of Park, was fought, about 1488, between the Mackenzies of Kintail and the Macdonalds of the Isles, in which the latter were completely defeated and their leader taken prisoner.

It was predicted by "Coinneach Odhar Fiosaiche," the far-famed Brahan Seer, that the time would yet come when this charming valley should be covered by an arm of the sea and when stately ships would ride at anchor in the immediate vicinity of the village.

DINGWALL TO ACHNASHEEN, ON THE SKYE LINE.

The train from Dingwall for Stromeferry parts with the direct line to Strathpeffer about two miles from Dingwall, proceeding to the right, across the valley, along a high and steep embankment, continuing in its course until it arrives at Achterneed Station, from which point, only a mile from the Spa, a fine view is obtained of Strathpeffer and its surroundings. Knockfarrel stands out conspicuously on the opposite side, forming the eastern terminus of a picturesque range of hills—the "Cat's Back"—which shelters Loch Ussie and the historic Castle of Brahan and policies on their northern side, while at the same time it forms the southern slope of the Strathpeffer Valley. Just below us is the ivy-covered, picturesque, and historic Castle Leod, the property of the Countess of Cromartie, who also owns the Spa, now seen ensconced at the top of the Strath, surrounded by a number of fine villas, hotels, and churches, which are fast raising Strathpeffer to the dignity of a town.

About a mile beyond Achterneed, the view of the Strathpeffer Valley seen to great advantage all the time, the train enters the striking gorge formed on the one side by the precipitous "Creag-an-fhithich," or the Raven's Rock, in

the recesses of which "Alastair Ionraic," sixth Baron Mackenzie of Kintail, then over eighty years of age, found shelter
from the enemy, while his valiant sons, Kenneth a Bhlair,
Duncan of Hilton, and Hector Roy of Gairloch, were
slaughtering the Macdonalds at the Battle of Park.   Until
this railway was made, a raven annually made his nest in
the face of this towering precipice, hence its name.

The grandeur and beauty of the scenery through which
the Skye Railway passes are most impressive, while the
historical and traditional interest of many points along
the route can scarcely be surpassed.

Having got through the Pass of the Raven's Rock, the
summit is reached, and the train runs along a singularly
bleak mile or two, leaving on the left the Falls of Rogie,
and the scattered remains of Tarvie Wood, notorious when
in its native prime for its highway robberies. Crossing the
Blackwater, in a few minutes the train skirts a high range
of hills, also on the left, and dashes along the shore of Loch
Garve, a fine sheet of water on the right, with the wooded
slope of Strath-Garve, and Mr C. A. Hanbury's beautiful
Highland residence, surrounded by its variegated hues, on
the same side.

Leaving Garve Station, there is a steep ascent of 1 in 50.
On the right will be seen, winding along, the Dirie Mor
Coach Road to Ullapool. Proceeding along the line, the
tourist soon comes in sight of Lochluichart on the left,
a sheet of water lying deep down between two ranges of
high hills, then passes along through charming woodland
scenery on the estate of Lady Ashburton, and, after stopping
at Lochluichart Station, leaves the Falls of Grudie on the
right. The train in its further progress skirts Loch Coolin,
a fine trouting loch, with the wooded slope of that name,
also famed in the traditions of the district for its highway
robberies, rising from its northern bank. The train soon
pulls up at Achanalt Station, where, and as it passes along
on its way to Achnasheen, a good view is obtained of the

towering Scuirvuillin and its attendant satellites as you skirt their base.

ACHNASHEEN TO LOCH-MAREE AND GAIRLOCII.

At Achnasheen, the next station, where there is a comfortable Hotel, passengers for Loch Maree and Gairloch leave the train and start on that glorious route by coach. On the left a series of well-marked and striking gravel terraces are passed, after which the coach bounds along the north bank of Loch Rosque for a distance of four miles over a level road, until it reaches Luib-Mhor at the west end of the lake, where for generations the "Black" House at the roadside on the right was a licensed hostelry, largely taken advantage of by the humbler class of travellers, but it is now a mere black dwelling-house.   At this point, the coach begins to climb, until all of a sudden, two miles further on, it comes in sight, at a considerable altitude, of the far-famed Loch Maree, that "mountain-set mirror," the grand and magnificent surroundings of which were so much admired and enjoyed by Her Majesty during her week's residence in the district.   An excellent view of its whole length, but by no means the best, is here obtained.   The features and surroundings of this lovely loch, eighteen miles in length, studded with 27 richly-wooded islands, including the famous Isle Maree, its endless promontories and creeks, walled round by lofty and precipitous mountain barriers, are magnificent and grand beyond description.

The towering Ben Slioch on the north, 3217 feet above the level of the sea, is peerless in its unique form and solid grandeur.   Its curiously-shaped rival Ben Aye, or File Mountain, opposite, on the south side of the loch, is in its own way equally striking and grand.   Between them, and with their huge and lofty attendants surrounding the placid lake, embosomed in their grip, they produce a panorama for combined beauty, magnificence, and granduer, unrivalled in the Highlands, and, according to far-travelled people, unsur-

passed in the world. This glorious district is full of historical
and traditional lore, but the visitor must be left to discover
this for himself.

Passing along the southern shore of the loch, through the
Kinlochewe forest, over one of the most interesting drives, and
amid the most varied and magnificent scenery in the Highlands, the coach comes in sight of the Loch Maree Hotel,
where the Queen and her suite lodged for a week in 1877—
" a home from home"—situated in a beautiful bay, immediately opposite a cluster of twenty-seven richly-wooded islands
in the lake, and sheltered on the south by towering hills
similarly wooded.

Horses are changed at the Loch Maree Hotel, after which
the coach winds along the variegated woods and wild steep
promontories of Stron-a-Choit. Crossing the River Garbhaig
by a substantial stone bridge, a fine cascade, called the
Victoria Fall, to commemorate Her Majesty's visit, is observed
a few yards to the left. About a mile further on, the Gairloch
road takes a turn to the left, while Loch Maree curves away
to the right. But still the view continues to improve, until,
after a stiff ascent, looking back upon the whole scene of
mountain, lake, cascade, and richly-covered islands, with the
giant Slioch towering to a height of over 3200 feet in
the distance, is completed the most magnificent and
grandest panorama which it is possible to conceive.

You soon leave Loch-Bhad-na-Sgalag, a fine sheet of
water, on your left, and begin to descend the rugged, steep,
and winding valley of the Kerry, with its waterfalls and
eddies, until, passing through the thickly-wooded and lovely
glens of Kerrisdale and Flowerdale, the coach pulls up at
the Gairloch Hotel. From here a splendid view is obtained
of the Torridon Hills, the Minch, and the Isle of Skye.
Gairloch is a fine sea-bathing place, and for the tourist who
is able to spend a few days in the district, there is excellent
sea and trout fishing, while the lovely walks all about the
district, and the centres of interest commemorated in song

and story within short walking distance of the Hotel, will prove most attractive to the lover of nature, the antiquarian, and archæologist.

THE ISLE OF SKYE.

From Gairloch the tourist is taken in one of Mr Macbrayne's steamers to Portree.   From the deck may be seen on the left the towering Ben Alligin, the mountains of Torridon and Applecross, the islands of Rona and Raasay and on the right, in the Isle of Skye, the famous Quairang, the Stoer Rock, and the entrance to Prince Charlie's Cave. Turning in to the narrow Kyle between Rona and Raasay on the one hand, and Skye on the other, the tourist soon finds himself sailing into the pretty, well-sheltered Bay of Portree, where, if he intends to see the lions of Skye, he will go ashore.

From Portree, where there are two good hotels, the Portree and the Royal, the visitor can visit Kingsburgh, where during his wanderings after the '45 Prince Charles slept for a night ; Uig Bay, where there is a most comfortable hotel, and from which Kilmuir, the burial place of the famous Flora Macdonald, over which a fine monumental Iona Cross is erected, and the Quairang, can be visited.   There are also Coruisk, the Coolin Hills, and many minor points of historic and romantic interest to be seen in the famous Isle of Mist. Two other excellent and central hotels are the Broadford and the Sligachan, the latter being the nearest to Coruisk and the most convenient to visit it from.

When at Dunvegan, the tourist should make a point of visiting Dunvegan Castle, the ancient seat of the Macleods of Macleod, one of the oldest inhabited strongholds in Scotland, and containing some very curious relics of the long, long ago.   There is a comfortable hotel within a mile of it.

THE OUTER HEBRIDES.

Those visiting the Lewis can get one of Mr Macbrayne's steamers twice a week from Kyleakin, Broadford, or Portree, and from Kyle of Lochalsh daily on the arrival of the south

mail train in the afternoon.   In good weather the sail is a
very enjoyable one, and there are three excellent hotels in
Stornoway, the Imperial, the Royal, and the Lewis, where
refreshment for the inner man and the best accommodation
can be found.   The most noted places of interest in the
Lewis are the famous Standing Stones at Callernish, and
Dun Carloway, 14 and 17 miles respectively by road, from
Stornoway.

The steamboat service between Skye and the other portions
of the Outer Hebrides has been much improved of late
years, and comfortable hotels can now be found in each of
the group which form what is generally termed " The Long
Island."   There is a commodious hotel in Tarbert, Harris,
the only licensed one in the island ; a very comfortable one
at Lochmaddy, in North Uist ; one in Benbecula ; another
excellent one at Lochboisdale, South Uist ; and one at
Castlebay, Barra.   Good fishing can be had at most of these,
but for all such information, and steamer sailings, the reader
must consult the Advertisement section of the Guide, as
they are repeatedly changing.

FROM SKYE TO INVERNESS.

Having seen all the wonders of Skye and the Outer
Hebrides the tourist may rejoin one of Mr Macbrayne's
boats at Portree, Broadford, or Kyleakin, continue his course
southward through the Kyles of Sleat and Bute, to Oban,
or proceed by the Dingwall and Skye Railway, *via* Kyle of
Lochalsh and Achnasheen to Inverness, getting a fine
parting view of the Coolins and the other glorious hills of
Skye, with the blue mountains of Kintail, Strathglass, and
Torridon ahead of him in the distance and on either side.
Passing Plockton, a thriving village, Duncraig Castle, the
principal West Coast residence of Sir Kenneth James
Matheson, Baronet of Lochalsh, with its picturesque surroundings, is soon left behind immediately below the line,
and in a few minutes more, after crossing the mouth of the
Fernaig Valley and closely skirting the shore of Loch-
carron the train pulls up at Stromeferry, where there is

a very good hotel and posting establishment. The ruined Castle of Strone, now Strome, is observed on an elevated promontory on the opposite shore of the loch. Four hundred years ago it was a stonghold of the Macdonalds of Glengarry, who for a time possessed also the lands in its neighbourhood, until driven out of it early in the seventeenth century by the Mackenzies. Next to it is the North Strome Hotel, a comfortable country hostelry. The view from the Stromeferry Hotel door is very fine, and if one cares to climb to the top of the hills behind it the panorama is simply magnificent in every direction, including Skye and the Outer Hebrides. The run from Stromeferry Station, skirting the seashore in sharp curves immediately below precipitous rocks in close proximity to the train is most interesting, and the opposite slope of Lochcarron parish, with the pretty village of Jeantown as a foreground, looks very pretty. The train soon pulls up six miles further on, at Attadale, close to which is observed on the right another of Sir Kenneth Matheson's West Coast residences. A minute later Strathcarron Station, having a comfortable hotel quite close to it, is passed, and the train in a few minutes enters the beautiful Valley of Achnashellach, and its extensive deer forest. The Lodge, ensconced by the surrounding plantations and sheltered by towering mountains, is left on the right, while the train climbs up the stiff ascent, with the pretty Burn of Achnashellach as its companion for a few miles, passing Glencarron Lodge on the left, until it reaches the watershed and pulls up at Achnasheen Station, where at page 79 the reader parted with the Railway on his way north for Loch Maree and Gairloch. From here he finds his way south to Dingwall and Inverness exactly reversing the route already described at pp. 56 to 59, and 77 to 79.

DINGWALL TO TAIN, BONAR-BRIDGE, HELMSDALE, WICK, AND THURSO.

DINGWALL TO TAIN.

RESUMING the journey from Inverness to the North on the main line the train going in the direction of Tain, Bonar-Bridge, Wick, and Thurso, on leaving the Dingwall Station, skirts the northern shore of the Cromarty Firth, and soon arrives at Fowlis Station, where a passing glimpse can be obtained of Fowlis Castle among the trees on the left. On the right, across the firth, the Black Isle slopes down to the shore. Here the ancient ruin of Castle Craig, at one time the summer residence of the Bishops of Ross, is a prominent object. Near the railway may be observed the farmhouse of Inchchoulter, built on the site of the historic Castle of Balconie, an ancient Easter Ross stronghold of the great Earls of Ross. Novar Station is soon passed, the principal objects of interest in the neighbourhood being the Black Rock, and Novar House, the Highland residence of Mr Munro-Ferguson, M.P., with a curious-looking arrangement of high standing-stones, representing an Indian temple, on the summit of the Hill of Fyrish, towering above it on the left. The village of Alness, chiefly famous for its distilleries, is next reached, after which, skirting the policies of Invergordon Castle, hidden away among the trees, the train pulls up at Invergordon Station. This is a thriving Police Burgh, having in 1891 a population of 1046. Possessing a fine harbour, it carries on a considerable trade in shipping. From here a good view is obtained of the burgh of Cromarty, situated on the opposite side of the entrance to the firth, chiefly distinguished as the birthplace of Hugh Miller, the famous mason-geologist.

The traveller now enters the region commonly known as Easter Ross, a flat and fertile district equal to any part of the Lothians. Passing Delny and Kildary Stations, near the former of which stands the Pollo Distillery, the roofs of Balnagown Castle and of Tarbat House may be seen above the surrounding trees. Nigg and Fearn Stations are successively left behind; but there is nothing in the course of this part of the journey which particularly strikes the eye except the extensive level reaches of enclosed land, and the high state of cultivation and fertility of the soil. Leaving Fearn, the ruined Castle of Loch Slin, the birthplace of Sir George Mackenzie of Rose-haugh, is a prominent feature in the distance. In a few minutes the Dornoch Firth comes in sight, the mountains of Sutherland towering away in the background, some of them rising to an altitude of more than 3000 feet. To the right, across the firth, the town of Dornoch lies low on the point of a peninsula, the tower of the Cathedral, built early in the thirteenth century, for many generations afterwards in ruins, and restored to its present position about sixty years ago, being its most prominent object. In a few minutes, and having passed the roofless ruin of the ancient Chapel of St. Duthus, close to the line, the train pulls up at Tain Station, 25¾ miles from Dingwall, and 44¼ from Inverness.

TAIN TO INVERSHIN.

Tain, situated on a high terrace above the station on the left, is a Royal Burgh of great antiquity, containing several buildings of historical interest. St. Duthus' Church, a very fine specimen of middle-pointed Gothic, founded in 1471, was in more recent times for many generations a ruin, until it was restored, through the liberality of a patriotic native, about thirty years ago. Here it was, within the Abbey of St. Duthus, that, in 1472-73, James IV. of Scotland was born. Afterwards he made at least seventeen annual pilgrimages to the venerable fane of the "blessed Bishop of Ross" at Tain, from 1496, if not earlier, to 1513, his last being in August of the latter, in which year he fell on the fatal field of Flodden.

Tain has a population of about 2000, and possesses an excellent Academy for higher class education. The town also boasts of two good hotels—the Royal and the Balnagown Arms.

Proceeding, the passenger, two miles and a half on the journey, will observe a road striking away to the right, leading to the Meikle Ferry, which in the good old coaching days was crossed by passengers for the north, instead of going round by Bonar-Bridge, thus shortening the journey by 11 or 12 miles. Skibo Castle, sheltered by its compact and beautifully-wooded policies, is here seen to advantage directly opposite.

From this point the train keeps close to the firth. Leaving the Free Church and Manse and then the Parish Church and Manse on the left, it pulls up at Edderton Station. The scenery here is strikingly varied and picturesque, the line running almost close to the water's edge, all along, until it arrives at Bonar-Bridge Station, the thriving village of that name being a mile distant on the other side of the Kyle. There is a railway refreshment room at Bonar-Bridge, the only one between Dingwall and Wick, more than a hundred miles distant. The Balnagown Arms, a comfortable country hotel, is close by. Leaving Bonar-Bridge, the train rushes along a terraced plain, with the Kyle, which again considerably widens above the village of Bonar, on the right. The whole of this estuary—which is tidal for several miles into the interior of the country as far as Invercassley—is, above Bonar Bridge, called the Kyle of Sutherland. About a mile before reaching Invershin the train crosses the River Carron by a stone bridge of three arches, almost immediately after which it is carried over the River Oykel, near Culrain platform, by a latticed iron girder viaduct of 230 feet span, and 55 feet above spring tides, with a continuation of five arches—two on the Ross-shire and three on the Sutherland side.

IN SUTHERLANDSHIRE.

The traveller now finds himself in the county of Sutherland, and the train almost immediately afterwards stops at Invershin Station. It next proceeds to Lairg, running due north,

along the east bank of the Shin. The course of the river
is very rocky, and in some places rough and wild, the falls,
a short distance from the station, being well worth seeing.
During the first mile beyond Invershin the line has a
gradient of 1 in 72. About half-way up the valley, Achany
House, the Sutherlandshire residence of the Mathesons of
the Lewis, is passed on the left, after which the glen widens
into a broad pastoral valley. In the course of this ascent
a fine view is obtained from the carriage windows, of the
Kyle of Sutherland, Strath Oykel, and the whole of the
surrounding country, with the great hills and mountains of
Ross-shire in the distant background. In a few minutes
the train stops at Lairg, within two miles of Loch Shin,
a magnificent sheet of water, 20 miles long. Here there
is a first-class hotel—the Sutherland Arms—very much
frequented during the season, not only by those who go
there to enjoy the splendid fishing on the lochs and rivers,
but who travel from this point by mail gig, or private conveyance, to Lochinver, to Scourie, to Tongue, and Durness
on the west and north-west coast of Sutherland, the roads
to which all converge at Lairg. At each of these places
there is a very good hotel, particularly at Tongue and
Lochinver.

Leaving Lairg Station, the line turns eastward, and shortly
after descends through the valley of Strath Fleet for several
miles by a gradient of 1 in 84, stopping at Rogart after a
run of ten miles. At the next Station, four miles farther
on, the Mound across Loch Fleet, from which the station
takes its name, strikes the eye. It is an embankment 1000
yards in length, over which the coach road was carried
across Loch Fleet, an arm of the sea, and was constructed
by the Commissioners of Highland Roads and Bridges at
a cost of £12,500. Before its construction, the passengers
by coach had to be ferried at the narrow entrance of the
Loch, known as the Little Ferry, seen several miles below.
On the opposite side are the ruins of Skelbo Castle, at

one time the Highland residence of the Sutherlands of Duffus.

DORNOCH.

Dornoch, the Capital of Sutherlandshire, seven miles distant from The Mound, is an ancient and interesting town, with a Cathedral dating from the beginning of the 13th century ; is pleasantly situated on the Dornoch Firth, with an amphitheatre of hills around, and possesses a beautiful sea beach and magnificent links which afford exceptional facilities for bathing and golfing.   The Links of Dornoch, the Northward Ho ! of Scotland, form one of the most extensive stretches of golfing ground in the British Isles.   The course consists of 18 holes, and is, according to a recent survey, slightly over 3 miles in length.   There are two comfortable hotels here.

GOLSPIE AND DUNROBIN CASTLE.

A mile and a half past Mound Station the village of Golspie is reached.   It has a population of between 1000 and 1100, and a first-class hotel—the Sutherland Arms—two branch banks, and two churches.   On the top of Ben Bhraggie, behind the village, at an altitude of 1250 feet, stands out conspicuously a colossal statue, 30 feet high, on a pedestal of 75 feet in height, of the present Duke's great-grandfather.   It is seen for a long distance in every direction, and from as far as Tain in the west.

But what will interest the tourist most in this locality is Dunrobin Castle, the Highland seat of the Duke of Sutherland, a magnificent structure, three-quarters of a mile beyond Golspie, on the right, between the railway and the sea, and surrounded by extensive and very finely wooded grounds.   It stands on a terrace about 80 feet above the level of the sea, which ripples but a very short distance from its walls.   The greater part of it is modern, but some portions, including the old keep, were founded as early as 1097.   It is a noble-looking building, worthy of the rank, position, and great opulence of its owner.   Visitors are always made welcome to visit both the mansion and policies when the family are non-resident, and generally even when they are at home. There are several monuments about the grounds, one fine full-length statue of the second Duke standing at the side of the public road.

Six miles from Golspie, Brora is reached, a thriving and growing village, in the neighbourhood of which are the Duke of Sutherland's coal mines, re-opened in 1872, after having been closed for many years. Loth Station is soon passed, five and a half miles further on, and after another run of equal distance, the train pulls up at Helmsdale, 82¾ miles from Dingwall.

HELMSDALE TO WICK AND THURSO.

Helmsdale lies down in a hollow, on the right, where the river of that name enters the sea. It is a village of considerable consequence, mainly on account of its herring fishing in the summer and autumn. In the immediate neighbourhood of the station are the ruins of an ancient castle, built by Margaret,' Dowager Countess of Sutherland, in the 15th century. It is chiefly memorable for a diabolical murder which took place within its walls in 1587. In that year it was visited by the Earl and Countess of Sutherland, and their son and heir, when Isabel Sinclair resolved to poison the three in order to open up the Sutherland succession to her son John, who was the next heir. She succeeded in the case of the Earl and Countess, but her own son by a providential mishap fell a victim to her iniquitous plot, while the heir of Sutherland escaped.

From Helmsdale the train proceeds up the valley of Kildonan, at one time occupied by a large population, but now, after the first two or three miles, quite desolate. Near Kildonan Station, which is next reached, the Helmsdale is joined by two mountain streams, the Kildonan and Suisgill, where the Sutherland gold diggings were carried on for a short time, and with varying success, in 1868 and

1869. Climbing up the valley, some 8 miles, Kinbrace Station is reached, from which point there is a direct public road, along the beautiful valley of the Naver, to Bettyhill and Tongue, from whence the tourist can proceed to either Thurso or Lairg by coach. Seven and a half miles further on is Forsinard Station. The only points of interest which will strike the eye here are Loch Ruar, on the left, fished free by visitors at the Forsinard Hotel, with Ben Griam Mor and Ben Griam Beg away in the distant background on the same side, at an altitude of 1930 and 1900 feet respectively; while still further, in the same direction, an excellent view is obtained of Ben Loyal, 2500 feet, and of Ben Hope, 3040 feet above the level of the sea. At Forsinard the line turns away to the east, and immediately afterwards the Caithness mountains—Morven, 2310 feet, Scaraven, 2060 feet, and the Maiden Pap, 1590 feet high—are observed prominently on the right.

The traveller now finds himself

IN THE COUNTY OF CAITHNESS,

and for miles passes through the most uninteresting country imaginable—nothing but a wide expanse of stunted heath and peat moss. Aultnabreac, famous for its winter snowblocks, is left behind, 8¼ miles from Forsinard. Next comes Scotscalder, 9¼; and Halkirk, 2½ miles further, situated on the Thurso River, is passed, after which cultivated fields again come in sight. Here a good view is obtained of Brawl Castle on the left, the origin of which is lost in the dim annals of antiquity. As early as 1375 it is referred to in charters of the period. Its style is very primitive, being only a stage removed from that of the round towers. In this vicinity is held the Georgemas Sheep Market in July of each year, just immediately before the great Inverness Sheep and Wool Fair. Georgemas Junction is reached 1½ miles further on, where a branch line breaks off for Thurso, 7 miles distant, but the main line goes direct to

Wick, passing through fine arable land, extending as far as the eye can reach on either side of the railway. Bower is first passed, 3 miles from Georgemas Junction, then Watten, 7; and finally Bilbster Station, 9 miles. Passing Loch Stemster on the left, and Loch Watten, a fine sheet of water on the right, the train pulls up at

WICK,

14 miles from Georgemas Junction, 161 from Inverness, and 305 from Perth. The ordinary population of Wick is about 8000, but during the herring fishing—from the beginning of July until the first week in September—it is nearly double that number. It is a Royal Burgh, its incorporation dating from 1589. Several most interesting excursions can be made from Wick—to the old Castles of Oldwick, Keiss, Girnigo, and Sinclair, to the Tower of Ackergill, and John O'Groat's House, the latter, however, being reached with about equal conveniénce from Thurso. The principal hotels in Wick are the Station and Caledonian, both comfortable.

The traveller, after visiting Wick, and the many places of historical, antiquarian, and archæological interest in its vicinity, can proceed by rail to

THURSO,

changing carriages at Georgemas Junction, 14 miles to the south on the main line, or, if he wishes to visit Thurso first, he can leave the Wick train at that Junction on his way north, and afterwards reverse the journey from Thurso to Wick, the distance between the two being 21 miles. Leaving Georgemas Junction the line runs due north, close to the famous fishing Thurso river. The town is a Burgh of Barony, containing a population of about 4000. In the immediate neighbourhood, to the east, is Thurso Castle, the modern residence of Sir J. G. Tollmache Sinclair, who owns the land on which Thurso is built. Further on, in the same direction, is Harold's Tower, commemorating the death of the Norse Earl of that name, who fell in battle

while defending himself against Earl ·Harrold the Wicked
in 1190. On the west side of the town the ruins of an
ancient castle, at one time the residence of the Bishops of
Caithness, can be visited.   Within two miles is the fine
anchorage of Scrabster Roads, while the Pentland Firth,
with its impetuous, dangerous, and eternal eddies and currents,
stretches itself in front between the mainland and the Orkney
Islands.   The famous John O'Groat's House, visited annually
by thousands from all parts of the world, is about twenty
miles distant by an excellent road through scenery of the
most beautiful and varied character.   At John O'Groat's
there is a very good hotel, and in Thurso, the Royal, Commercial, and St. Clair.

INVERNESS TO BEAULY AND THE FALLS OF
KILMORACK, BY COACH.

FROM Inverness to Lentran the coach road runs along the side of the railway, and a full description of all the points of interest on that part of the journey will be found at pages 56 and 57. The coach road, a short distance beyond Lentran railway station takes a detour to the left, passing, a mile further on, Bogroy Inn on the right.

A few yards past, and half way between the inn and the Free Church and manse on the left, a road strikes off to the right which leads to the Established Church and manse of Kirkhill, and terminates, two miles distant, at the Churchyard, which contains a curious old mortuary Chapel in which several of the old Lovat Chiefs are buried. The most interesting object in this ancient building, next to the decapitated remains of Simon of the 'Forty-five, is a memorial bearing a curious inscription, partly in English and partly in Latin, erected by that extraordinary man, ostensibly to his father, Lord Thomas of Beaufort, but really to commemorate his own transcendant virtues! The inscription, couched in eulogistic terms, will be found at length in Mackenzie's *History of the Frasers*, under Lord Simon.

Soon after the memorial was erected, Sir Robert Munro, killed at Falkirk in 1745, was on a visit to Lord Lovat, when they proceeded to have a look at the monument. Upon reading the inscription Sir Robert addressed his lordship, saying, " Simon, how the devil came you to have the assurance to put up such a boasting and romantic inscription?" to which the latter at once replied—"The monument and inscription are chiefly calculated for the Frasers, who must believe whatever I, their Chief, require of them, and their posterity will think it as true as the

Gospel "—a prediction which it is feared has not been verified.

Continuing the coach route by the main road, and passing the Free Church, with the manse a little distance behind it, we reach, a mile further on, a small stone bridge, where we observe Reelick House immediately on the left, and Moniack Castle, a portion of which is very old, a short distance further west, both snugly sheltered on either side of the gorge formed by the Moniack Burn, so interesting to the geologist and the botanist. At once after crossing this bridge, the road takes a sharp turn, first to the right, then to the left, and continues up a gentle ascent until the highest altitude on the route is reached. From this point a magnificent view is obtained in every direction. The whole stretch of the Aird, extending for miles, is seen from east to west, Beaufort Castle, a massive modern erection, forming the most striking object, is observed on the left, with the Strathglass hills rising to a height of more than 3400 feet right in front. The extensive low-lying and fertile lands of the Beauly district come gradually in sight on the right, until, as the coach rattles down the declivity leading to the bridge, the village itself, the picturesque ruins of the ancient Priory, and the Church of Cilliechriost, come fully into view. The coach, after crossing Telford's famous bridge, partly carried away by the great floods of 1892, and re-built in 1894, drives first into Beauly, in order that the passengers may visit the Priory and other places of interest, and also, if so disposed, refresh the inner man at the Lovat Arms Hotel, after which the drive is resumed to the Falls of Kilmorack, where ample time is given for the exploration and full enjoyment of the glorious scenery and romantic surroundings of that far-famed locality.

THE FALLS OF KILMORACK AND THE DRUIM.

Visitors who go by rail must either hire or walk from Beauly, a distance of two miles, to see the Falls, and two to three miles farther to get a view of the remarkable gorge cut out of the Druim, and of the marvellous beauties of Eilean Aigas. The scenery here is unsurpassed by anything of its kind in the Highlands, and will well repay the very moderate trouble and expense of seeing it. The "Druim" (which really means the ridge through which this great gorge had been cut by the river; not, as has been supposed by non-Gaelic speakers, the gorge itself) has been poetically and graphically described by the late Dr Charles Mackay, the poet, as follows :—

> In Lomond's isles the rowans grow.
> In sweet Glennant the lintocks tarry,
> And grand is Cruachan by Loch-Awe,
> And bonny are the birks of Garry.
> Beloved spots !—yet dearer far,
> And cherish'd in my heart more truly,
> Are sweet Kilmorack's lingering falls,
> The lovely "Dream" and banks of Beauly.
>
> The joyous river runs its course,
> Now dark and deep, now clear and shallow ;
> And high on either side the rocks
> Rise, crown'd with mosses green and yellow ;
> And birks, the "damsel of the wood,"
> So slim and delicately shaded,
> Stand in the clefts, and look below,
> With graceful forms and tresses braided.
>
> And rowans flourish on the heights,
> With scarlet bunches thickly studded,
> And brambles, heavy-laden, trail
> Their luscious berries purple-blooded ;
> And on the bosom of the hills,
> Wooing the bees, the modest heather
> Waves to the wind its hardy bells,
> And blossoms in the wildest weather.

The coach does not proceed beyond the Falls, and it takes

8

its passengers direct to Inverness without calling at Beauly
on the return journey.

STRATHGLASS, GUISACHAN, AND GLENURQUHART.

Those who can afford the time and expense should continue this route through the Strathglass valley to Cannich
and Guisachan, cross into Glenurquhart, and drive to Drum-
drochit Hotel at the foot of that charming glen, proceeding
to Inverness by one of Mr Macbrayne's Caledonian Canal
steamers. For a description of Glenurquhart and the Canal
portion of this route see " Inverness to Oban " section,
beginning at page 110.

Eilean Aigas, with its sylvan scenes, was for many years
the favourite residence of the brothers Sobieski Stuart, who
claimed to be the lawful successors of Prince Charles Edward,
the hero of the 'Forty-five ; and, at another period, of the
great Sir Robert Peel. Further up the strath the scenery,
though changed, is beautiful in the extreme, all the way to
Guisachan. The wooded surroundings of Erchless Castle,
the ancient seat of the Chiefs of Chisholm ; the magnificent
scenery of Glenstrathfarrar, Glencannich, and Glenaffric ;
Guisachan House, the Highland residence of Lord Tweed-
mouth, and its policies can all be seen or explored on this
tour. The various and diversified attractions of Strathglass—
its sylvan valleys and towering mountains, its rushing rivers
and endless lakes, its wooded groves and heather-clad
slopes—must be seen, not adequately described.

INVERNESS TO CULLODEN MOOR, DALCROSS, KILRAVOCK, AND CAWDOR CASTLES.

THIS is a fine Excursion by road. Visitors going all the way to Cawdor Castle will find it much cheaper, as well as more convenient and pleasant, to go by Messrs Macrae & Dick's four-in-hand coach, which leaves Inverness on alternate days three times a week, proceeding by Culloden Moor and Kilravock to Cawdor Castle, returning by Dalcross and other places of interest which cannot be seen on the outward journey. Those who can only spare the time to see the battle field, five miles from Inverness, Cumberland's Stone, and the Clava Stone Circles, respectively a quarter of a mile and a mile farther, will have to hire or walk.

Leaving Inverness, the coach will proceed along Petty Street and the Millburn Road, which run parallel with and quite close to the Inverness and Nairn section of the Highland Railway. In a few minutes Millburn House is passed on the left, and the Millburn Distillery and the Cameron Barracks on the right. Immediately afterwards the Perth and Edinburgh coach road, which is the route for Culloden, leaves the Inverness and Nairn road and strikes suddenly to the right—leaving Raigmore House and grounds on the left—and proceeds through a narrow valley until, about a mile and a half from Inverness, it passes the village of Culcabock on the right. Soon after, Inshes House and grounds, for centuries until a few years ago, the family residence of the Robertsons of Inshes, is passed on the same side. Almost opposite the entrance to this mansion house the Culloden road strikes eastward and to the left from the old Perth and Edinburgh Road, along a gentle ascent until the top of the ridge is reached.

Here a magnificent view is obtained in every direction. The town of Inverness is beautifully and peacefully situated on a low-lying and flat peninsula behind ; the Ross-shire hills rise beyond, prominent among them Ben Wyvis, with the Black Isle in the foreground ; while the Sutherland and Caithness mountains extend away to the north, far as the eye can reach. Below, on the left, about three miles distant, is the Moray Firth, Fort-George, and the Point of Chanonry, which appear almost to meet, with Fortrose and Rosemarkie behind, the latter on the north shore, and the Soutars of Cromarty farther east, forming most striking and picturesque objects in the glorious panorama ; while away to the south-west, Mealfourvonie, towering majestically above its neighbouring satellites, on the west side of Loch Ness, completes a picture impossible to surpass anywhere for extent, diversity of scene, variety of colouring, and beauty.

THE BATTLE FIELD OF CULLODEN.

We are soon in sight of a larch plantation, which did not exist at the date of the battle. Passing through it, we all at once drive into an open space and come in sight of an imposing cairn, twenty feet high by about eighteen in diameter, raised a few years ago by Mr Duncan Forbes, proprietor of Culloden, from a shapeless heap of stones gathered together, half a century earlier, with the view of erecting a monument to the followers of Prince Charles who fell on this fatal field on the 16th of April, 1746. The money originally collected for the purpose was shamefully squandered, but the genial owner of Culloden has not only wiped out the disgrace, so far, by collecting the stones together, erecting them in the form in which they now are and cutting an inscription on a slab on which is recorded the date and object of the battle, but he has also placed head-stones at the end of the long graves or pits—the Mackintosh trench being fifty-four feet long—in which the Highlanders are interred, with boldly cut inscriptions giving the name of each of the clans whose members lie buried beneath. As recent as 1846—a hundred years after the battle—the graves are described as "large, green grassy *mounds*," but for many years past they have, by the complete decay of the bodies which they contained, become green grassy *hollows.* The place, its history, and surroundings are full of pathos and interest, particularly to those who have any Highland blood in their veins.   But it is impossible in the space at our disposal to enter into any extended detail.   A few incidents may, however, be mentioned.

On that eventful day Prince Charles had only about 5000 men, ill-fed, ill-clad, and but poorly armed, in the field, while his opponent had nearly double that number—8811—of Royal troops, fed, clad, and armed to perfection, supported by the best cavalry and artillery.   But even then, the general opinion is that had not the Macdonalds sulked and refused to charge, the day would have been won by the Highlanders.   Chambers says that a Lowland gentleman who was in the line, and who survived to a late period, used always in relating the events of Culloden to comment with a feeling like awe upon the more than natural expression of rage which glowed on every face and gleamed in every eye as he surveyed the extended Highland line immediately before the charge.   "The action and event of the onset," he says, "were throughout quite as dreadful as the mental condition which urged it. Notwithstanding that the three files of the front line of English poured forth their incessant fire of musketry—notwithstanding that the cannon, now loaded with grapeshot, swept the field as with an hail-storm—notwithstanding the flank fire of Wolfe's regiment—onward, onward went the headlong Highlanders, flinging themselves into, rather than rushing upon, the lines of the enemy, which, indeed, they did not see for smoke till involved among their weapons. All that courage, all that despair could do, was done.   It was a moment of dreadful and agonising suspense, but only a moment—for the whirlwind does not reap the forest with greater rapidity than the Highlanders cleared the line.   Nevertheless, almost every man in the front rank, chief and gentleman, fell before the deadly weapons which they had braved; and although the enemy gave way, it was not till every bayonet was bent and bloody with the strife." When the Highlanders had thus swept aside the first line of the Royalist troops they still continued their impetuous and irresistible charge until they were quite close to the second. But ere this they were almost annihilated by the terrible. and well directed fire of the English, and the shattered remains of what but an hour before had been a compact and courageous band began to waver. Still a few of the heroes rushed headlong on, resolved rather to die than forfeit their well acquired and dearly-estimated honour. "They rushed on ; but not a man ever came in contact with the enemy. The last perished as he reached the points of the bayonets" of Cumberland's troops.

It is related of Alastair Mor Macgillivray, commanding the Mackintoshes in the absence of their own chief, who was fighting on the Royalist side, that he fought his way a gunshot past the enemy's cannon, and that he killed no less than a dozen of the enemy with his claymore, although some of the English halberts were driven deep into his body before he fell. One of the stones recently erected by Mr Forbes marks the spot on which he expired while crawling to obtain a drink of water from the well, since named after him—which he never reached—after he had been left for dead on the field.

Among numberless other heroic actions on this fatal day must be mentioned the final glorious act in the life of Alexander Macdonald of Keppoch. Chambers, describing the cowardly conduct of the other Macdonalds who, on a false and baseless point of punctilio, refused to charge, insisting that they were entitled to the place of honour on the right—they undoubtedly fought on the left at Killicrankie—says, "From this conduct there was a brilliant exception in the chieftain of Keppoch, a man of chivalrous character and noted for private worth. When the rest of his clan retreated, Keppoch exclaimed with feelings not to be appreciated in modern society, 'My God, have the children of my own tribe forsaken me?'—he then advanced with a pistol in one hand and a drawn sword in the other, resolved apparently to sacrifice his life to the offended genius of his name. He had got but a little way from his regiment when a musket shot brought him to the ground, and a clansman of more than ordinary devotedness who followed him and with tears and prayers conjured him not to throw his life away, raised him, with the cheering assurance that his wound was not mortal, and that he might still quit the field with life. Keppoch desired his faithful follower to take care of himself, and, again rushing forward, received another shot and fell to rise no more." This engagement, the last fought on British soil, and in which an ancient Royal dynasty came to an end, lasted less than forty minutes.

The conduct of Cumberland and his troops after the battle was so savage, cruel, and cowardly as to secure for him ever since the appropriate title of "The Butcher." We shall, however, not soil these pages by giving more than one infamous instance of his horrid inhumanity. Riding over the field, attended by some of his officers, immediately after the battle, the Duke observed a young wounded Highlander resting on his elbow and staring, half dazed, at the monster and his friends as they passed along. Cumberland asked the wounded man to what party he belonged, when the youth at once replied, "To the Prince." The Butcher instantly ordered one of his staff to shoot "that insolent scoundrel." This officer, Major Wolfe, who afterwards died so gloriously on the Heights of Abraham, near Quebec, refused to execute the brutal order, saying that his commission was at the disposal of his Royal Highness, but that he would not become his executioner. The Duke asked several other officers in succession to "pistol" the Highlander, but with a similar result. He then commanded one of his common soldiers to empty the contents of his musket into the wounded officer's body, an order which was immediately obeyed. The young man thus brutally slain was Charles Fraser, younger of Inverallochy, Lieutenant-Colonel in the Master of Lovat's regiment; and it is commonly said that the Butcher ever after frowned upon the heroic Wolfe for refusing to carry out his cowardly Royal commands to shoot the gentle and wounded Highland youth in cold blood. The same blood-thirsty and inhuman spirit governed the conduct of the Butcher after all was over; for he spared neither wounded, old, nor young that came in his way, whether engaged in the battle or not, but had them mercilessly slaughtered in cold blood. "A broad pavement of carnage marked four out of the five miles intervening betwixt the battlefield and Inverness," the last of the slain being found at Millburn within half-a-mile of the town.

Leaving the open space and proceeding eastward a few head-stones will be observed in an arable field on the right, marking where the English slain were interred. About a quarter of a mile further on, at the cross roads, we come upon

CUMBERLAND'S STONE,

from the top of which the Duke is said to have directed the movements of his army during the battle. It is an imposing boulder, and Mr Forbes of Culloden, when marking out the graves had the following inscription cut into it :—

"THE POSITION
OF THE DUKE OF CUMBERLAND DURING THE
BATTLE OF CULLODEN."

For Continuation of Coach Route see p. 104.

For Continuation of Coach Route see p. 104.

THE CLAVA STONE CIRCLES.

Three quarters of a mile from this point, by the road turning to the right, are, on the opposite side of the River Nairn, the ancient stone monuments of Clava. In going to see them the visitor gets a fine view of the great Railway viaduct which here, quite close to him, spans the Nairn Valley. No time is allowed to those going by coach, but no one visiting Culloden Moor should fail to see these pre-historic remains, described as "the most splendid series of circles and cairns on the eastern side of the Island." The whole extent of the

The Culloden Cairn.

plain is covered with them.   Each of the principal cairns, surrounded by great sandstone pillars or standing stones, has in the centre a chamber, formed of ordinary uncemented masonry, 12 feet high by 12 to 15 feet in diameter.   The largest and most perfect one was opened in 1830, when it was found to contain a central circular chamber, five yards in diameter, "lined at the base with a ring of 14 large stones in an upright position, and surmounted by crosses of uncemented masonry, the stones of which incline inwards and overlap one another, so as to have met at the top in a sort of rude dome."   Eighteen inches below the floor of the cell the workmen discovered two small earthen vases or urns of the coarsest workmanship, containing calcined bones.   The urns were accidentally broken and the ashes which they contained were thus scattered and lost.

Continuation by Coach.

Resuming the journey by coach, beyond the Cumberland Stone, the drive is continued along the ridge of the moor, which commands a splendid view of the Nairn valley, all the way to Cawdor and far beyond it, on the right.   Cantray is soon left behind, but is not in sight, and, after it, Holme Rose, on the same side.   By the generous courtesy of Major Rose, the proprietor of Kilravock, which place is next reached, the coach is allowed to drive a distance of two miles through his private policies, entering the grounds through the West Lodge at the village of Croy, and passing right in front of the Castle—a most agreeable and pleasant treat.

KILRAVOCK CASTLE.

This ancient family residence is one of the finest and most picturesque castellated buildings in the North of Scotland.   It is a square keep, with a range of high-roofed additions, perched on a rocky bank overlooking the Nairn, embosomed in thick woods and tall ancient trees.   Inigo Jones, the famous English architect, is said to have designed the principal additions to the original tower, and it has been admitted that the elegant proportions of the public rooms are worthy of

From Photo. by]

Kilravock Castle.

[J. Valentine & Sons

From Photo. by]   **Cawdor Castle.**   [J. Valentine & Sons.

his fame. Cochrane, the minion of James III.—by whom he was afterwards created Earl of Mar—is supposed to have planned the original structure, about the middle of the fifteenth century. The gardens and policies are laid out with extreme good taste, and kept in splendid order, and they contain some of the rarest shrubs and choicest flowers.

The family of Rose is one of the oldest in the Highlands. Formerly proprietors of Geddes in the same county they, in 1280, acquired the lands of Kilravock by the marriage of the head of the house, Hugh de Rose, to Marie, daughter of Sir Andrew de Bosco of Eddyrtor, or Redcastle, a Norman knight, by his wife Elizabeth, daughter of Sir John Bisset of the Aird. The seventh of the family, Hugh Rose, having obtained the required license from his superior, John, fourth Lord of the Isles, dated the 18th of February, 1460, and confirmed by James III. in 1475, erected the original tower. Hugh, known as "the Black Baron," and tenth of his line, who died in 1597, at the age of 90, entertained Queen Mary in the tower in 1562 on the occasion of her visit to Inverness, and Her Majesty's room is still pointed out to visitors. It is in its original state, with an arched roof and without a fireplace. It is neither lathed nor plastered, and the floor " consisted of great coarse boards roughly sawn and nailed together." The present proprietor, Major James Rose, is the 23rd Baron in direct male descent from the first of the family.

In the Castle have been preserved several very fine pictures, old armour, and manuscripts, the most valuable among the latter being a copy of the now well-known " Kilravock Papers," mainly written in 1683-84 by the Rev. Hew Rose, minister of Nairn, and a member of the family. These papers were carefully edited by the late Mr Cosmo Innes, and published by the Spalding Club in 1848. Anciently the family was one of the most powerful in the North, and though the Barons of Kilravock had neither clan nor numerous following they held their own through all the changes of Governments and dynasties, "amid Church schisms and Celtic rebellions," always keeping aloof from faction and shunning the crowd. "They had felt the charms of music, and solaced themselves with old books, and old friends, and old wine." The Castle itself "is embowered in fine old timber—beech, oak and Scotch fir, mixed with the remains of the native birch forest, and a beautiful undergrowth of juniper," altogether making one of the most interesting old residences still occupied, in one of the most picturesque situations, in the Highlands.

A mile beyond the Castle, the coach leaves the grounds by the eastern or principal entrance, gets into the Clephanton or Fort-George and Cawdor road, turns sharply to the right, crosses the Nairn by the high-arched White Bridge, and after a drive of two miles, through a beautiful country, rattles across the bridge which spans the Cawdor Burn, within a few yards of the prettily-situated, picturesque, and ancient Highland residence of the Earls of Cawdor

CAWDOR CASTLE.

This fine baronial Castle was built in 1454 by Thane William of Calder, or Cawdor, by license from James II. This fact, now fully authenticated, completely disposes of the fiction that the tower was the scene of Shakespeare's Tragedy of Macbeth, which took place four centuries before the foundation of the castle was laid. Thane William married Isobel Rose of Kilravock, and by her had an only son, John, in whom the male line became extinct. Dying in 1498, he left an only child —a posthumous daughter, Muriel. The story of how she was carried away by the Campbells and afterwards, in 1510, married to Sir John Campbell, third son of Archibald, second Earl of Argyll, and progenitor of the present family of Cawdor, is too well known to need repetition.

There are several versions of the curious tradition which relates the manner in which the site of Cawdor Castle was originally chosen. According to one, Thane William was directed by a dream, and to another by a wizard, to build his castle at the third hawthorn tree at which an ass laden with a chest full of gold—the family treasury—should stop. These directions were duly acted upon. The ass was loaded with the chest of gold. It rested at one tree, then went on and halted at a second, and finally stopped at a third, round which the ancient tower was subsequently erected. The tree stands firmly rooted in the donjon, the lowest vault of the tower, the old chest which contained the treasure by which the original building was erected occupying the place of honour beside it. To this day when one wishes prosperity to the family the sentiment is usually expressed in the words, " Freshness to the hawthorn tree of Cawdor." Anderson says that if " its name be not sufficient to excite curiosity, the beauties of the situation, the freshness in which all its appurtenances of ancient feudal gloom and grandeur and means of defence remain, will recompense the tourist for the trouble he may be put to in visiting it. Perched upon a low rock, overhanging the bed of a Highland torrent, and surrounded on all sides by the largest sized forest-trees, which partly conceal the extent of its park, it stands a relic of the work of several ages, a weather-beaten tower, encircled by comparatively newer and less elevated dwellings, the whole being enclosed within a moat, and approachable only by a draw-bridge, which rattles on its chains as in years gone by." It is still inhabited ; the staircase, the iron grated doors and wickets, the large baronial kitchen, partly formed out of the native rock ; the hall, the old furniture, the carved mantelpieces, the quantity of figured tapestry (purchased at Arras in 1682) and even the grotesque family mirrors, in use 200 years, are still cherished and preserved by the family. The drawbridge and gateway are particularly worthy of notice. On one of the mantelpieces, dated 1510, there is the figure of a fox smoking a cutty pipe, 75 years before the introduction of tobacco to this country by Sir Walter Raleigh, in 1585. The gardens are very fine, and the policies contain several large oaks, sycamores, elms, walnuts, pine, and ash trees—one of the latter being 23 feet in circumference.

After the Battle of Culloden, Simon Lord Lovat found refuge

for several days concealed in a small low-built attic immediately underneath the roof of the tower, having a single window, close to the floor.   So many of his enemies came to visit the castle that he began to feel unsafe in his hiding-place, and effected his escape by means of a rope.   He subsequently found his way to the west, but was arrested on the 8th of the following June in an island on Loch Morar "wrapped about with blankets in the trunk of a (hollow) tree."   In March, 1747, he was tried and condemned at Westminster on a charge of high treason, and was beheaded on the 9th of April following, on Tower Hill, in the 80th year of his age.

Ample time is allowed for visiting the castle and exploring the grounds.   Sixpence, devoted to charity, is charged for admission.

On the return journey the route is considerably varied. Instead of driving through the policies of Kilravock, the coach, after recrossing the Nairn by the White Bridge, keeps the public highway until it comes to the village of Clephanton. There it turns sharply to the left and proceeds westward, outside Kilravock grounds, for some distance through a richly-wooded country, and on through the village of Croy, after which it once more drives for a short time over the route traversed in the morning, straight in the direction of Culloden Moor, until it reaches the cross roads at Croy Free Church.   At this point it leaves the direct course to Inverness and turns to the right along the road which leads to Dalcross Railway Station passing, soon after, a few hundred yards on the right,

DALCROSS CASTLE,

which was built in 1620 by Simon, eighth Lord Lovat.   The lands on which it was erected had then been for some time in possession of the Frasers, but before that they formed part of the Mackintosh estates.   Soon after the castle was built Lord Simon gave it as a marriage portion to his third son, Sir James Fraser of Brea, who in turn bestowed it as a marriage portion upon Major Bateman who married his daughter Jean. This gentleman subsequently sold it to James Roy Dunbar, one of the bailies of Inverness, who, in 1702, sold it to Sir Lachlan Mackintosh of Mackintosh who died in it in 1704, and whose descendants now possess it. The castle consists of two towers joined at right angles ; the inner corner where they meet being covered by a projecting turret and large entrance gate. Anderson, writing some fifty years ago, says that many of the appurtenances of an old baronial residence were then entire. Water was still raised from a deep draw-well in the front court. The windows were all stanchioned with iron. The huge oaken door, studded with large nails, and the inner iron gratings, still turned on their rusty hinges. The kitchen, with its enormous vaulted chimney, like the arch of a bridge, the dungeon and the hall were quite entire. The ceiling of the latter was of fine carved oak, in part rudely painted ; but its most interesting feature was the *dais* or portion of the floor raised above the rest "for the special use of the lord of the manor, his family, and principal guests." The roof of one of the bedrooms was painted all over with the coats-of-arms of the principal families in the country, and those of Robert Bruce, the Earls of Huntly, Marischal, and and Stuart "are still quite distinct." There is, however, no trace of them now. Even the roof itself has disappeared. The castle was partly restored some years ago, by one of the Chiefs of Mackintosh, but it is now fast going to ruin.

The passengers having visited the castle, if so disposed, the coach rattles down the hill until it reaches the main road from Nairn to Inverness, about a half-a-mile westward from Dalcross Railway Station, and 6½ from the Highland Capital, by which it proceeds, almost close to the line, leaving Castle Stuart, in the hollow on the right, all the way to Inverness. For description of this part of the route, by rail, see the "Inverness to Elgin and Aberdeen" section.

INVERNESS TO FORT-AUGUSTUS, FORT-WILLIAM, AND OBAN, BY THE CALEDONIAN CANAL.

THIS on a fine day is one of the most enjoyable sails which it is possible to imagine, and during the summer season Mr David Macbrayne runs one or more of his commodious and well-found fleet of steamers both ways. The scenery all along the route is unsurpassed anywhere, and various places of unique and striking interest, such as the Falls of Foyers, Ben Nevis, the highest mountain in Great Britain, and Glencoe, are passed and seen on the way.

The passenger steamers leave Muirtown Wharf, below Craig Phadruig, a mile from Inverness. It almost immediately passes Tomnahurich Cemetery (for a description and illustration of which see page 52), on the left—a lovely view—and glides gently through a swing bridge—the paddle boxes almost touching it on either side—over which the Inverness and Glenurquhart Road crosses the Canal at the southern end of the Cemetery. In another minute the boat skirts the base of

TOR-A-VEAN

a high wooded hill on the right, while the Ness rushes along on the left in the opposite direction, on a level considerably below the Canal, the view opening up in front being beautiful beyond description. Tor-a-Vean, as well as Craig Phadruig, has been pointed to as the residence of King Brude, where that monarch was visited in 565 by Saint Columba. It is 275 feet high, and there are distinct traces of fortification on the conical eminence in which it terminates at the rear, also of ramparts, "one of them forming a sort of circumvallation about 40 feet from the top."

In 1808, the workmen engaged in constructing the Caledonian

Canal found at the base of the hill a massive silver chain of 33 circular double links neatly chanelled round with a prominent astragal, and having at each end two rings larger than the others. It is 18 inches long, and weighs 104 ounces. It is now the property of the Society of Antiquaries of Scotland. The chain is alleged to have been the badge of office of Donald Bane, a Hebridean Chief, said to have been killed and buried where it was found, in 1187, on the occasion of a skirmish between him and a party of troops from the Castle of Inverness.

In more recent times the top of Tor-a-Vean was used as a moot hill or seat of justice, and according to tradition there was an ancient burying-place on a small plateau on the north side of it. The hill is said to have derived its name from Beathan or Baithne, a cousin and follower of Saint Columba, who afterwards became Abbot of Iona.

The boat soon after leaving Tor-a-Veán arrives at

DOCHGARROCH LOCKS.

Here a good peep is obtained of Dochfour House, a fine modern mansion, in the Italian style, in which its owner, the late Mr Evan Baillie of Dochfour, had the honour of entertaining the Prince Consort on the occasion of the visit of his Royal Highness to Inverness in 1846. After leaving the Locks the boat passes through Loch Dochfour, connected with Loch Ness by a cutting of the Canal about a quarter of a mile long and now practically an extension of the larger lake. Here, until recently, could be seen the ruins of the old church of Bona, and on the peninsula which marks the division of Loch Dochfour from Loch Ness are the remains of an encampment, described as "An oblong square, rounded at the corners, and encircled with an irregular ditch, which is believed to have been a Roman encampment, pitched on the site of the British Boness, or foot of Loch Ness, a name Latinised by the Romans into Bonessia, and by Ptolemy into Banatia," but now familiar

to all as Bona. In the immediate vicinity of this encampment, on a square mound stood the ruins of

CASTLE SPIORADAN,

an old stronghold or keep, "which in ancient days commanded the passage of the fords across the river in the
neighbourhood." It is said to have been built by Charles
Maclean, progenitor of Clann Thearlaich or the Macleans of
Urquhart and Dochgarroch, early in the fifteenth century.
All his sons, except one, were killed in the Castle soon
after its erection, and if tradition be credited, this was
only one of many violent scenes and slaughters which it
has witnessed.

A glorious view is here obtained of the whole of Loch
Ness, extending for 24 miles right in front. The boat calls
by signal at Aldourie pier, and in passing, a peep of the
fine turretted mansion-house of Aldourie, the residence of
Mr Fraser-Tytler, is obtained through an avenue in the
plantation in which it is embosomed. Aldourie is interesting
as the birthplace of Sir James Mackintosh, the historian,
philosopher, and statesman. The steamer also stops by
signal, going and coming, at Abriachan Pier, on the west
or right-hand side of the Loch, to take in and discharge
passengers or goods, and after a delightful morning sail
turns in to the beautiful Bay of Urquhart and calls at
Temple Pier, on its northern side, 14 miles from Inverness.
The view which here opens up is one of the most charming
in the Highlands.

GLENURQUHART

stands unrivalled for its beauty, fertility, and sylvan loveliness, and would require at least a long day well spent to
explore its delightful retreats and manifold objects of historic
and antiquarian interest. On the southern promontory of
the bay towers the massive ruin of

URQUHART CASTLE,

the history of which extends far back into the unknown

annals of the past. It is the most interesting object in the glen. The date of its origin is unknown, but it is said to have been erected in the eighth century, some placing it as far back as the sixth. In 1303 it was occupied and stoutly defended against the army of Edward I., but after a long siege it was taken, when the Governor, Alexander de Bois, and the whole garrison were put to the sword. In 1334 Sir Robert Lauder, the Constable, gallantly maintained it against Baliol. In 1509 it was granted by James IV. to the ancestor of the Earls of Seafield. It covered a very large area, the rock on which it stands being 600 feet long by 200 broad in an irregular rectangular form, the walls of the Castle following the contour of the rock. The remains of the drawbridge are yet to be seen, and so are the towers of a handsome gateway which opened into the courtyard. A considerable portion of the outer walls are still standing, and the strong square keep, 50 feet high, and measuring 21 feet by 26 feet internally, of three storeys surmounted by four square hanging turrets, are in good preservation and a most striking feature of the great ruin. The walls are 8 feet thick, and when habitable the Castle is said to have had accommodation for 600 men. The moat by which it was protected on the land side was 25 feet deep and 16 wide, while on its other sides the rock on which it stands is washed by the waters of Loch Ness. The Castle has also been the scene of many a tale of love, romance, and chivalry, a good example of which is portrayed in *Tales of the Heather* under the title of "William Grant of Glenurquhart," as well as in other publications of the same kind. The lake, directly opposite, is 125 fathoms or 750 feet deep, and in consequence of its great depth it was never known to freeze in any part.

Balmacaan House, the modern local residence of the Seafields, is situated in a charming spot in the centre of the valley, westward from the old Castle, under the protecting shadow of the neighbouring Craig-Mony, around which centres so much local tradition and romance, and can be seen among the surrounding woods from the deck of the steamer as it enters or leaves the Bay of Urquhart.

THE FALLS OF DIVACH.

Tourists who go ashore at Glenurquhart are sure to visit the Falls of Divach, formed by the stream of that name which flows from the shoulder of Mealfourvonie and after a bound over the precipice of about 100 feet forming the Fall, joins the Coilltie, a rough and, when in flood, dangerous rivulet which passes through the southern side of the glen past the village of Lewiston on its way to Loch Ness. The Fall of Divach is even higher than Foyers, and although the volume of water is much smaller, when the burn is in flood it is highly picturesque and well worth going a long way to see. It is about four miles from Drumnadrochit Hotel, and most of the distance can be driven over, but the remainder must be traversed on foot through a deep and thickly-wooded ravine. Immediately above the Fall is Divach Cottage, for many years the summer residence of the late John Phillips, the famous artist, and more recently of Arthur J. Lewis and his wife, the latter better known by her maiden name of Kate Terry.

Climbing up by an excellent path from the bed of the ravine to the higher level, the visitor can there meet his carriage, and drive or walk to the old Castle by the upper road, about a mile distant. Other places of antiquarian and romantic interest abound in this lovely glen, but the reader who resolves to spend some time in it must be left to find them out for himself. Its unique beauties have been celebrated in prose, in verse, and on canvas, by Shirley Brooks, John Bright, John Phillips, and many others. Mr Bright, writing in the famed Drumnadrochit Hotel Visitor's Book, says—

> In Highland glens 'tis far too oft observed,
> That man is chased away and game preserved ;
> Glenurquhart is to me a lovelier glen—
> Here deer and grouse have not supplanted men.

The steamer having discharged and taken on board passengers

From Photo. by]   Urquhart Castle.   [J. Valentine & Sons

From Photo. by]   At Foyers Pier.   [J. Valentine & Sons.

at Temple Pier, proceeds on her way, passing close to the ruins of Castle Urquhart, as she leaves the bay, to Inverfaragaig, her next place of call.

THE PASS OF INVERFARAGAIG.

This is one of the most romantic and wildest passes in the North of Scotland. It is very narrow at its entrance, not much wider than the road which runs through it. Its sides are very steep, especially the northern one, which is formed of an almost perpendicular and rugged precipice—the Black Rock, on the summit of which are the vitrified remains of Dun Jardil. About a mile from the Pier, on the bank of the roaring mountain torrent, which brawls and tumbles through this grim gorge, is a granite monolith erected by the Inverness Scientific Society and Field Club to commemorate the death, in July, 1877, of Dr James Bryce of Edinburgh, a well-known geologist, by the fall of a rock, while in pursuit of his favourite science among the precipices opposite. Both sides of the Pass are covered with wood, principally birch, except where the Black rock exposes its rugged and knarled face to the countless ages.

THE FALLS OF FOYERS.

Passengers desiring to see the magnificent Falls can do so by taking one of Mr Macbrayne's steamers from Inverness or Fort-Augustus, the only difference between the new and the old arrangement being that the boat by which the parties arrive does not wait to take them away. There is thus longer time to enjoy the grandeur of the Falls and the magnificent scenery by which they are surrounded in comfort, ample time being afforded in which to catch the next steamer either going North or South. As there are two steamers daily each way this arrangement causes no inconvenience, but increases the comfort of the traveller. Mr Macbrayne's steamship "Gondolier" is shown on the opposite page.

The Foyers, which takes its rise in Loch Killin in the Monadhliath mountains, runs a course of thirteen miles before it takes its first great plunge of 30 feet over the perpendicular rock which formed the first or Upper Fall, within one and a half of its mouth. Another quarter of a mile and it got compressed through a narrow gorge from which it bounded over a yawning precipice of 90 feet into a seething cauldron, far down between the surrounding rocks, sending up volumes of misty foam from which the Fall derives it Gaelic name of "Eas-na-Smuid," or the smoking Cataract. It is quite impossible to give any adequate description of these cascades and their surroundings as we remember them, and we shall not make the attempt. Robert Burns on first seeing them wrote the following lines on the Lower or principal Fall, when in its glory, as shown in our illustration—

> Among the heathy hills and rugged woods,
> The roaring Foyers pours his mossy floods,
> Till full he dashes on the rocky mounds,
> Where through a shapeless breach his stream resounds.
> As high in air the bursting torrents flow,
> As deep recoiling surges foam below,
> Prone down the rock the whitening sheet descends,
> And viewless, echo's ear astonished rends,
> Dim-seen through rising mist and ceaseless showers,
> The hoary cavern, wide-resounding, low'rs.
> Still through the gap the struggling river toils,
> And still below the horrid cauldron boils.

Professor Wilson says :—"The Fall of Foyers is the most magnificent cataract out of all sight and hearing, in Britain. The din is quite loud enough in ordinary weather, and it is only in ordinary weather that you can approach the place from which you have a full view of its grandeur. In ordinary Highland weather—meaning, thereby, weather neither very wet nor very dry—it is worth walking a thousand miles to see the Fall of Foyers. The spacious cavity is enclosed by complicated cliffs and perpendicular precipices of immense height, and though, for a while, it wears to the eye a savage aspect, yet beauty fears not to dwell even there, and the horror is softened by what appears to

From Photo. by]   **Fall of Foyers.**   [J. Valentine & Sons.

be masses of tall shrubs, or single shrubs almost like trees.   And they are trees, which on the level plain would look even stately; but as they ascend, ledge above ledge, the walls of that awful chasm, it takes the eye time to see them as they really are, while, on first discernment of their character, serenely standing among the tumult, they are felt on such sites to be sublime."   Another and more recent writer says :—" As we approach, we feel the ground tremble with the roar and din of the falling waters, from which a thick cloud of spray constantly ascends.   Having gained the point of observation the visitor beholds the whole extent of the Fall, the terrific gulf beneath and the lofty and precipitous rocks around, fringed with luxuriant birch and tangled masses of shrubs and small plants nourished by the vapour which ever and anon floats around.   Oak and pine trees are also abundant, adding grace and beauty to the scene."   When the river was in flood the effect was truly sublime and the spectator was deeply impressed with feelings of awe and admiration.   From Foyers the towering Mealfourvonie, rising to an altitude of 2284 feet, directly opposite on the other side of Loch Ness, will be seen to great advantage.

Leaving Foyers' pier the steamer proceeds on her journey and almost immediately passes the point at which the Foyers enters Loch Ness in the calmest and most placid serenity.   Here is a green fertile spot of great beauty once occupied by the mansion-house for many generations inhabited by the cadet family of Fraser of Foyers, but now used for the purposes of the Aluminium Company. On the opposite side of the lake, first Allt-Giuthais, and next, two miles further on, Allt-Sigh are observed, deeply indented between the rocks, finding their way to Loch Ness. Soon we reach Invermoriston, where the impetuous mountain stream of that name, after traversing the whole length of Glenmoriston, enters Loch Ness, the old family residence of the Grants showing its roof among the trees beyond.   Those

who desire to visit this beautiful glen will go ashore and
proceed to the Hotel, passing o · their way the fine Falls
on the river, and the salmon ladder recently erected to
enable the fish to pass up to the higher reaches of the
Moriston, some years ago stocked with salmon fry by the late
Mr Dunbar of Brawl Castle, Caithness.

From Invermoriston there is a good country road through
Cluanie forest, to Glenshiel, Glenelg, or Balmacarra, at each
of which there is an excellent Hotel.

Leaving Invermoriston, the boat proceeds on her way to

FORT-AUGUSTUS,

the scenery on all sides, in front and in rear, being of the
most magnificent and varied character, the Abbey of St.
Benedict forming an imposing and massive structure, the
building of which cost £80,000, in the foreground, on the
site of the old fort to the left of the village and on the right
bank of the Canal. The cost of the Church when finished
will be about £50,000 additional. Here we pull up, in the
entrance to the first of a series of five locks at the end of
the lake.

The old ·military fort which has given place to the Benedictine Abbey was erected by General Wade in 1729 to overawe
the Highland clans who took part in the Rising of 1715
under the Earl of Mar. It was a square building, with four
bastions, mounting twelve six-pounders and containing accommodation for one field officer, four captains, twelve subalterns,
and 280 rank and file. It was taken by the followers of
Prince Charles in 1745, and after the battle of Culloden was
for a short time the head-quarters of the Duke of Cumberland.
In 1773 it was visited by Dr Johnson and Boswell, on their
tour to the Hebrides.

The site of the old fort, which was occupied until the
Crimean War, and the land surrounding it were bought
from the Government by Thomas Alexander Fraser, Lord
Lovat, in 1867, for £5000, and in 1876 was presented by

his son, the late Simon Lord Lovat, to the Benedictine order of Monks to erect this noble pile of ecclesiastical buildings upon it. The Abbey is a quadrangle of four distinct buildings, containing a College, Monastery, Hospice, and Scriptorium, connected with cloisters, in the purest early English Gothic style of architecture.

Fort-Augustus is becoming very popular with visitors, especially anglers. There are two good Hotels, the Temperance being one of the most comfortable of its kind in the Highlands. There are also several new villas in which accommodation can be arranged for in advance by those who intend to remain for any time in the district.

The boat takes about three-quarters of an hour passing through the Locks, and passengers who care to walk can proceed on foot along the banks of the Canal to Kyltra Locks, two miles further on, and be there in good time before the boat arrives. The walk in fine weather is a most enjoyable one. Another two miles and the boat enters Loch Oich through Cullochy Locks, near Aberchalder, where Prince Charles mustered his forces before proceeding on his memorable march to the Lowlands, on the 27th of August, 1745. The road just passed, and which crosses the Canal by a swing bridge, and the River Oich by an elegant suspension bridge on the right, leads from Fort-Augustus to Invergarry and Fort-William, and also from Invergarry, the residence of Mrs Ellice, to Glenquoich, for many years occupied as a deer forest by Lord Burton, to the head of Lochourn, and Glenelg, where there is a first-class Hotel, on the West Coast of Inverness-shire.

The scenery round Loch Oich, which is 3½ miles long by about a furlong in average width, 100 feet above the level of the sea, and the highest reach of the Canal navigation, is varied and beautiful in the extreme, dotted here and there with little wood-covered islets, and surrounded by a combination of Alpine grandeur and sylvan loveliness, which cannot fail to leave a pleasing impression on the imagination.

The district has also many romantic and historical associations. About half-way along the Loch the ruin of the old Castle, for ages the stronghold and home of the warlike Chiefs of Glengarry, stands out hoary and prominent to the right, on "Creagan an Fhithich," which became the war cry of this branch of the Macdonalds, and which, with the old burying ground, is the only portion which now remains to the representatives of that ancient Highland family of their once enormous possessions. In this Castle Prince Charles spent part of the night of the 26th of August, 1745, just before he started on his journey south to meet Sir John Cope, and subsequently, a few days before it was burnt by Cumberland's soldiers after Culloden, the same Prince found shelter in it, though then deserted, the first night after the battle, and after he had an interview with Simon, Lord Lovat, at Gortuleg House, Stratherrick. A little to the right of this grim old ruin is the elegant modern mansion erected by the late proprietor of the estate, the Hon. Edward Ellice, for many years M.P. for the St. Andrews Burghs. The situation is very fine, and the scenery at this point has been favourably compared with some of the most picturesque parts of the Rhine.

Near the south-west end of Loch Oich on the right, will be observed a monumental pyramid which was erected by the notorious Glengarry of George IV's time, over a well, known as "Tobar nan Ceann," or the Well of the Heads. The apex of the monument represents seven human heads, and it has the following inscription upon its four sides in as many languages :—

"As a memorial of the ample and summary vengeance which, in the swift course of feudal justice, inflicted by the orders of the Lord Macdonnell and Aross, overtook the perpetrators of the foul murder of the Keppoch family, a branch of the powerful and illustrious clan of which his lordship was the Chief, this monument is erected by Colonel Macdonnell of Glengarry, XVII. Mac Mhic Alastair, his successor and representative, in the year of our Lord,

1812. The heads of the seven murderers were presented at the feet of the noble Chief in Glengarry Castle, after having been washed in this Spring ; and ever since that event, which took place early in the sixteenth century, it has been known by the name of 'Tobar-nan-Ceann,' or 'The Well of the Heads.'"

In one important respect this inscription is historically inaccurate. In point of fact Lord Macdonell and Aros, though urged with all the intensity of passion which Ian Lom Macdonald, the Keppoch bard—who took the execution of vengeance in hand—was able to bring to bear upon him, refused to interfere. The Bard then proceeded to Skye and succeeded, after composing one of his best songs to Sir James Macdonald of Sleat, in inducing that Chief to take the matter up. Sir James at once applied to the Government, obtained a commission of fire and sword, signed by the Duke of Hamilton, the Marquis of Montrose, and other seven Privy Councillors, against the murderers, and then sent his brother, Archibald, known as "An Ciaran Mabach," poet and soldier, at the head of a trusty band led by "Ian Lom," to punish the assassins. They fell upon them during the night, while in their beds, inflicted summary vengeance, and next morning, having cut off their heads, washed them in this well and laid them at the feet of Lord Macdonell and Aros at Invergarry Castle, more to show him what they had succeeded in doing without his aid than for any assistance he had given them. The murder of the Keppoch brothers took place in 1663, and on the 15th of December, 1665, a letter was addressed to Sir James Macdonald, signed by the Earl of Rothes, Treasurer and Keeper of the Great Seal of Scotland, thanking him "for the singular service" he had done to the country by punishing the murderers, and assuring him that he would not be allowed to remain long unrewarded.*

Three quarters of a mile after leaving Loch Oich, through

* See *Mackenzie's History of the Macdonalds and Lords of the Isles*, pp. 217-218.

a charming winding avenue formed by a thick and very pretty plantation on either side, Laggan Locks are reached, and on the right will be observed the old burying-place of Kilfinnan, where the Macdonalds of Glengarry had been buried for generations.

Just at the end of Loch Lochy, which is entered a mile further on, the most sanguinary battle ever fought among the Highland clans was fought on the 15th of July, 1544, between the Macdonalds of Clanranald, under John Moydertach, and the Frasers, under Lord Lovat. Out of about a thousand men—six hundred Macdonalds and four hundred Frasers—only ten left the scene of conflict alive, among the slain being Lord Lovat himself, the Master of Lovat, and eighty leading gentlemen of the clan, as well as Ranald Gallda Macdonald, the legitimate chief of Clanranald, whose cause the Frasers had espoused. The battle is still known in Gaelic as " Blar-nan-Leine," or the Battle of the Shirts, from the fact that the combatants on both sides stripped themselves of all their upper garments and fought in their shirts and kilts.*

The scenery on both sides of Loch Lochy, ten miles long, with an average width of one, is exceedingly fine, the first half of the distance being walled in by high hills on both sides, some of them rising to an altitude of more than 3000 feet. On the left is Letterfinlay, at one time fully populated by a fine race, the MacMartins, said to be the oldest branch of the Camerons, but now forsaken and desolate. As the southwest end of the lake is approached, the mouth of Glen-Arkaig opens up to the right, the fine farm house observed on the same side, near the loch, being Clunes House, for many generations occupied by the Camerons of Clunes, cadets of the family of Lochiel, one of whom ferried Prince Charles across the River Lochy in a ricketty boat during his wanderings after he escaped from the Long Island to the mainland.

* For a fully detailed and graphic account of this sanguinary conflict see Mackenzie's *History of the Frasers.*

A little further on, and about a mile higher up the glen, Achnacarry Castle, the residence of Lochiel, chief of the Camerons, is seen among the trees, and in its immediate neighbourhood, but not seen from the boat, still stands the ivy-covered ruins of its predecessor, where Prince Charles Edward slept the second night after Culloden, and burnt a few days later by the Duke of Cumberland's red-coats.. There are several points of interest here, such as the Dark Mile, one of the most remarkable avenues of trees in the kingdom, Prince Charlie's Cave, and Loch-Arkaig, which extends from Achnacarry fourteen miles inland, through a fine district once thickly populated by a comfortable and contented tenantry, but now a deer forest. But as these places cannot be seen from the deck of the steamer, we shall follow the plan of this Guide throughout and pass on without making any further reference to them.

On the left the mansion of Invergloy, flanked by lofty and recently-planted hills, on the east side of the loch, is soon passed, and then Glenfintaig House. Immediately behind the former there is a water beach at an altitude of 1278 feet above the present level of the sea, and a few miles eastward are the famous parallel roads of Glenroy, which have proved such a puzzle to the geologist. In a few minutes the boat arrives at Gairlochy Locks, at the south-western extremity of Loch Lochy, and passes through them into the last stretch of the Canal before reaching its terminus at Banavie. At this point a good road cuts across country to Glenroy and Spean Bridge, where the Glasgow and Fort-William Railway may be joined.

Proceeding along the Canal, Glenloy soon opens up on the right. Erracht House—the birthplace of the famous General Sir Alan Cameron, K.C.B., who in 1793, in the remarkably short space of three months, raised and for many years commanded the 79th Cameron Highlanders, now known as "The Queen's Own," and the Inverness-shire County Regiment, having most appropriately its headquarters in the

Highland Capital—is seen on the east side of the river, while Strone House, for several generations occupied by a well-known family of Camerons, stands on the promontory which forms the western shoulder of this very picturesque and lovely glen.

The country now begins to open up and the massive Ben Nevis comes into view slightly to the left, surrounded by other giants, with the effect that from this point the highest mountain in Britain is somewhat disappointing, but as the steamer gets nearer to it, its great height and massiveness rapidly grow upon us. The wall, which is soon seen striking up the hill to the right, is the march dyke between the counties of Inverness and Argyle. Winding along the remainder of the Canal in the most pleasant fashion, and gradually approaching closer to the mighty Ben Nevis, 4406 feet above the level of the sea, we observe on a high and projecting precipice, on the west bank of the River Lochy, a short distance eastward from the Canal, the ruin of Banquo's House, or Tor Castle, an ancient seat of the Chiefs of Mackintosh, who at one time owned the whole of this district, and fought with the Camerons for possession of it for more than three hundred and forty years, a final settlement of the dispute having only been arrived at in 1681, when it was given up to the Lochiels on payment to Mackintosh of 72,500 merks. Away in the distance on the plain, on the other side of the Lochy, within three and a half miles of Fort-William, is the imposing modern mansion of Lord Abinger, Torlundy House, where Her Majesty resided for some time during her visit to the Highlands in 1873, and still further away, in the neighbourhood of Fort-William, the extensive ruin of Inverlochy Castle, a quadrangular building, with massive towers at each angle, surrounded by a wide and deep fosse. In a few minutes more the steamer arrives at Banavie, at the top of "Neptune's staircase," formed of a series of eight locks, which at its western terminus connect the Caledonian Canal with the sea at Corpach.

BANAVIE AND CORPACH.

From here a glorious view is obtained of Ben Nevis, and there is a first-class Hotel under excellent management at Banavie, and another on a smaller scale, recently re-built, re-furnished, and very comfortable, three quarters of a mile distant, at Corpach, at both of which those who desire to remain for any time in the district can find first-rate accommodation at reasonable rates, have every facility for ascending the mountain, and for visiting the many other places of interest which abound in the neighbourhood, such as Prince Charles' monument in Glenfinnan, at the head of Lochsheil, where he first raised his flag in 1745; Achnacarry Castle; the scenes of the Prince's wanderings in its vicinity; the Parallel Roads of Glenroy; and Glen Nevis with its two fine waterfalls. Close to the Corpach Hotel, outside the Churchyard of Kilmallie, will be observed a tall obelisk erected to commemorate the valiant and highly distinguished Colonel John Cameron of Fassifern, who for so many years commanded the 92nd Gordon Highlanders, and fell at their head on the 16th of June, 1815, at Quatre Bras, and is buried in the ivy-covered ruin inside the Churchyard, his body having been brought home in a Government ship. Another notable Highlander interred in this Churchyard is Mary Mackellar the Gaelic poetess, a native of Lochaber.

Passengers going further South leave the steamer here and proceed by rail to

FORT-WILLIAM,

lying at the base of the majestic Ben Nevis. Fort-William in 1891 had a population of 1870 souls, but since the introduction of the West Highland Railway in 1894 it has been increasing by leaps and bounds. A large number of new houses and villas have been built in recent years at both ends of the town, now an important Police Burgh, governed by a Provost, Magistrates, and Town Council. It contains several good Hotels and the number, demanded by the extra tourist traffic introduced by the Railway, are being much improved and increased. The Station Hotel, built in a beautiful and commanding situation near the station in 1896, provides first-class accommodation for 100 to 120 guests, and is altogether one of the most palatial and best equipped tourist hotels in Scotland. . It is electrically lighted throughout. The West End Hotel has also been very much extended and improved of late. The only places of special interest in or in the immediate neighbourhood of the town are, the Fort at the east end, first erected by General Monk during the English Commonwealth, and subsequently rebuilt on a more limited scale in the reign of William III. It was unsuccessfully besieged in the 'Fifteen and the Forty-five and it continued garrisoned by troops until 1864, when it was sold by the Government to Mrs Cameron Campbell of Monzie, the superior of the rest of Fort-William. Another stronghold, the ancient Castle of Inverlochy, already mentioned, is of still greater interest. It also is to the east of the town on the right, between the road and the river.

From Fort-William the new line to Mallaig, extending to about 40 miles, opens up a district of great natural beauty and historic interest, which has hitherto been practically inaccessible to the tourist because of the total want of railway accommodation. To the fishermen and agriculturalists in the outer islands, the pier at Mallaig and the railway will be of immense advantage, as the former will enable them to land their produce without delay, and by the line it will be rapidly conveyed to the southern markets. To the tourist the extension will prove equally valuable. The rugged grandeur of the route is excelled by no district in Scotland, and every mountain, stream, and loch, calls up memories of Prince Charlie and the '45, and of the grim old warriors of the Cameron Clan and the Macdonalds of Clanranald.

Fort-William is the nearest point from which to ascend

Ben Nevis, and since a bridle path was constructed in recent years, starting at Achintee, on the road from the town to Glen Nevis, the ascent is comparatively easy, and can be made riding or on foot. The Meteorological Society in November, 1893, opened an Observatory on the very summit of the mountain, erected at a cost of £6000, and placed it under the charge of Mr R. F. Omond, F.R.S.E., and two assistants. For the use of this path tickets are issued to pedestrians for one and to persons on horseback for three shillings, the distance from Fort-William to the Observatory being 7½ miles. These tickets entitle the holders to the privilege of despatching telegrams from the highest pinnacle of the mountain, at ordinary rates, to any part of the world. The panorama from the summit for extent, variety, and grandeur on a clear day must be seen, not described, and many ascend in the evening and remain on the top all night to see the sun rising over the German Ocean, and lighting up the incalculable number of mountain summits which are seen from this altitude. Sleeping accommodation is provided for twelve persons in the Observatory, and refreshments are supplied, all at reasonable rates, considering the situation and circumstances. As the future centre of a great railway system Fort-William is destined to become one of the most attractive and flourishing towns in the Highlands.

FORT-WILLIAM TO BALLACHULISH (FOR GLENCOE) AND OBAN.

The steamer, leaving Fort-William, sails at the rate of sixteen knots an hour down Loch Aber, or Upper Loch Linnhe, passing Conaglen, the Highland residence of the Earl of Morton, a few miles along, on the right, and close to the shore is pointed out the rock on which Alastair Ranaldson Macdonell, XV. of Glengarry, was killed in the heyday of his glory by recklessly jumping ashore from the stranded steamer "Stirling Castle," at Inverscaddle, on the 14th of January, 1828. From this point another fine view is obtained of Ben Nevis.   Soon Ardgour Pier is reached, and having called there the boat passes through the narrows of Corran Ferry and enters Loch Linnhe proper.   Ardgour House (Maclean's) is left on the right.   In a few minutes Onich Point—from which the upper workings of the Ballach-ulish slate quarries, the largest in Scotland, can be seen ahead in the direction of Glencoe—is rounded and we enter Loch Leven.   Turning to the left a call is made at Onich Pier, from which, a short distance round the bay, Onich Manse, the residence of the Rev. Alexander Stewart, LL.D., so widely and popularly known all over the world as a dis-tinguished literateur, naturalist, and Celtic scholar, under his *nom de plume* of "Nether-Lochaber," is observed.   Sur-rounded by a fine clump of trees, near the Point, is Cuilchenna House, occupied for generations by a branch of the Camerons descended from the ancient family of Callart. Of the Camerons of Cuilchenna were the distinguished Colonel Sir John Cameron, K.C.B., and his more celebrated son, General Sir Duncan Alexander Cameron, K.C.B., Colonel of the 42nd Royal Highlanders, Black Watch.   Sir Duncan dis-tinguished himself in the Crimea, in Australia, and in New Zealand against the Maories, and was in 1865 appointed Governor of the Royal Military College at Sandhurst.

From Onich the boat steams straight across to Ballach-ulish Pier in Argyleshire, where those going to Glencoe will disembark and proceed by either of the opposing coaches to visit that far-famed modern Valley of the Shadow of Death.   There are two comfortable hotels at Ballachulish, one of them Temperance, and a third on the north side of the narrows, which divide Upper from Lower Loch Leven, where, on St. Mun's Isle, there is an ancient ruin of a church and a burial-place, in which on one part of the island the Camerons of Callart had been buried for ages, and the Macdonalds of Glencoe on another.   Callart House stands on the opposite shore of the lake.   From this point the entrance to Glencoe can be seen, a few miles distant, guarded by a high conical hill called the Pap of Glencoe. Immediately below it, in a clump of trees, near the modern mansion of Invercoe, stand the ruins of Mac Ian's house, where the old Chief and his family were so treacherously massacred by the orders of Breadalbane and King William III. in February, 1692. The sad and terrible tale is too well known to need recapitulation here, and to describe the scenery would require the power and pen of a Gilfillan. It must be seen for one to have any idea of its awe-inspiring magnificence, utter loneliness, and savage grandeur, unique and altogether peculiar to itself.

The steamer having turned round after leaving Ballach-ulish Pier, in a few minutes again enters Loch Linnhe, and proceeds on her way to Appin and Oban, with the mountains of Ardgour, Kingairloch, and Morvern in the distance on the right, and the hills of Appin on the left. Ardsheal House, at one time a seat of the Stewarts of Appin, is passed almost immediately, also on the left, and the mouth of a cave is pointed out in Ardsheal Hill, where Colonel Charles Stewart was in hiding after Culloden, until he was able to effect his escape to France. Looking across to the opposite coast of Morvern a glimpse is obtained of Caisteal-a-chuirn, on the summit of a conical hill at the entrance to Glen Sanda. Looking backwards from where we now are a fine view is got of Ben Nevis, perhaps the best of it that can be obtained anywhere. Shuna Island, with its ruined castle, is rounded a little on our left, and on the mainland further away, almost concealed in a thick wood, is Appin House. Stalker Castle, an ancient stronghold of the Stewarts of Appin, on a small rocky island, and once occupied by James VI. while on one of his Highland hunting expeditions, is passed, and the boat in a few minutes pulls up at Appin pier, from which their is a ferry to Lismore, the large fertile island which stretches along on the right, and which shall now keep us company on the same side until we turn into the beautiful bay of Oban.

Proceeding, we soon pass Airds House, snugly sheltered at
the head of Airds Bay, and then the entrance to Loch
Creran, and the island of Eriska, with its peculiar looking
red stone mansion-house.   On the right at this point may
be observed, on the island of Lismore, Tirafuar Castle, said
to be an ancient Scandinavian watch tower, and in the far
distance ahead across the Sound of Mull, in line with the
Lismore Lighthouse, the old Castle of Duart, frowning
on the mountains of Morvern on the opposite coast.   Soon we
pass Lochnell and Lochnell House, and cross the mouth
of Loch Etive on the left, getting a good view in front of
Dunstaffnage Castle, prominently situated on a wood-covered
peninsula which juts out into the sea, the great Ben Cruachan,
with its two gracefully formed peaks, 3689 feet above sea level,
in the distance, making up a glorious background to the fine
scenery by which Loch Etive is surrounded.
    Dunstaffnage Castle, said to be of Pictish origin, at one time
contained the famous Coronation Stone of Scotland, originally
taken from Ireland by King Fergus, and deposited in Iona.
It was carried away from this castle to Scone by Kenneth II.
about 805.   Later on it was removed by Edward I. to
Westminster Abbey, where it now remains, supporting the
historic chair in which the sovereigns of the United Kingdom are crowned on their accession to the throne.   Robert
the Bruce took possession of Dunstaffnage Castle after he
defeated the Macdougalls of Lorn in the Pass of Brander,
and in 1746 the famous Flora Macdonald was detained in it
for about ten days, while on her way as a State prisoner to
London, for the part which she took in the escape of Prince
Charles from the Long Island, through Skye, to the mainland
after the Battle of Culloden.   In a few minutes a prominent
and picturesque object, the ivy-clad, green-mantled Dunolly
Castle, the ancient residence of the Macdougalls of Lorn,
towering on a rocky eminence, is passed, and the boat turns
in to the pretty Bay of Oban, almost land-locked, fully protected from the Atlantic waves by the island of Kerrara on

the right, on which King Alexander II. of Scotland died while on a visit to the Western Isles in 1249.

Oban has been very appropriately described as the Charing Cross of the West Highlands.   It is a most convenient centre from which to reach any part of the Western Isles or the West Coast mainland by sea, including Staffa and Iona, the Outer Hebrides, Coruisk, and all other parts of Skye, Gairloch (for Loch Maree), Lochewe, Lochinver, and Stornoway, as well as the places just described on the route from Oban to Inverness.   It is conveniently connected with Edinburgh, Glasgow, and the south by railway *via* Callander, Dunblane, and Stirling ; *via* Crianlarich, Dumbarton and Glasgow ; by Mr MacBrayne's splendid steamers, through the Crinan Canal, the Kyles of Bute, and the Firth of Clyde, to Rothesay, Greenock, and Glasgow ; or *via* Loch Awe, Ford, and Ardrishaig.   There is also a very fine excursion by rail, coach, and steamer, from Oban to Lochawe, calling at Portsonachan—where there is a first-class hotel—and back in one day.   It has made great progress in recent years.   In 1790 it was non-existent.   In 1847 its annual rental was only £1719, while in 1894 it was—in less than half a century—considerably over £35,000, with a normal population of 4902, very much increased in the season.   It has a large number of excellent Hotels, with sufficient accommodation for more than a thousand persons, seven or eight churches, five or six branch banks, three weekly newspapers, and a whisky distillery of good repute.   There is not a prettier sight anywhere than Oban and its bay by night or by day in the summer season, the latter always swarming with steamers and pleasure yachts of every sort, size, and description.   The situation of the town is unique, of great natural beauty, and commanding views of the very finest scenery, far and near, and unsurpassed in Scotland.

INVERNESS TO NAIRN, FORRES, ELGIN, KEITH, AND ABERDEEN.

INVERNESS TO NAIRN AND FORRES.

LEAVING Inverness the first object that strikes the traveller is a large and imposing building on the 100 feet terrace on his right—the Cameron Barracks, erected by Government a few years ago at a cost of £60,000—forming the territorial head-quarters of the county regiment, the Queen's Own Cameron Highlanders, and providing accommodation for 300 officers and men. The Barracks are built on "Cnoc-an-Tionail," or the Gathering Hill, and not, as has been said, on the site of Macbeth's Castle, which was further west on the Crown lands. On the next terrace further east is Raigmore House, the residence of Mr Æneas Mackintosh, Chairman of the Highland Railway Company, and an ex-M.P. for the Inverness District of Burghs. Proceeding eastward the line skirts the southern shore of the Moray Firth—passing through a level and fertile country, and commanding a fine view of the Black Isle on the opposite coast, and of the Sutherland and Caithness mountains far away to the north—until it reaches Culloden Station, 3½ miles from Inverness. Culloden House is a mile to the south but cannot be seen from the railway in consequence of the extensive woods by which it is surrounded. Culloden Moor, on which was fought in 1746 the ever-memorable battle between the followers of Prince Charles and the Duke of Cumberland, is three miles to the south, on the wooded ridge ; but in order to see it properly the visitor must accompany us in our Excursion, by road, pp. 97-109, *via* the battlefield to Cawdor Castle. A short distance from the station we pass the small village of Turlies Point, sheltered on the south side by a prominent hill, and,

From Photo. by]

Castle Stuart.

[J. Valentine & Sons.

in the hollow beyond it on the same side, 5½ miles from Inverness, is

CASTLE STUART,

belonging to the Earl of Moray. It is described as "a fine example of the castellated mansion intermediate between the baronial keep and the plain modern house." It was built about 1606, but it is often confused with Hal-hill, a structure of much earlier date, which stood on a hill a little further east, but of which not a vestige now remains. It is mentioned in Gordon's *Earldom of Sutherland* as having been taken from the Earl of Moray by the Mackintoshes in 1624. It had a splendid orchard, which was famous for its geans, and the tall forest trees which adorned its grounds were among the finest in the north. The Castle had again fallen into disrepair, but a late Earl of Moray had it restored as near as possible to its original beauty.

Dalcross Station is soon reached and left behind, the low-lying land between it and the next stoppage being altogether uninteresting. But as the train is nearing

GOLLANFIELD JUNCTION,

the station for Fort-George, the fort is seen to the left on Ardersier Point, below the village of Campbelltown, 3½ miles distant. It covers about sixteen acres of land, and upwards of £160,000 were expended upon its construction. It is an imposing, elegant, and substantial-looking structure, and was erected soon after the 'Forty-five in continuation of a plan in terms of which Fort-Augustus and Fort-William were built at an earlier date, for the purpose of overawing and keeping down the Highland clans. Conveyances for passengers run in connection with all trains between the station and the fort, which is still maintained, although dismantled, as the depot of the Seaforth Highlanders. About a mile past Gollanfield Junction, the train passes through a peat moss of considerable extent, but nothing of interest can be seen from the railway until within a quarter of a mile of Nairn, when on a slight eminence on the right the traveller observes Balblair House situated on the identical spot on which the Duke of Cumberland and his army encamped the night preceding the battle of Culloden. In another instant the train pulls up at Nairn Station, a few minutes' walk from the centre of the town.

NAIRN

is a Royal Burgh, with a population in 1891 of 4014, governed by a Provost, Magistrate, Dean of Guild, and Town Council. It occupies a beautiful and highly favoured position on the southern shore of the Moray Firth, and has a splendid sandy beach, largely taken advantage of for bathing. There are also extensive public indoor salt water swimming baths for the use of those who prefer them. The Links cover a large area, and being open to the public are freely taken advantage of for amusements and recreations of all kinds. There is also an excellent golf course, which not only proves a great attraction for the usual summer visitors, but to golfers from the neighbouring burghs of Inverness and Forres, who often go to Nairn to enjoy their favourite game. The most prominent architectural feature of the town is the graceful spire of the Free Church which stands near the Railway Station. The climate is very dry, and altogether Nairn is one of the most attractive places of summer resort in Scotland. It is visited every year by thousands of people from all parts of the world, who find the most ample provision made for their accommodation and comfort in Sutherland's Marine and Shaw's Private Hotels, both on the Links, close to the beach; in King's Royal Hotel in the centre of High Street, and in the numerous villas of all sorts and sizes in which the town abounds.

NAIRN TO FORRES.

Starting from Nairn, the train almost immediately passes over a fine stone bridge of four arches 70 feet span each and 34 feet high. About a mile further on, the village of Auldearn is noticed on the right. Here in 1645 a sanguinary battle was fought between Montrose and the

NOTE.—For more detailed description of Nairn see page 167.

Covenanters, at which the latter, under the Earl of Seaforth, were signally defeated and then fled to Inverness. Three miles from Nairn, on the right, the reader will observe a small cluster of trees on a knoll, said to mark the "blasted heath" immortalised by Shakespeare, where Macbeth met the famous witches. Looking to his left the traveller will get occasional glimpses of the Culbin Sands, which cover, to a depth of 100 feet in some places, 10,000 acres of land, at one time cultivated and supporting a considerable population. This land was buried during a terrific storm, about 200 years ago, by the drift sand from the sea. The desert extends on an average to two miles in breadth, and stretches along the coast from the mouth of the river Findhorn to within two miles of Nairn. Arriving at Brodie Station, six miles from Nairn, the reader will notice on his right an extensive forest in which is embosomed Darnaway Castle, the Highland residence of the Earl of Moray, a historic and most interesting ancient mansion well worth a visit, but from the density of the great forest surrounding it it cannot be seen from the railway. It contains a magnificent hall erected by Sir Thomas Randolph, Earl of Moray, nephew of King Robert the Bruce, 95 feet long, by 35 broad and 30 feet high, and capable of accommodating a thousand men under arms. In this hall Queen Mary, at the time a young widow only 20 years of age, held a Council in 1562, while on her way to Inverness. A few seconds after leaving the station, a glimpse is obtained on the left of Brodie Castle through the extensive wooded policies and dense shrubbery by which it is surrounded. A little further on Dalvey House, the residence of Captain Norman Macleod, with its luxuriant flower gardens, is observed on the same side, after which the train crosses the Findhorn by a fine tubular girder bridge of three spans, 150 feet each, and in a few minutes pulls up at the Forres Railway Station, where there is a good Refreshment Room, belonging to the

Highland Railway Company, 24¼ miles from Inverness.

FORRES.

Forres is a town of considerable importance, with a population in 1891 of 3971, and, built on a gravel terrace, it boasts of a climate and surroundings admitted to be unsurpassed in Scotland. The rainfall being very low it is free from damp and surface evaporation. It is mild in winter while cool and bracing in summer. In addition to the Hydropathic, which is situated on a considerable elevation, but at the same time well sheltered and commanding a very picturesque and extensive view, there are two good Hotels in the town, the Royal Station and the Commercial.

The principal object of interest in the immediate vicinity is Sweno's Stone, a pillar 23 feet high, with curiously carved figures of men on foot and on horseback, of animals and birds, surrounded by runic ornamentation. It commemorates a battle fought between the Danes and the Scots in 1014.

Everyone who breaks the journey here should visit the Banks of the Findhorn, the most striking combination of mountain, river, and wooded scenery it has ever been our privilege to see. By driving to the end nearest Forres, and back from its farthest extremity, it can be overtaken comfortably in an afternoon, and should on no account be missed. There are also some very pleasant drives in the vicinity of Forres, through the most charming country—to Altyre, Dunphail, and Relugas. Darnaway Castle, already referred to, is only a few miles distant, and should be visited.

FORRES TO ELGIN, KEITH, AND ABERDEEN.

Leaving for Elgin and the east, the first station is Kinloss, three miles distant, where the remaining ruin—a single tower and the bottom storey—of the Cistercian Abbey of Kinloss, a beautiful structure founded by David I. in 1150, will be seen. It was destroyed by Cromwell, who carried most of the stones to Inverness and used them in the construction of his short-lived fort. After passing through a most fertile

district, known as "The Laigh of Moray," the train pulls
up at Alves Station, four miles further, where a branch line
of seven miles breaks off for the important fishing villages
of Burghead and Hopeman, through a fine agricultural district,
along the right bank of the river Lossie. On the Lochty,
a tributary of the Lossie, are the ruins of the Priory of Pluscardine, in good preservation, founded in 1230 by Alexander
II. The walls are still entire, and the ruins, covered with
ivy to the very top, form a most exquisite picture. The
architecture is in the early pointed style, the later portions
being slightly decorated. The windows have deservedly been
very much admired. The ancient Parish Church of Birnie,
the oldest in Moray, built in the eleventh or twelfth century,
exhibiting a feature quite unique in the north—a distinct
and separately roofed chancel and nave—the first bishop's
church in the diocese, strong and complete as when first
erected, also stands on a reach of the Lossie, and is still used
as the parish kirk.

The train on the main line having crossed the Lossie,
soon arrives at Elgin Station, 12 miles from Forres.

ELGIN.

In 1891 Elgin had a population of 7799 souls. Everyone
should visit the splendid ruin of its Cathedral—"The Lan-
thorn of the North." What still remains of this noble
building measures 282 feet by 86. It is 115 feet across
the transept, and the central spire was 198 feet high. The
original building was founded on the 19th of July, 1224, in
terms of a Papal bull by Andrew, Bishop of Moray. It was
set on fire in 1270, and all that remains of the original is a
mere fragment of the south transept. It was, however, soon
after rebuilt, but was again burnt in 1390 by the "Wolf of
Badenoch," for which sacrilege he had to do penance at
the door of Blackfriars' Church, Perth. It was again rebuilt
early in the fifteenth century, and subsequent additions were
made to it until about the middle of the sixteenth century.

* For a description of Moray Firth Coast Line and the Craigellachie
route of the Great North of Scotland Railway see pp. 143-148.

In 1568, after the Reformation, the lead was stripped from the roof by order of the Privy Council, with the result that its interior fell rapidly into decay, culminating in its present ruinous condition. It must have been a magnificent structure when in its glory ; for the highest authorities on ecclesiastical antiquities describe it as the most beautiful building even yet of its kind in Scotland. There are also the ruins of the Bishop's Palace, the Dean's House, and the Greyfriars Church.

Elgin has a very good local museum and a tastefully laid out cemetery in the immediate neighbourhood. . Anderson's Educational Institution is a most important acquisition to the town. There are many fine modern churches, several banks, an infirmary, lunatic asylum, a large number of pretty villas, with everything that go to make up a prosperous and growing city, including two very good Hotels.

On the way towards Lhanbryde, the next station, some 3 miles farther, on the main line, near the Loch of Spynie, is conspicuously situated the ruins of the Bishop's Palace and Chapel, erected by Bishop David Stewart of Moray in 1475, and past the station, on the right, Coxton Tower, one of the old residences of the family of Innes, and subsequently the property of the Earls of Fife. It is a tall specimen of the ancient castellated mansion. Another 3 miles, and old Fochabers Station, now Orbliston Junction, is reached, about 3 miles from the village of that name, now connected by a branch line, and close to which stands Gordon Castle, the principal Scottish residence of the Duke of Richmond and Gordon, and anciently known as the " Bog o' Gight." It is a very noble structure, comprising a great central building of four storeys, a square tower of six storeys in the rear, with a spacious wing of two storeys on either side, and connecting galleries of similar height, surrounded by an embattled coping, in a fine park extending to 1300 acres, formerly a marsh, but now adorned with every variety of gigantic forest trees, principally limes, horse-chesnuts, and walnuts. The gardens occupy about ten acres. Proceeding on the main line to Orton, a fine view is obtained down to and along the Banffshire coast, across the Moray Firth—which, opposite this point, is about 30 miles wide—to the Ord of Caithness. The red perpendicular cliffs by which the east side of the Spey is lined are very striking objects in front. They rise to about 400 feet above the bed of the river, and are formed of a great deposit of boulder clay, gravel and sand, which in course of ages has become nearly as hard as the solid rock, while the cliffs are so marked, cut up with watercourses, and so impregnated with iron as to give them the red mural sandstone strata appearance which is so prominent a feature of them.

Orton Station reached and passed, the train proceeds through a large cutting and then over an extensive embankment connected by a series of dry arches with a plate-iron viaduct of 230 feet span constructed on the tubular principle, by which it crosses the Spey. Within a short distance is the Boat o' Brig Bridge, a very handsome iron suspension bridge of 235 feet, over which the ordinary carriage road is carried. From the river the train proceeds up a steep ascent of 1 in 60, for about 2 miles, through the bold and wooded ravine of the Mulben Burn, and pulls up at Mulben Station. Another good run of 5 miles on a level road and the train stops at

KEITH JUNCTION,

the terminus eastward of the Highland Railway system, where it meets the Great North of Scotland Railway, 18 miles from Elgin, 30¼ from Forres, and 55 from Inverness. The three towns of Old, New, and Fife Keiths, are clustered together on an eminence on both banks of the River Isla, with an aggregate population of something like 4500. There is a good Refreshment Room at the station, belonging to the Great North of Scotland Railway Company, and there are two comfortable Hotels—the Gordon and the Grant Arms—in the town.

THE KEITH AND BUCKIE BRANCH.

From here the Keith, Buckie, and Portessie line, 13½ miles, branches off. While a very useful railway for local traffic, there is nothing on the route of any particular interest to the ordinary tourist. There are stations at Forgie, Enzie, Drybridge, Rathen, and Buckie, the latter with a fishing population of over 4000 and a commodious harbour, constructed and opened in 1880 at a cost of £60,000, which is the north-western terminus of the branch, and from which it turns in the opposite direction, proceeding for another mile and a half, along the sea coast eastwards to the village of Portessie.

KEITH TO HUNTLY, INVERURIE, KINTORE, DYCE, AND ABERDEEN.

Leaving Keith by the Great North of Scotland Railway Company's main line, the train, 4½ miles on, makes the first stop at Grange Station, which is the junction for the Banff-shire and the Moray Firth coast railways. Running through Strathisla, for 3½ miles, the next station is at Rothiemay, where the line crosses the river Deveron by a stone bridge of five arches, 70 feet in height, leaves Banffshire, and enters the County of Aberdeen. Another 4½ miles and Huntly is reached. This is a Burgh of Barony, and the Capital of Strathbogie, with a population in 1891 of 3760 souls. It is neatly built, has several thriving industries, good streets, and a spacious Market Square. It stands on an angle at the juncture of the rivers Deveron and Bogie. Huntly Castle, now in ruins, but once a famous stronghold of the Gordons, stands on an eminence near by, and is well worth a visit. Of the walls and towers sufficient remains to give the visitor a good idea of its former strength and appearance.

On the way to Gartly and Kennethmont, the next two stations, the Hill of Noth, rising from the left bank of the Bogie, is observed. On its summit is to be found "the most remarkable specimen of a vitrified fort either as to altitude, extent, or area, or preservation, extant in Great Britain." Wardhouse Station is next passed, and then Insch, near which stands, on the top of a conical hill, over looking Christ's Kirk, the vitrified remains of Drumideer. ____ Station comes next, and then Pitcaple. Pitcaple

Castle, partly built early in the sixteenth century, surrounded by beautiful trees, is seen in a hollow on the left. Queen Mary spent a night in it and planted a tree, still called after her, in the grounds to commemorate her visit, and in 1650 the great Montrose rested a night within it while being taken south as a State prisoner after his capture in Assynt.

At Inveramsay junction, the next station reached, the Turriff and Macduff linebreaks off to the north coast. Close to Inveramsay, on the east side of the line, is the scene of the great battle of Harlaw, fought in 1411 between Donald of the Isles and the Royal forces under the Earl of Mar, the question in dispute being Donald's claim, after this battle decided in his favour, to the Earldom of Ross in right of his wife Margaret Leslie, Countess of Ross in her own right. The ruined Castle of Balquhain, built in 1530, the square tower of which is still standing, will be observed on the west side of the line, opposite the field of Harlaw. Inverurie, an ancient Royal Burgh, situated at the juncture of the Don and the Urie, is next reached. Here the Old Meldrum branch breaks off to the left. In the immediate neighbourhood King Robert the Bruce secured in 1308 his well-known victory over the Comyns of Badenoch, afterwards pursued them to Buchan, despoiled their lands, and proscribed their name Near the station, also on the left, is Keith-Hall, the residence of the Earls of Kintore, surrounded by its prettily laid out lawns, gardens, extensive grounds, and wooded policies. On the same side stands the Bass of Inverurie, a curious conical-shaped mound between 50 and 60 feet high, at the base of which flows the Urie, and in its immediate vicinity are several antiquarian remains of Roman camps, stone circles. and ancient tombs. Leaving Inverurie, the train crosses the Don over a fine wrought iron viaduct supported on stone piers, and passing, a little further on, Messrs Tait's Paper Mills at Port Elphinstone on the left, in a few minutes pulls up at Kintore Station, the junction for the Alford Valley line. Kintore is a quiet, little Royal Burgh, of great antiquity,

said to have had its original charter of incorporation from
Kenneth II. in the ninth century. Its population in 1891
was 3105. Kinaldie and Pitmedden stations are passed, and
the train stops next at Dyce, the junction for the Buchan
line to Peterhead and Fraserburgh. Passing the small local
stations of Buxburn, Woodside, and Kittybrewster, it proceeds through a thickly populated and enterprising manu-
facturing district, along the western slope facing the river
Don, which has a number of pretty villas along its wooded
banks, and finally pulls up at Aberdeen Central Station,
108½ miles from Inverness. Within the station, with a covered
entrance from the platform, stands the commodious and
excellently-managed Palace Hotel, owned and carried on by
the Great North of Scotland Railway Company. There is
also a first-class Restaurant at the Station. Aberdeen has
several other first-class Hotels.

ELGIN TO KEITH *via* THE MORAY FIRTH COAST LINE.

AN alternative route from Elgin to Aberdeen in connection with the Highland is by the Coast Line of the Great North of Scotland Railway. This line for a considerable distance runs along the shore of the Moray Firth. About a mile from Elgin the branch for Lossiemouth, a well-known summer resort for golfers and bathers, leaves the Coast Line. The latter then runs –passing on the left the ruins of Spynie Palace, the ancient residence of the Bishops of Moray—from Calçots to Urquhart, leaving Innes House, one of the seats of the Duke of Fife, on the same side, along a fine undulating partly-wooded country, on its way through a very pretty district, with several plantations almost continuous on the right, the broadening and exhilarating Moray Firth on the left and in front, all the way to Garmouth, 8¾ miles from Elgin, a quaint and clean-looking village the streets of which are delightfully odd, intricate and irregular and characteristic of an old time town. Charles II. landed here in 1650 from Holland and signed the Solemn League and Covenant. Garmouth was at one time a busy shipping, and ship-building centre, but it is now best known as a favourite bathing resort for which the situation is all that can be wished. Immediately on leaving it the line crosses the Spey by an iron viaduct built on piers of solid masonry. This fine structure is about 950 feet in length. The central span, measuring about 350 feet, is said to be the longest single line bridge in the Kingdom. The piers of the central span are founded on cast iron cylinders filled with concrete and sunk 50 feet below the river bed.

After crossing the viaduct the Fochabers Station of the Great North is reached, and a magnificent view of the Spey Valley is here obtained as well as of the far hills which bound it, the most prominent being Benaigen, 1500 feet high, and Benrinnes, 2747 feet. Portgordon Station is next reached. Here there is a rising seaside town and a very good harbour.

Passing the small station of Buckpool the train pulls up at Buckie, one of the largest and most prosperous fishing towns in the North, possessing a substantial and convenient harbour, built by the Superior at a cost of £70,000. A flourishing seaport, with a rapidly increasing population, it contains several handsome churches, prominent among them the Roman Catholic Cathedral, an ornate and imposing structure. Since the opening of this line the commerce of Buckie has made great strides and the town is rapidly becoming an emporium for the whole of the surrounding district.

Leaving Buckie the line runs close to the sea, past the fishing stations of Portessie, Findochty, and Portknockie, affording fine views of the precipitous and rock-bound coast until, passing along a high embankment skirting the links of Cullen, it enters that Royal Burgh by a handsome stone viaduct. Cullen stands almost without a rival amongst the North East Coast fishing towns in attractions for the visitor. It combines the charm of antiquity with the advantages of a picturesque situation on a rising ground, overlooking the bay and the sea town in which the fishing population reside. The hills of Sutherland and Caithness are seen across the Moray Firth. Cullen House, one of the seats of the Seafield family, is in the immediate vicinity, but hid from the Railway by the beautiful woods by which it is surrounded. The ancient and interesting Church of Cullen was built in the reign of Robert I. Documents bearing the date of 1543 record that Elizabeth, the Queen of Robert Bruce, died in the Burgh when on a visit to the North, and that "her bowels were erdit in the Lady Kirk thereof." Mary, Queen of Scots also visited the town on the occasion of an expedition to the North to settle a dispute which had arisen between the Gordons and the Ogilvies, and it was amicably settled in her presence in the Old Kirk. Cullen suffered severely during the wars of Montrose, having been plundered three times. Since the opening of the railway it has become quite a fashionable sea-bathing resort. Favoured with beautiful scenery, a salubrious climate, and a bracing atmosphere, combined with the advantages offered by the Railway facilities, it is destined in the near future to become one of the most popular watering places on the Moray Firth. The Bin Hill of Cullen, a prominent object, clothed with wood far up its sides, serves as a landmark for seamen a great distance out at sea.

After passing through a long and heavy rock cutting Tochieneal and Glassaugh Stations are passed on the way east, and then Portsoy is reached 5½ miles from Cullen. This is a growing town of over 2000 inhabitants, picturesquely situated on the headland occupying the inner bend of and projecting into a large bay formed by the promontories of East Head and -Redhythe Point. The district round Portsoy is rich in minerals, steatite, chrysolite, asbestos, and enstatite being found, while diorite and serpentine are also largely developed.

The train next pulls up at Tillynaught, the junction for the branch line, 6 miles in length, to Banff—a busy thriving seaport and a Royal Burgh. It is of great antiquity, and contains the remains of a castle once a Royal fortress, and visited by Edward I. in 1296 and 1303. In 1645 the Marquis of Montrose paid it a visit. He plundered it "pitifully ; no merchants' goods nor gear left : they saw no man on the street but was stripped naked to the skin." In 1746 the Duke of Cumberland's army passed through the Burgh on its way to Culloden. Near to the town is Duff House, one of the seats of the Earl of Fife, a fine modern mansion in the Roman style of architecture. Its erection cost £70,000, and it contains a very valuable collection of paintings and portraits by Vandyke, Titian, Sir Joshua Reynolds, Raeburn, Murillo, Velasquez, Corregio Quintin Matsys, and other famed masters. From Tillynaught junction the main line proceeds in a Southerly direction through an interesting and pretty district past the stations of Cornhill, Glenbarry, and Knock to Grange, the junction of the two Great North routes from Elgin to Aberdeen.

ELGIN TO KEITH *via* CRAIGELLACHIE.

ANOTHER route from Elgin to Keith and Aberdeen is by the Great North via Craigellachie, through a charming inland country affording an endless variety of characteristic and very fine Scottish scenery. Sweeping round the ascending curve by which the line leaves Elgin Station a splendid view of the Cathedral City is obtained. The next stoppage is at Longmorn, 3 miles distant. For about 3 miles after leaving this station the scenery presents all the wild and rugged grandeur so character-istic of the Highlands. This is succeeded by the beautiful glen of Rothes. On the right hand immediately on entering it will be seen the fine mansion of Birchfield. Rothes itself, 9¼ miles from Elgin, is a place of considerable antiquity. It stretches along an alluvial plain, surrounded by lofty hills. From some points near the town a magnificent view can be obtained of the valley of the Spey and the bold dark crystalline hills of the district.

Between Rothes and Craigellachie—a distance of 3 miles—the line runs along the beautiful valley of the Spey. Passing the small Station of Dandaleith it crosses the river by a substantial iron bridge immediately before entering Craigellachie Station. Here is the junction for the Speyside line which runs thence along the Strath of Spey surrounded by the most lovely and variegated scenery on all sides, touching Aberlour, Carron —where it passes the largest and one of the best malt distilleries in the Kingdom, the famous Dailuaine-Glenlivet Distillery—Ballindalloch, Grantown, and Abernethy stations, until the line joins the Highland Railway at Boat of Garten.

Craigellachie in the summer, when the heather is in full bloom, the sloping fields rich with grain, and the dark woods echo to the songs of numberless birds, presents a picture never to be forgotten. Turn where you may beauty meets the eye on every hand. Looking up the Spey Valley the bright and bounding river sweeps onward by crag and wood, its waters glistening in the sunbeams. Downward towards Rothes are the lovely hill-girt plains. On the heights above and over-looking the river stands the hamlet of Craigellachie, yearly becoming more and more the popular resort of the tourist and sportsman. Craigellachie Rock is a mass of granite and gneiss, rising from the river bed to a height of over 150 feet, and is thickly clothed to the summit with trees of every hue. Near it was erected by Telford in 1814-15 that beautiful bridge across the Spey, 150 feet span, the oldest iron bridge in Scotland, and known far and near as " Craigellachie Brig." There is in this village a very comfortable, recently built hotel, fitted up with all modern requirements, and beautfully situated over-looking the Spey.

From Craigellachie to Dufftown the line threads a sinuous course following the Fiddich, which it crosses and recrosses. Pine and birch climb the heights on either side and crown the beetling crags through which the line is cut. Dufftown, an interesting and thriving town, is situated on a slope on the right, a mile from the railway station and surrounded by a crescent of hills. The Old Castle is about half a mile past the station on the same side and occupies the flat summit of a steep eminence overhanging the Fiddich, a very picturesque situation. Near the fine old ruin, the origin of which is lost in antiquity, Malcolm II. defeated the Danes in 1010. On the left stands what is known as the New Castle of Balvenie, a spacious building of imposing size, part-erected by the first Earl of Fife but never finished, and now converted into a distillery.

About a mile before Drummuir—the next station—is reached, the line passes on the left the Loch of Park, a narrow sheet of water, skirting it on a narrow ledge between the water and the steep hillside. The lake, which is more than a mile long, but only about a hundred yards broad, occupies the bottom of a con- tracted mountain gorge, forming, with its steep, richly-wooded banks on either side, a most picturesque feature of this route.

On the left of Drummuir Station is Drummuir Castle, situated on a commanding height surrounded with fine trees and forming one of the most imposing sights in the neighbourhood.   It is a magnificent building in the Tudor Gothic style, with castellated and embrasured roof.   The entrance is protected by a spacious porch, above the centre of which, looking to the east and west, are two armorial shields with the motto—

> ·· Kind heart be true,
> And you shall never rue. "

Leaving Drummuir, and passing through Strathisla, the small stations of Auchindachy and Earlsmill—the nearest station for the town of Keith, a thriving town in Banffshire, Keith Station, formerly the terminus of the main line from Aberdeen, is reached.   It is the junction of four railway lines, possesses several manufactories and a distillery, is the centre of a large agricultural district, where a considerable trade is carried on in butcher meat, grain, flour, and other agricultural products. Here the Craigellachie route of the Great North again joins the direct main line from Inverness to Aberdeen.

At Grange, the junction with the Moray Firth coast line from Elgin, 4½ miles from Keith, the two Great North trains are united to form the through connection from both routes Eastward to Aberdeen.

FORRES TO GRANTOWN, KINGUSSIE, BLAIR-ATHOLL, PITLOCHRY, DUNKELD, AND PERTH.

FORRES TO GRANTOWN AND AVIEMORE.

LEAVING Forres the most prominent object is the Nelson Monument on the summit of Cluny Hill on the left, and below it facing the south, the Cluny Hill Hydropathic, a well-managed and popular institution sheltered from the north and east winds. Further on in the distance, on the same side, on a hill stands conspicuously the old tower of Blervie. The train now proceeds over the Rafford embankment, containing the great aggregate quantity of 308,000 cubic yards, after which it passes through a deep cutting of 291,000 cubic yards, ascending a steep gradient towards Dunphail, in course of which looking backward a very extensive view is obtained of the fertile district which is being left behind and of a long and wide stretch of the Moray Firth, with the Ross and Cromarty, Sutherland, and Caithness mountains rising from its northern shores. Passing through the Altyre pleasure grounds, the train soon reaches and leaves behind Dunphail Station, 614 feet above the level of the sea, and then Dava, first climbing and then descending. Along this district nothing striking or of any particular interest can be seen from the carriages—only occasional stunted trees and bleak moors—until the train gets within a few miles of Grantown, towards which it descends, for the last 5 miles, a gradient of 1 in 80 to 1 in 84. About half way between Dava and Grantown the wooded policies of Castle Grant begin to make their appearances on the left, and the Castle itself, a lofty quadrangular pile of several storeys, with leaden roof, comes fully into view, surrounded by extensive grounds, well stocked with fine old trees and shrubbery. In a few minutes more the train pulls up, 48 miles from **Inverness**, 23¼ from Forres, and 713 feet above sea level, **at**

GRANTOWN-ON-SPEY.

This pretty and beautifully situated village, three-quarters of **a** mile from the Railway Station, is rapidly extending in every direction, and at the present rate of progress it **will** very soon develop into a large and important town as the Capital of Strathspey. It is a favourite resort for summer visitors. In fact, fast as it is spreading out on all sides **by** the constant erection of substantial and beautiful villas, **it is** necessary to secure accommodation for those intending **to** remain in it for any time several weeks in advance. It is surrounded by pine forests and the most varied and beautiful scenery, and the walks round about it and in the neighbourhood are good, pleasant, and plentiful. It has several branch banks, and two first-class Hotels, the Grant Arms in which the Queen slept for a night in 1860, and the Palace, originally the Black Bull, re-built and re-furnished in 1894. In 1891 Grantown had a population of 1423.

Proceeding on the journey south, a few yards after leaving Grantown Station the old ruined church and burying-place of Inverallan is passed. Crossing the river Dulnan 2 miles further on, the old Tower of Mucherach, a beautifully-situated and picturesque ruin, is observed about a mile to the right, close to the river, on the brow of a hill, and visible from a long distance east and west. It was built in 1598 by Patrick, second son of John Grant of Grant and Margaret Stewart, his first wife, a daughter of the Earl of Atholl of the day, and was the original family seat of the Grants of Rothiemurchus. Two miles more and Broomhill Station is reached, opposite the village of Abernethy, whose Established and Free Churches and manses, a little across the Spey, and on the east side of the Nethy, stand out conspicuously among the less pretentious buildings by which they are surrounded. On leaving Broomhill the train immediately passes through the farm of Tullochgorm made famous by the celebrated Strathspey tune, song, and reel of that name. At Boat of Garten, the next station, the Highland line is joined by a branch of the Great North of Scotland Railway, which follows the course of the Spey for a considerable distance, connecting with Elgin and Keith on the main line from Inverness to Aberdeen. The Boat of Garten Hotel, much enlarged in recent years, is, for cleanliness and comfort, second to none in the district. Passing along an undulating plain, overhanging the Spey, partly arable and partly a deep peat moss, the remains of an extensive old fir plantation, one of the first in the Highlands, is entered.

Aviemore Station is soon reached, 5 miles further on. From here the new and much shorter line through Slochd-Muic direct to Inverness commences (see page 177.)

AVIEMORE TO KINGUSSIE, BLAIR ATHOLL, PITLOCHRY, DUNKELD AND PERTH.

Soon after leaving Aviemore Junction for the south the train skirts Tor Alvie, a prominent hill to the left, on the summit of which stands on the end nearest a tall monumental pillar erected to the memory of George, the last of the old Dukes of Gordon. On the other end is a huge cairn, standing out against the sky, erected to commemorate Sir Robert Macara, Colonel of the 42nd Royal Highlanders, and Colonel John Cameron of Fassifern, who commanded the 92nd Gordon Highlanders in the peninsula and fell mortally wounded at Quatre Bras. A little further on, on the right, is passed the prominent birch-clad hill from which the Grants take their slogan or war cry of " Stand fast, Craigellachie." On the opposite bank of the Spey Invereshie House, the residence of Sir George Macpherson Grant of Ballindalloch, is seen, and the train almost immediately pulls up at Kincraig Station. Presently we are climbing a gentle ascent through a singularly beautiful and interesting country combining mountain, forest, lake, and river, and from the top—near Belleville House, the Highland residence of Mr Brewster Macpherson, the representative of his namesake, James Macpherson of Ossianic fame, erected on the site of the old Castle of Raits, and passed on the right—is obtained a fine and extended view of the Cairngorm Mountains, which form a prominent section of the great Grampian range. Among the most striking and imposing are Ben Macdui, 4296 feet high; Braeriach, 4248; Cairntoul, 4241; and Cairngorm, 4084 feet high. Close to Belleville House stands a monument erected to James Macpherson, its original owner. Soon the train leaves the parish of Alvie and enters that of Kingussie. Before pulling up at

KINGUSSIE STATION

the ruins of the barracks of Ruthven, built in 1718, are observed on the right bank of the Spey, situated on the spot where the notorious "Wolf of Badenoch," a natural son of Robert II., King of Scotland, had one of his castles in the fourteenth century, and subsequently a residence of the Gordons, standing out prominently on a gravel terrace about a mile distant from the village. Five minutes are allowed here by all trains, north and south, for refreshments.

Kingussie is a growing and thriving village, 764 feet above the level of the sea. It is a modern Burgh, with Provost, Magistrates, and Police Commissioners. In 1891 it had a population of 740. The climate is delightful, and the district is deservedly highly popular as a place of summer resort. The hotel accommodation is good, and the number of villas which can be had furnished during the season, or in which accommodation can be found, are numerous and increasing more and more every year. A coach runs between Kingussie and Fort-William daily, through a most charming country. Some very pleasant excursions can be made from the village; one to the ancient British hill fort of Dun-da-lamh, in the parish of Laggan, considered to be the most perfect specimen of its kind in the kingdom. Another to Gaick Forest, famed for its wild grandeur, and for the catastrophe which occurred there on Old Christmas Day, in 1799, when Captain Macpherson of Ballachroan and several others who accompanied him on a hunting expedition, met their death by an avalanche of snow which during the night buried the bothy in which they were asleep.

The ruined chapel and the site of the old monastery of St. Columba are close to the burgh on its north side.

The train, proceeding on its journey, soon leaves the parish of Kingussie and enters that of Laggan, the first stoppage being at Newtonmore, three miles further on. Passing along, the line soon crosses the Spey, which the Truim almost immediately joins. Glentruim House, is noticed on the right in the picturesque valley of that name, embosomed in fine plantations of larch and fir, mixed with natural birch, altogether very extensive. Climbing along the west side of the Truim, Dalwhinnie Station is soon reached, the painted snow-posts observed by the side of the coach road, which runs parallel with the railway, and other striking indications, reminding the traveller of the fact that in winter this is the wildest and coldest part of the Highlands. There is not much to be seen here of any particular interest except bleak moors and lofty mountains, the latter rising to an altitude of from 1800 to 2000 feet above the level of the line which itself, at Dalnaspidal, is 1484 feet above the level of the sea. A glimpse is obtained of Loch Ericht, 17 miles long, on the right, and in the distance is seen the top of Ben Alder, 3767 feet high, in the face of which Prince Charles took refuge for a time in "The Cage," with Cluny and Lochiel, after Culloden. The Pass of Dalnaspidal, bounded on the right by the "Boar of Badenoch," followed immediately on the same side by the "Sow of Atholl" is entered, and the traveller is reminded by these names that he has just left Inverness-shire and entered the County o' Perth. Here the line reaches its highest altitude, 1484 feet above the level of the sea, in a pass only 300 feet wide, and said to be the greatest height of any railway in Great Britain, and in less than a minute the train pulls up at Dalnaspidal Station. The mountain streams now begin to run to the south instead of the north as hitherto. Loch Garry, from which the river which shall now for several miles be our companion takes its rise and its name, is seen away to the right. The river Garry is then crossed, and the train dashes down a gradient of 1 in 70 to 1 in 80 for the next ten miles, skirting the great deer forest of Atholl the whole way as it rushes along and leaves the giant Grampian mountains behind, through a wild and bleak country, abounding mainly in heather and wild mountain grasses. Having reached and passed Struan Station, and after recrossing the deep and rocky channel of the tumultuous Garry, with its series of falls and rapids, at Calvine, by a handsome stone bridge of three arches, one of which is 80 feet span and 40 feet above the bed of the river, and two of 40 feet span—looking westward through Glen Errochie, the top of Schiehallion, in Rannoch, 3547 feet high, is seen in the far distance. The altitude of 1484 feet above sea level at Dalnaspidal is reduced at Struan, the next station, to 615! In a few minutes more the Falls of Bruar, immortalised by Burns, are passed. Bruar Water is then crossed, the Manse of Blair left behind, the Atholl policies reached and skirted on the left for two miles, with the Garry, now subdued and quiet, running through a level broad valley, close on the right. Blair Castle, the ancient feudal stronghold of the Dukes of Atholl, is now in full view on a slight elevation in the entrance to Glen Tilt, on the left, and in a couple of minutes more the train stops at

BLAIR ATHOLL STATION,

immediately at the back of the commodious and well-managed Atholl Arms Hotel, which possesses one of the finest and most elegant coffee-rooms in the Highlands. The room was planned and built by the late Duke of Atholl for a private ballroom, but since his death it has been added to the hotel

There is another smaller but comfortable Hotel, the Glentilt, about a quarter of a mile from the railway station.

Blair Castle is a huge heterogeneous pile, built at different periods. It was originally turreted but was subsequently dismantled, and its battlements and upper storeys removed. It has, however, been partly restored and much improved in appearance by the present Duke. Portions of it are very old, and it has many stirring historical associations. Montrose held it in 1644; Viscount Dundee, immediately before the battle of Killiecrankie, in 1689; and some of the Duke of Cumberland's troops were besieged within its walls by Lord George Murray, brother of the Duke of Atholl, on behalf of Prince Charles, in 1746. The grounds are fine and extensive. Visitors are admitted by the main entrance between 9 A.M. and 6 P.M., on signing their names in a book, and paying a shilling each to a guide, who accompanies them through the policies and explains the various points of interest as they proceed. One of the walks through the grounds is along the banks of the river Tilt, on which a succession of very fine falls 70 feet high will be much admired. In Blair-Atholl the climate is very bracing and consequently it is one of the favourite resorts of health-seekers.

Several fine excursions can be conveniently made from Blair-Atholl—such as the Pass of Killiecrankie, 3 miles; the Falls of Tummel, at the other end of the Pass; the Queen's View, on Loch Tummel; the Falls of Bruar, 4 miles; the Rumbling Bridge, Taymouth Castle, Loch Tay, Loch Rannoch, and several other places of interest more or less distant.

Leaving Blair-Atholl Station, the train is almost immediately carried over the Tilt by a handsome girder bridge, and at this point a view of Ben-y-gloes, 3671 feet high, is obtained on the left. On the same side, the fine and beautifully situated mansion house of the Macinroys of Lude on an elevated undulating slope, surrounded by its pretty wooded policies, is observed. The train rushes along the level Atholl Valley, several handsome residences, surrounded by natural woods or modern plantations, being prominent on both sides of the line, which here runs parallel to the public road, and is lined by a series of fine old trees—oaks, elms, ash, and beech singly and in curiously arranged separate groups. The train proceeds through a level plain, which was occupied by a portion of Dundee's army in charge of the baggage, while on another plain, on the terraced ground higher up, to the left, General Mackay was engaged with the rest of his army, 4000 strong, hopelessly contending with the renowned Viscount Dundee at the famous battle of Killiecrankie, in July, 1689, at the head of a comparatively small force of 1800 Highlanders. On the plain below, close to the railway, a tall standing stone is seen from the carriage window, on the left, erected on the spot on which General Halliburton of Pitcur was killed while in charge of General Mackay's baggage, when the Highlanders rushed down from the terraced height above, after having routed Mackay's army, killing or driving before them everything that stood in their way. Those interested in such matters will drive or walk to this historic spot from Blair-Atholl or Pitlochry, and examine the scene of the famous battle for themselves. The spot at which the valiant Dundee fell mortally wounded is on a knoll in the garden of Urrard House embosomed in a cluster of trees on the terrace, 150 feet above the level of the railway, on the left. He was at once carried to Blair Castle and was interred in a vault in the old Church of Blair, where the late Duke of Atholl was also buried, being the first occasion on which the vault was opened since the famous battle and brilliant victory, and it is said that several skulls with sabre cuts were discovered.*

Leaving Killiecrankie station behind the train enters a tunnel

* By far the best, most complete and accurate account of this memorable battle will be found in Mackenzie's *History of the Camerons*, pp. 184 to 199, the famous Sir Ewen Cameron of Lochiel having taken a leading part in it.

gloes, towering on our left to the north, and the junction of
the Tummel and the Tay, close by on the right.   We are
now in the parish of Logierait, and passing through the
Haughs of Tullymet, just after the train leaves Guay Station,
the pretty farm buildings of St. Colme's, the model dairy
farm of the Dowager Duchess of Atholl, form a striking
object on an elevated plateau on the left.   The Tay is
soon crossed, over a graceful iron girder viaduct of 360
feet span, and a mile and a half further, Dalguise Station is
reached, where the valley narrows up.   We now pass through
very pretty oak and birchen woods, and obtain charming
glimpses of the Tay, on the left, all along at this point.   The
train then enters a tunnel of 360 yards, a mile before it pulls
up at Dunkeld, getting pretty peeps of the Tay, the village
of Inver, and the town of Dunkeld, until the station, really

AT BIRNAM.

although named Dunkeld, which is half a mile distant by road,
is reached.   Here the tourist who wishes to examine the points
of historical association and the picturesque surroundings of
this most beautiful and interesting locality, will break his
journey.   Within one minute's walk of the railway station
he will find all the comforts that his heart can desire in the
recently extended, sumptuously furnished, and tastefully decorated Birnam Hotel.   It is the only Hotel in Birnam, is
built in the Saxon-Gothic style, and, with its castellated
towers, impresses the traveller more with the idea of a
gentleman's private residence than a house of public entertainment.   The internal arrangements are in keeping with
its external appearance.   Every room in the house combines
comfort and elegance.   The windows on all sides command
the most magnificent views of the surrounding scenery.   The
house contains one of the most spacious dining-rooms iu
Scotland, and a good billiard room.   The grounds and gardens
are extensive, and have a convenient entrance from the Hotel,
or through two handsome Cyclopian iron gates, which lead
to a long avenue of trees extending from the front to the

river Tay, on the banks of which will be found two huge trees, the last of the old forest of Birnam, and said to be more than a thousand years old. One of them is a majestic oak, having, five feet from the ground, a girth of 18 feet, while the other, a sycamore, at the same height, measures 19 feet 8 inches. Six miles of the Tay can, by arrangement with the proprietor, be fished by visitors at this Hotel. The climate of the district for salubrity and invigorating health-giving qualities cannot be surpassed. The locality is beautifully sheltered, closed in as it is by wooded eminences on all sides, the classic Hill of Birnam, 1324 feet high, on the south, and the loftier masses of Craig-y-barns to the north and Craig-y-vinean to the west, their sides thickly covered with pine to their summits.

Birnam Hill, in the immediate vicinity of the Hotel, has been made classic in "Macbeth"—

"Fear not, till Birnam do come to Dunsinane."

From Skakespeare's references to these and other places in the district, it is certain that he was there and personally well acquainted with its surroundings.

From the Birnam Hotel several places of great beauty and interest can be conveniently visited. One of these is Murthly Castle and grounds, through which the proprietor of the Hotel has the privilege of driving his guests. On the way the carriage passes through the famed pass of Birnam, and soon after entering the grounds the visitor on his left notices Birnam Hall, the favourite autumn retreat of Sir John Millais, the celebrated artist, whose residence and reproduction on canvas of some of the finest views in the neighbourhood have rendered this lovely district for ever classical. There are also, in an opposite direction, the Falls of the Hermitage and the Rumbling Bridge, the latter worth going any distance to see. On the way to these Falls the village of Inver—where still stands intact the cottage where Neil Gow, the famous fiddler and composer, was born and died—is noticed

a little distance away on the right, where the Braan joins
the Tay. Everyone will, of course, visit

DUNKELD CATHEDRAL,

a mile from Birnam. On the way the traveller passes over
the graceful stone bridge of seven arches erected by John,
fourth Duke of Atholl, between 1805 and 1809, at a cost of
£40,000. From the centre arch of this noble and elegant
structure a glorious view in every direction is obtained of
the surrounding landscape. During the Pictish period Dunkeld
was a Royal residence. In the sixth century it was visited
by St. Columba and Kentigern. The choir of the Cathedral
was commenced in 1318 by Bishop Sinclair, and in 1406
Bishop Cardney founded the nave, the whole edifice being
completed by Bishop Thomas Lauder in 1460. Exactly a
hundred years later it was despoiled of all its best ornaments
by order of the Scottish Privy Council, and it continued in
ruins until the choir was converted into the present parish
church by Duke John at a cost of £6000. The other portions
of the Cathedral are ruinous and roofless. It contains several
monuments, the most notable of which are a recumbent effigy
of the "Wolf of Badenoch" in full armour, and a marble
tablet erected in the vestibule a few years ago by the officers
and men of the 42nd Royal Highlanders (Black Watch)
to commemorate the death of their comrades who fell in
battle since the regiment was first embodied in 1740, down
to the close of the Indian Mutiny in 1859. The monument
is surmounted by the old colours of the regiment, "all tattered
and torn," having been through many a sanguinary and
hard won fight.

In the immediate vicinity of the Cathedral, and within the
grounds, is the Highland residence of the Dowager Duchess
of Atholl, where she had the honour of entertaining Her
Majesty on three different occasions.

During the summer, coaches leave the Hotels in the morning
for Blairgowrie and Braemar, where they arrive between five

and six in the afternoon, a distance of 46 miles. Various other excursions can be made by coach or rail, particulars of which can be obtained at the Birnam Hotel, at the Duke of Atholl Arms, or at the Royal, the two last being also well-found and excellently-conducted Hotels in Dunkeld. In 1891 the population of Dunkeld, without Birnam, was 613.

Having satiated himself with the historical associations and scenery of the place and district, the tourist, who has broken the journey here on his way south, rejoins the train where he left it at Dunkeld Station, one minute's walk from the Birnam Hotel, and in a few seconds more finds himself on a gradient of 1 in 80 skirting the famous Hill of Birnam on his right. Here he should look back and take a last look at the magnificent panorama just left behind him, this being by far the best point from which to see the whole picture at a glance closed in on all sides by richly-wooded eminences, crowned in the distance by the mountains of Craig-y-barns, in the north, and Craig-y-vinean, to the west, a bold and charming background to one of the prettiest combinations of scenery in the Highlands. In a few minutes Murthly tunnel, 300 feet, is entered and a mile further on will be seen on the right the Malakoff Arch, originally designed as the approach to the new Castle of Murthly, of which a glimpse may be obtained on a terrace on the same side, through its thickly-wooded policies, as the train rushes along. It is an imposing modern structure, in the Elizabethan style, commenced in 1826, roofed in 1838, but never finished, the death of its then proprietor, Sir John Stuart, having stopped its further progress. Quite close to it is the old Castle, forming three sides of a square. It has recently undergone a complete overhaul and is occupied by the proprietor. The grounds and gardens are very fine, but in order to see them parties must drive or walk through them. A mile and a half further and Murthly station is passed. The large building on the left, surrounded by a half-grown plantation and extensive grounds is the Murthly Lunatic Asylum. The country now begins to get gradually flat and tame, as the train rushes through the fertile Valley of Strathmore. Three and a half miles further, through extensive plantations of larch, fir, and spruce, Stanley Junction is reached, where, on the left, the Caledonian Railway branches off to the right for Aberdeen. Luncarty Station, in the neighbourhood of which in the tenth century, during the reign of Kenneth III., a desperate battle was fought between the Scots and the Danes, when the former, almost overcome by their opponents, were encouraged and rallied by a common country peasant and his two sons whose only weapons were their plough-yokes, whereupon the Scots again charging secured a decisive victory over their enemies. From this valiant peasant, named Hay, descended the Hay Earls of Errol. From this point the train proceeds through a level, flat country along the right bank of the river Tay, in some places quite close to it. On the left bank of the river, among the trees, the ancient Palace of Scone, now the residence of the Earl of Mansfield, is seen in the distance. Here Robert the Bruce was crowned in 1306, while in the Church adjoining it Charles II. was crowned, the last in Scotland, on the 1st of January, 1651. We now pass through the North Inch of Perth, on which was fought in 1396, in the reign of Robert III., the sanguinary clan battle celebrated in Scott's " Fair Maid of Perth," and which, as regards those engaged in it, has been the theme of controversy ever since. In another minute the train pulls up at PERTH GENERAL STATION, 144 miles from Inverness, and from this central point passengers can find their way conveniently to Edinburgh, *via* the Forth Bridge, to Glasgow, *via* Stirling, to London, *via* either, and to all parts of the United Kingdom, north and south, east and west. The population of Perth in 1891 was 29,899 souls.

BALLINLUIG TO ABERFELDY, LOCH TAY, KILLIN, CALLANDER AND OBAN.

THIS is one of the most interesting tours in the Highlands. A branch of the Highland Railway, 9 miles, connects Ballinluig with Aberfeldy. In less than a minute after leaving the junction the train crosses, first the Tummel and then the Tay, by long viaducts of latticed iron girders, and immediately enters the picturesque valley of Strath Tay. Having crossed the river, leaving the Duke of Atholl monument on the hill to the right, a row of small cottages are observed on the same side, the thatched one being that in which the late Hon. Alexander Mackenzie, Premier of Canada, was born. The scenery of Strath Tay is lovely and varied all along.

Aberfeldy is famed principally for its Tartan and Tweed Mills belonging to Messrs P. & J. Haggard, who manufacture the native wool, clan tartans, plaids, tweeds, crumbcloths, blankets, plaidings, winceys, and the other materials for which this firm has long been noted. There are two good Hotels in the village, the Breadalbane Arms and the Station. From the former a four-in-hand coach runs regularly during the summer season in connection with the Loch Tay steamers at Kenmore, six miles distant.

Leaving Aberfeldy, the tourist observes on the right a substantial stone bridge of five arches across the Tay, erected by General Wade after the '45, and beyond it some little distance is the Weems Hotel. At the near end of the Bridge is observed a fine monument erected to commemorate the formation of the Black Watch. The coach, however, keeps to the left along a lovely drive which follows the river until it reaches the entrance lodge to the policies of Taymouth Castle, where it turns still further to the left. Several pretty mansion-houses are seen embosomed along the face of the slope on the opposite bank of the river. The road throughout is richly-wooded on either side, and in summer the foliage is so dense that Taymouth Castle, the principal Highland residence of the Marquis of Breadalbane, can only be seen from one particular point—the summit of a slight ascent, within the policies, called the Vista Fort, from which a splendid view is obtained. The Castle is one of the most magnificent and palatial residences occupied by any of the Scottish nobility. Its predecessor was known as Balloch Castle, or Baile-Loch, and originally belonged to the Macgregors. The present noble structure is a great quadrangular pile of four storeys, with round corner towers, a central pavilion mounting to a height of 150 feet, and wings of two storeys at opposite corners. The grounds are most extensive, and the varied beauty of the surroundings baffle description.

From the Vista Fort a very fine view is obtained of Loch Tay, stretching for 16 miles immediately in front, hemmed in by gigantic mountains on both sides. Ben Lawers, on the right, mounts to an altitude of 4000 feet, while the lofty Schiehallion, to the north, rises to 3547 feet above sea level.

The Queen and Prince Albert were guests at the Castle during their visit to Scotland in 1842. Her Majesty re-visited the district incognita in 1866 along with the Princess Louise, the Dowager Duchess of Atholl, and Miss Mac-gregor, and viewed the grand panorama from the Vista Fort.

Having enjoyed the comprehensive and enchanting view from this point, we return to the coach, which then dashes down hill to the end of Loch Tay, where passing through the village of Kenmore, it turns sharply to the right, crosses the river as it emerges from the lake by a fine stone bridge of five arches, and in a few seconds pulls up at the Breadal-bane Arms, a plain but commodious and well-managed Hotel.

Taymouth Castle gardens are situated a little past the Hotel, on the northern shore of the lake, and further on still, in the loch, is a small island, said to be artificial, in which lies buried Sybilla, daughter of Henry I. of England, who became the Queen of King Alexander I. of Scotland. This trip is continued by a delightful sail on

LOCH TAY TO KILLIN

by the steamers which ply daily on this fine lake. Immediately on the arrival of the coach at Kenmore, either of the swift steamers, "Lady of the Lake" or "Sybilla" is waiting at the pier, ready to start for Killin, at the other end of the loch, 16 miles distant.

The scenery along this route is picturesque and beautiful in the extreme. Calling at Fernan; at Ardtaluaig, on the south side, from which a good view of Ben Lawers is obtained; at Lawers, on the north, and at Ardeonaig on the south side, the boat arrives at Killin, a prettily-situated village at the south-west end of the lake, where there is an excellent Hotel. The Breadalbane mausoleum is in the vicinity and Finlarig Castle, an ancient seat of the same family, now a picturesque ivy-covered ruin, is close by. By the kind permission of the Marquis visitors may see every Wednesday the Kinnell Vine, said to be the largest in the world.

KILLIN TO OBAN.

The tourist may now proceed by rail to Oban *via* Crianlarich, Tyndrum, and Dalmally, past the head of Lochawe; to Fort-William, changing at Crianlarich; to Glasgow, by the West Highland line, *via* Dumbarton and Helensburgh; or to Stirling, Edinburgh, Glasgow, and the south, *via* Callender and Dunblane. There are excellent Hotels all along the route to Oban—at Crianlarich, the nearest station for Loch Lomond; at Tyndrum; at Dalmally, charmingly-situated at the head of Glenorchy; and at the head of Lochawe, close to the station and to the pier erected for the steamers which ply on the lake. Continuing the journey to Oban, Taynuilt—where there is a good Hotel—is soon passed, and from Oban the traveller can find his way, over the most delightful routes, to any part of the Highlands. For a description of the district from Oban to Inverness see pages 110 to 131.

NAIRN

AS A

HEALTH RESORT

From Photo. by]

High Street, Nairn.

[J. Valentine & Sons.

NAIRN AS A HEALTH RESORT.

THE Royal Burgh of Nairn stands on the southern shore of the Moray Firth, and on the west bank of the River Nairn. In olden times, however, the river seems to have been rather undecided as to where it should join the sea, sometimes flowing to the west of the town, but in 1820 it was helped to a decision and confined to its present channel. The old name of the town was Invernairn, and under this name it appears as a Royal Burgh in manuscripts of the 13th century. The oldest existing charter was granted by James VI. and is dated 1597. It makes mention of former charters granted by Alexander I. and his immediate successors, and confirms the privileges conferred upon the burgh by these older deeds. This charter was ratified by the Scottish Parliament in 1661. The oldest minute-book of the Burgh Council begins on the 16th November, 1657; but a list of Provosts, given in *The History of Nairnshire*, goes back as far as 1450.

POPULATION. The population of Nairn Parish is about 5000, and of these about 1200 are supported by the fishing industry. The fishermen live by themselves in the part of the town nearest the river mouth, and, apart from business relations, they have but little intercourse of any kind with the rest of the people. They seem to belong to one original family; for " Main " is almost the only surname among them. They are a sober, steady race, and most enterprising in pursuit of their calling. During the herring season they sail far, and their boats visit all the fishing grounds of the British Isles, following up the migratory herring shoals. The various occupations connected with the building trade afford employment to almost all the rest of the working class.   There are no manufactures.

Nairn, like Inverness, has been a "lowland" town from time immemorial, English being the general tongue of the people, though Gaelic was, and is still, spoken by many, chiefly immigrants from the neighbouring Highlands.   This use of two languages suggested King James' boast that his Scottish town of Nairn was so large that the folk at one end did not understand the language spoken at the other.

BUILDINGS AND INSTITUTIONS. Nairn has three Presbyterian Churches, including Established and the United Free; one Episcopal Church, and Congregational and one Roman Catholic.   The United Free High Church is a fine Gothic building, to the right hand as one enters the town from the Railway Station.   Its beautiful spire is a landmark for miles around. The new Established Church has also a fine appearance, and its square tower is a striking object in any view of the town.   Nairn has long been very much alive to the necessity of having good facilities for education.   Excellent provision has been made in the Board Schools for ordinary standard work, while the Academy, which is under a special Board of Governors, devotes its curriculum mainly to the higher departments of study, pupils who have passed the sixth standard being admitted free.   The Academy possesses several endowments, and awards a number of free scholarships by open annual competition.   The Nairn Museum, of which the members of the Literary Institute are the curators, is accommodated in the Public Hall Buildings.   It is especially rich in the Geological department, containing well-chosen specimens illustrative of Scottish Geology and also that of Norway and Greenland.   Among these are many fossils from the old red sandstone strata of the Nairn district.   In the section of Mineralogy its collection is of considerable value, and contains many rare and precious crystals from all parts of the world.   The Museum also possesses many things of scientific, antiquarian and foreign interest.

NAIRN AS A HEALTH RESORT. For over fifty years Nairn has enjoyed a high reputation as a watering-place and general health resort. It is popularly called the "Brighton of the North," for it is the chief "City of Refuge" north of the Grampians for those whose constitution compels them to take anxious thought about climate and situation. Apart from its great natural advantages, to which we shall presently refer, both the Corporation of the burgh and its private citizens spare neither pains nor expense to make the town worthy of its popular name. A copious supply of good water has been introduced, special attention is paid to the street-cleaning department, and the drainage problem—always a matter of first importance in a health resort—has been thoroughly dealt with by the formation of a sewage farm on the farther side of the River Nairn, and at a sufficient distance from the town. None of the sewage is discharged into the sea.

CLIMATE. "The climate," says a medical report, "in its character possesses a combination of the bracing element with dryness, sunshine and moderate warmth. Nairn has hitherto enjoyed the reputation of being one of the driest counties in Scotland. The average rainfall is a fraction over 20 inches annually. This is owing to its geographical position, being bounded by hills to the north, south, and west. The average maximum temperature is 52.55, and the minimum 39.17, temperatures which compare favourably with places much further south. During March, April, and May north and east winds are in some seasons troublesome, while the rest of the year south and south-west winds prevail. With few exceptions the winters are not severe; very little snow falls, and frost does not hold long sway, while mist and fog are seldom seen." An earlier writer enthusiastically observes, "Although this country is in a climate considerably northern, yet no country in Europe can boast of a more pure, temperate and wholesome air. No part of it is either too hot and sultry in summer, nor too sharp and cold in winter; and it is gener-

ally, and, I think, justly, observed that in the plains of
Moray they have forty days of fair weather in the year more
than in any other county in Scotland." From another
medical report we quote the following :—" Greater attention
is now being paid to different localities within the British
Isles, presenting soil, climate and arrangements suitable for
winter quarters ; and it is certain that, sooner or later, the
claims of Nairn as a residence in winter will become as well
known and appreciated as its advantages as a sea-bathing
resort in summer already are."

SITUATION.   The town of Nairn stands on two ancient
sea-beaches. The upper of these terraces,
on which the greater part of the town is
built, is from 50 to 60 feet above the sea level ; the fisher-
town, which stands on the lower terrace, being about 30 feet
above the sea. These beaches are composed mainly of
extensive deposits of fine sand and gravel, interspersed in
places with patches of boulder clay, the whole resting upon
the old red sandstone. Thus the porous nature of the soil
adds materially to the dryness of the locality, even a heavy
rainfall being absorbed almost as quickly as it falls.

A magnificent view of land and sea may be had from
almost any part of the town. Right opposite and about
nine miles away, the rampart rocks of Cromarty rise boldly
from the Moray Firth, the massive line of rock broken only
by the entrance to the Bay of Cromarty. The cliffs on
either side of the portal are known as the Sutors, and within
them a splendid and secure harbour opens out—the only
good natural harbour on the East Coast—where the largest
ships afloat could find safe anchorage. To the left and
inland, the huge mass of Ben Wyvis arrests the eye, and
further west the distant peaks of Strathglass and Glen Farrar.
North-east from the Sutors of Cromarty the rugged coast-line
recedes past Easter Ross, Sutherland and Caithness, until
sea and sky meet far out in the German Ocean, and the
gazing eye turns homeward, drawn by the sandy coast of
Moray on the east.

ACCOM-
MODATION.

Ample provision has been made for the accommodation of visitors, and of a nature to suit all reasonable requirements. The Hotels are numerous and well-appointed. The Royal Marine Hotel is on the beach, and the Nairn Hotel close to the Golf Course. More centrally situated are the Royal, the Station, and the Caledonian Hotels, all in High Street, the Star Hotel in Church Street, the Waverley Temperance Hotel and others. For those who prefer semi private accommodation there are several well-conducted Boarding Houses, such as Shaw's Private Hotel, Clifton House, Washington House, Golf View, and Johnstone's Private Hotel. Visitors who prefer private lodgings or furnished houses rented by the month can readily find something to suit them from among the scores of villas and other houses which have been built to meet this demand. The charges are moderate on the whole.

SEA-
BATHING.

In no other watering-place in Scotland, and in but one or two in England, are there such excellent bathing facilities as in Nairn. For miles upon miles along the margin of the sea stretches an expanse of smooth clean sand, soft as a carpet and firm underfoot, gently sloping into the deeper water. Thus, although a large tract of tidal shore is uncovered at low water, the perpendicular rise and fall of the tide is not great. There are no dangerous currents, no quicksands, no sudden descents into deep water. To guard, however, against the rare contingency of an accident, a boat provided with life buoys is always kept at the bathing station. A sufficient number of comfortable bathing coaches are employed during the season. From Shaw's Private Hotel eastwards, the beach is reserved for ladies.

There is also a splendid covered salt-water swimming-bath, 80 feet square, with a swimming course of one hundred yards. This is a great convenience in wet or windy weather when it would be uncomfortable to bathe in the sea. The floor of the bath is hewn out of the solid rock, and the depth of water slopes from 18 inches at one to six feet at the other.   A competent teacher is always at hand to give instruction in swimming if required.   In the same building there is a suite of single baths with all conveniences for every description of bathing, including pine, ozone, and peat baths. There is also a bathing establishment in connection with the Marine Hotel, where plunge, shower, spray and douche baths may be had in fresh or sea-water, and at any temperature.

RECREATIONS.   Clubs are in existence for the encouragement of cricket, bowling, tennis, rowing, swimming, etc., and their privileges are open to visitors on fair conditions.   There is a Reading Room in connection with the Literary Institute.   Nairn is especially fortunate in possessing a fine Golf Course which attracts increasing numbers of those who love the ancient and loyal game.   The Club House, presented by Sir R. B. Finlay, on whose ground it stands, is within a mile of the town, and the course of 18 holes stretches westward from there for three miles along the shore of the Moray Firth. It is very varied in character and gives good practice in negotiating all kinds of golfing problems.   The course is in the hands of a large and influential club, and is open to members only, but membership for definite periods is accorded to visitors on easy terms.   A professional is employed as caretaker, and the greens are kept in splendid order.   Another course of nine holes has been laid out on the east side of the town, and it affords considerable variety of play.

PLACES OF INTEREST   Though Nairn itself is a very old town, it contains no building of historical or antiquarian interest.   The old castle, built by William the Lion about 1291, occupied the high bank of the river known as the Constabulary or Castle Hill, but not a trace of it now remains except the name. Balblair, which stands on rising ground to the south-west, marks the place where the Duke of Cumberland's army encamped on the night before the battle of Culloden.   The

From Photo. by]

Nairn Golf Course.

[J. Valentine & Sons

Duke himself rested for the night in a house in Nairn belonging to Rose of Kilravock and now known as Macgillivray's Buildings.   About three or four miles south of Nairn, and to the right of the Grantown road, is the picturesque ruins of Rait Castle.   A magnificent view of the countryside may be obtained from the summit of the hill behind.   This hill is scattered over with huge travelled boulders, and its rocks show distinct traces of glacial action. Glenferness and Dulsie Bridge, about 12 miles out, are well worth a visit.   Dulsie is considered to be "one of the most beautiful and romantic spots in the world."   Between Dulsie and Glenferness is the Rock Walk, perhaps the finest bit of scenery on the river.

> " The primrose pale and violet flower
> Found in each cliff a narrow bower . . .
> Aloft, the ash and warrior oak
> Cast anchor in the rifted rock ;
> And higher still the pine tree hung
> His shattered trunk, and frequent flung,
> Where seemed the cliffs to meet on high,
> His boughs athwart the narrowed sky."

Sir Thomas Dick Lauder writes of Glenferness, "At Ferness, about two miles below Dulsie Bridge, the river sweeps for three miles round a high peninsula, through some of the wildest scenery imaginable, between lofty and precipitous rocks, towering in some places into castellated shapes, where the natural pine shoots out its tortuous and scaly form, mingled with birch and other trees.   In the middle of a beautiful holm which the river embraces before it enters this romantic part of its course, stands a lonely cairn with a rudely sculptured obelisk rising from it.   Tradition tells us that this is the grave of two lovers. . . . . . . This solitary spot is perfectly beautiful."   Other places of interest within easy walking, driving, or cycling distance are mentioned or described elsewhere, as follows :—

Auldearn,	- - - -	$2\frac{1}{2}$ miles	- -	page 134.
The Blasted Heath,	-	3 ,,	- -	,, 135.
Darnaway Castle,	- -	8 ,,	- -	,, 135.
Brodie Castle,	- -	6 ,,	- -	,, 135.

The Culbin Sands,	- 10 miles	- -	page	135.
Cawdor Castle,	- - 5 ,,	- -	,,	106.
Kilravock Castle, -	- 6½ ,,	- -	,,	104.
Culloden Moor, -	- 12 ,,	- -	,,	98.
Clava, Druidical Cir- cles and Standing Stones, - - -	} 13 ,,	- -	,,	102.
Fort-George, - -	- 8½ ,,	- -	,,	133.

INVERNESS TO AVIEMORE.

SHORTLY after leaving Inverness Station the train crosses first the Railway line and then the high road to Nairn and the east, passing Stoneyfield House on the left and Raigmore House and grounds on the right, as it begins to turn away from the sea. About two miles out, and close to the line on the right, is Cradlehall, at one time the residence of a certain Major Cauldfield who succeeded to General Wade's office of road-builder in the north. The place took its name from his ingenious device for the accommodation of guests who had partaken of his generous hospitality " not wisely but too well." He had a number of boxes or cradles constructed in his dining hall, into these the helpless guests were bundled and then hoisted up to the rafters by means of block and tackle, there to remain until sober enough to find their several ways home, and not scandalise the community by lying promiscuously along the roadside. A little beyond Cradlehall, the line, hitherto on high embankments, passes through a deep cutting into Culloden woods. To the left hand, but concealed by fine old trees, is

CULLODEN HOUSE,

which used to be a perfect museum of relics of Prince Charlie and the '45. These, however, were sold by auction after the death of the last laird of Culloden in 1897, and so scattered all over the country, but the whole neighbourhood is still full of historical interest. The President's Tree, a large oak which stands out prominently on the left, is so called after Lord President Forbes whose influence among the Highland chiefs was so powerful at the time of the Rebellion. It was owing to his efforts alone that fully half the Highlands remained loyal to the Government at that critical time. Not far from this tree is St. Mary's Well, one of the many wishing wells of the country, to which many young people still make pilgrimage on the 1st of May. Steel's Mount is also close at hand, the place where a number of Prince Charlie's officers were slaughtered after a loathsome imprisonment in the dungeons of Culloden House. To the right, as the train leaves the wood, notice a hollow where some of the clans rested on their return from the fatal march to Nairn on the night before the Battle of Culloden. Presently the train draws up at

CULLODEN MOOR,

the first station on the line.   The battlefield is about a mile westward of the station.   A description of the battle is given elsewhere (page 98 *et seq.*) and need not detain us here.   In a few minutes after leaving Culloden the train passes over the Nairn valley by a fine viaduct 600 yards long.   It consists of 28 arches of 50 feet span, and one of 100 feet, the latter being across the river bed.   The structure is one of the largest and loftiest stone railway bridges in the kingdom, substantial and yet graceful.   From here is obtained a splendid view of the Nairn valley.   On the south bank of the river, between it and the railway, are the circles and standing stones of Clava, to which reference is made on page 102.   Many of the stones here and in the neighbourhood bear those indentations which are known as cup-marks, one stone in the ring having as many as twenty of them grouped in clusters.   Further up the river the Doon of Daviot stands forth prominently, its summit crowned by a vitrified fort, and in the distance rise the rugged mountains that sentinel the sources of the Nairn.   Eastward are the woods of Cantray, Kilravock and Cawdor, with the blue of the Moray Firth beyond.   This whole district is of considerable geological interest.   Some huge specimens of travelled boulders, fine beds of boulder clay and strata of the old red sandstone rich in fossil remains, may be seen in the immediate neighbourhood.

Leaving the viaduct the train ascends the hillside on a gradient of 1 in 60, passing through deep cuttings and over high embankments, affording many a fine outlook upon the scenery of the Inverness district.   Just across the Nairn, a young pine wood hides the battlefield of Culloden, the haze of smoke rising above the trees shows where Inverness lies,

From Photo. by]   **Nairn Viaduct (Culloden Moor).**   [D. Whyte.

From Photo. by]   **Findhorn Viaduct (Tomatin).**   D. Whyte.

with the Moray Firth stretching away to the north and east, the great mass of Ben Wyvis rises in front, and far to the west may be seen the dome-shaped Mealfuarvonie overlooking the Great Glen.   Two or three miles beyond the viaduct, as we pass under the shadow of Meall Mor, we note a house lying near by the river.   This is Daltullich where a fight took place in 1495 between the Calders and the Campbells for the possession of Muriel Calder, the infant heiress of Cawdor. The Campbells lost the fight but kept the girl.   She was afterwards married to Sir John Campbell, son of the then Duke of Argyle, and they became the progenitors of the present Cawdor Campbells.

Rounding the shoulder of Meall Mor we pass Daviot Station and presently enter the

MACKINTOSH COUNTRY.

The narrowest part of the pass which marks the watershed between the Nairn and the Findhorn is called the "Threshold of the Highlands," and is the scene of the "Rout of Moy," well known to Highland Ballads.   On an April evening in 1746, Lord Loudon set out from Inverness with 1500 men to attempt the capture of Prince Charlie who was lying at Moy Hall that night almost unattended.   Word of the expedition came to Donald Fraser, blacksmith of Moy, and with four other men he arranged to ambush the soldiers in this pass.   The five disposed themselves at intervals along the hillside, and as the head of the column appeared, raised such a noise with firing and shouting that the soldiers thought that all the Highland clans were sweeping down upon them. They were seized with a panic and fled back to Inverness rather faster than they came.

The next stop is at Moy Station, opposite the entrance lodge of

MOY HALL,

the seat of the Mackintosh.   The mansion is a fine example of the Scottish baronial style of architecture, its chief feature being a massive square tower which stands boldly out from the dark green of the woods.   Some most interesting relics of Prince Charlie and his day have found a resting-place here with many other historical antiquities. The loch beneath is rather over a mile long by half a mile wide. The larger of its two islets contains a fine granite obelisk 70 feet high, erected to the memory of Sir Æneas Mackintosh, the 23rd Chief of the clan. On this island stood the old castle of Moy together with a number of smaller houses. During an ancient feud the Cummings invested the place and, not being able to come to close quarters, tried to drown out the Mackintoshes by building a dam across the outlet at the south end of the loch. One of the latter, however, on a dark night made his way to the dam on a raft and managed to destroy it, letting loose the waters upon the unsuspecting Cummings encamped below. Many of these were drowned, and it is said that the bold Mackintosh also perished with them.

As the train passes the south end of the loch, note a small stream directly opposite. On the bank of this stream, about a mile away, the last wolf in this district was killed by Macqueen of Pollochaig as late as about the end of the 17th century. His own account of the adventure was:—"As I came through the Slochd, by east the hill there, I fore-gathered with the peast; I buckled with him, and durkit him, and whuttled his craig, and brccht away his head for fear he might come alive again."

About a mile further, and to the left hand, the river Findhorn passes roaring down into the Pass of Pollochaig on its way to the sea.

TOMATIN

is the next halt, a pretty little village embowered in trees. Here the Freeburn Hotel affords good accommodation, and trout fishing may be had by permission up to the 1st August. Just beyond the station a beautiful viaduct carries the railway line across the deep ravine of the Findhorn. The viaduct, 445 yards long, is built on a curve and is 144 feet above the river bed. It consists of 9 spans of 130 feet each, with landward arches, of 36 feet span at either end. The view from here, both up and down the river, is wild and impressive. At this point we pass out of the Mackintosh country, and ascending the hillside, presently strike into Drumbain cutting about a mile and a half from the viaduct. The cutting is over 50 feet deep for a great part of its length, and at its upper end there is a great depth of peat moss in which three successive forests of fir can be traced. As the train emerges from the cutting the highest point in the line is passed (1723 feet); and looking forward, we get our first view of the Grampian range, while to the west are the Monadhliath hills, a bleak expanse of moss, rock and heather. Leaving this short open tract, the train dashes into the gloom of the

SLOCHD MOR

or Great Pass, sometimes called Slochd Mhuic or the Wild Boar's Pass. This place was a veritable den of robbers for many years after the '45. The secret leader of one of their bands was a son of "Old Borlum," a Mackintosh laird. The history of this freebooter is given in Sir Thomas Dick Lauder's novel, "Lochandhu." Emerging from the pass we come into full view of Strathspey and the Badenoch district, Cairngorm looming large in front, with the Braemar mountains beyond. The line crosses the Aonaich burn by a fine viaduct of 8 arches of 37 feet span and 105 feet above the stream. Then, after swinging round the hillside and four times crossing the Bogbain burn, it passes along a series of cuttings and embankments into the Dalrachy cutting, one of the heaviest pieces of work in the construction of the line. The excavations took about 3 years to accomplish, the material cut through being clay for the most part. From this cutting the line passes over a high embankment, crosses the Dulnan river on a span of 180 feet and immediately stops at

CARR-BRIDGE.

The village of Carr-Bridge is about 900 feet above the sea-level, situated among great heath-clad hills and dense pine woods. The climate is good, the air is pure and bracing, and the place is a favourite resort of summer visitors. The accommodation is good, consisting of a large new hotel and numerous villas. Trout fishing may be had in the Dulnan river, and there are many beautiful walks by river, wood and hill, accessible to the public.   Duthil, about 2 miles down the, river, contains the burial place of the Grants of Seafield. Near the Free Church is a pine wood where the congregation worshipped in the open air, summer and winter, for years after the Disruption of '43.

Immediately after leaving Carr-Bridge we enter the Crannich woods where considerable trouble was caused by the peat moss when the line was being made.   Load after load of material amounting in the end to 50,000 cubic yards, was cast into the Slough ere the embankment was rendered secure.   Breaking from the wood we find ourselves in the valley of the Spey, and passing a Druidical circle close to the line on the right, the train pulls up at

AVIEMORE.

The total length of line between Inverness and Aviemore is 34 miles, and in that distance we have crossed no fewer than 150 bridges and 4 viaducts.   The continuation of the line south from Aviemore will be found on page 151.

GLASGOW AND THE HIGHLANDS.
ROYAL ROUTE
VIA CRINAN AND CALEDONIAN CANALS.

THE Swift Steamers, "GONDOLIER" or "GAIRLOCHY," sail from INVERNESS as under, conveying Passengers in connection with Steamers "Columba," "Iona," "Grenadier," "Chevalier," &c., &c.

For Banavie, Fort-William, and Ballachulish (for Glencoe), Oban, Greenock, and Glasgow.

Daily (ex Sunday) during June, July, August, and September, and every Monday, Wednesday, and Friday, till about 9th of October........................ ....at 7 a.m.

Banavie, Fort-William, and Ballachulish to Glasgow.

Daily (ex. Sunday) during June, July, August, and September, from Fort-William, 5.10; and Ballachulish, at 6.0 a.m.

Oban to Glasgow.

Daily *via* Crinan, during June, July, August, and September..................at 8.20 a.m.
          Also daily *via* Lochawe during June, July, August, and September.

The Royal Mail Steamer, "COLUMBA" or "IONA," sails daily at 7 a.m. (Sunday excepted) from GLASGOW BRIDGE WHARF for Ardrishaig and intermediate places, conveying passengers from

Glasgow to Oban.

Daily *via* Crinan, during June, July, August, and September....................at 7 a.m.
          Also daily *via* Lochawe during June, July, August, and September, at 7 a.m.

Glasgow to Ballachulish, Fort-William, and Inverness.

Daily during June, July, August, and September............. ....at 7 a.m.

Oban to Inverness.

Daily in June, July, August, and September, at 6 a.m., arriving at Inverness same day; and at 4.50 p.m., arriving at Banavie same evening. and Inverness following day.

Oban Ballachulish (Glencoe), Fort-William, and Banavie.

From Oban daily during June, July, August, and September, at 6 and 9.15 a.m., 12.30 and 5.5 p.m., and all the year round, daily at 12.30 p.m.

From Fort-William daily during June, July, August, and September, at 5.10 and 9 a.m., 1.0, 3.30, and 6.15 p.m.; and during the year, daily at 9 a.m.

Oban to Loch Scavaig.

Every Tuesday during June, July August, and September.....................at 7 a.m.

Oban to Skye and Gairloch.

Every Tuesday, Thursday, and Saturday, during June, July, August, & September at 7 a.m.

Oban to Staffa and Iona.

Daily in June, July, August, and September................................at 8 a.m.

Glasgow to Oban, Tobermory, Portree, and Stornoway.

"CLAYMORE" or "CLANSMAN," every Monday and Thursday (during the greater part of the year), at 12 noon; leaving Stornoway Monday and Thursday, Portree same evening; and Kyle af Lochalsh Tuesday and Friday, at 4 a.m., for Glasgow, &c.

Portree, Kyle of Lochalsh, and Inverness.
Calling at Raasay. Broadford &c., daily (to and from) during the year.

Stornoway (Mail Route) to Inverness and the South.
Via Kyle of Lochalsh. Daily (to and from) during the year.

Portree, Tarbert (Harris), Rodel, Lochmaddy, and Dunvegan.

Mail Steamer from Portree every Tuesday, Thursday, and Saturday morning, returning every Monday, Wednesday, and Friday morning, calling as above going and returning.

Oban (Railway Pier) to Tobermory, Castlebay, Lochboisdale, Lochmaddy, and Dunvegan.

The Royal Mail Steamer leaves Oban daily, except Sunday. For arrangements and hours of sailing see Handbills.

INVERNESS.

MACGILVRAY'S

TEMPERANCE HOTEL,

QUEENSGATE BUILDINGS.

Adjoining Post Office and Close to Railway Station.

Large Dining-Room and several Bedrooms added.

TARIFF.—BEDROOM, Single, 2/- ; Double, 3/-. BREAKFAST, 1/6 and 2/-. DINNER from 2/-. TEA from 1/3. ATTENDANCE, 6d.

Hot and Cold Baths,　　　　*Conveyance awaits Canal Steamers.*

RECOMMENDATIONS.

" I am pleased, though not surprised, to hear of your having to enlarge premises. Having stayed at your Hotel I was much impressed by the constant attention of Mrs Macgilvray and yourself to the comfort of your visitors. This, I think, is the secret of your success, and you can certainly use my name in recommending your Hotel."—Editor, *Scottish Reformer.*

" Shall recommend all my friends going to Inverness to your Hotel, with the assurance that they will find such kindly and hospital treatment as can only be expected at home and seldom at Hotels."—Bailie A. Hay, Peterhead.

" This little Hotel has won golden opinions for the care and attention given to visitors. Mr and Mrs Macgilvray have the happy art of making their patrons feel at home."—*Christian Union.*

" Mr and Mrs Macgilvray have during their tenancy done much to popularize this little Hotel. It is really a very comfortable house. Everything is most satisfactory and charges exceptionally low."—*Highland News.*

Sir Jas. and Lady Colquhoun—" Exceedingly comfortable, and every attention."

THE VICTORIA

HAIRDRESSING SALOON,

25 ACADEMY STREET, INVERNESS.

(Nearest the Railway Station. Opposite Macrae & Dick's.)

Cleanliness and Workmanship Guaranteed

Manager, STEPHEN HANDLEY.

NAIRN.
STATION HOTEL.

THIS MAGNIFICENT HOTEL, in convenience of arrangements and perfect appointments, ranks with the first establishments in the kingdom. Families, Tourists, and Commercial Gentlemen will find this First-class Hotel replete with every comfort and convenience, combined with strictly moderate charges.

Handsome Drawing Room, Coffee Room, Private Parlours, Commercial Room, Billiard Room, and Superior Bedrooms,

Furnished in first-class style and lighted throughout with Electric Light.

Parties Boarded by the Week and Month.   Cook's Coupons Accepted.

FIVE MINUTES' WALK FROM THE STATION AND TEN MINUTES' FROM THE GOLF LINKS. 'BUS AND HOTEL BOOTS AWAIT ARRIVAL OF ALL TRAINS.

C. MACPHERSON, Lessee.

(Under New Management.)

FOYERS HOTEL,

LOCH NESS.

Near the celebrated FALLS OF FOYERS. Beautifully situated, and commanding Finest Views of Loch Ness and the Great Glen.

Redecorated and most Comfortably Refurnished. *Electric Light Throughout.*

Salmon and Trout Fishing on Loch Ness, Farraline, Garth, and Bran Free to Visitors.

Foyers is the best place for Passengers down the Caledonian Canal to break their journey, as Steamers from Inverness arrive about 5.15 p.m., leaving Foyers about 9 a.m. next morning, thus avoiding the early start from Inverness.

POSTING. Telegrams—"HOTEL, FOYERS."

Post and Telegraph Office. *Charges Strictly Moderate.*

S. TILSTON, Proprietor.

LOCHCARRON HOTEL,

LOCHCARRON, ROSS-SHIRE.

THE attention of Tourists and the Public generally is respectfully invited to this comfortable and well-known Hotel. It is delightfully situated on Lochcarron, within three miles of Strathcarron Station. Commands a very beautiful view of Strathcarron and Attadale. The drives to Stromeferry, Shieldaig, Achnashellach, and Applecross, are almost unrivalled.

Sea Fishing and Boating most convenient.

All the conveniences of an Hotel are to be found combined with the comforts of a private dwelling.

at Moderate Charges.

JOHN MORRISON, Proprietor.

Hawkhill Marine Hotel,

FORTROSE, N.B.

THIS new Hotel, three quarters of a mile from Fortrose Station, is situated on one of the finest parts of the northern shore of the Moray Firth. The facilities for SEA BATHING are unique. There is a magnificent GOLF COURSE at hand. The surrounding country abounds in pleasant Walking and Driving Routes, including the Romantic Glades of Fairy Glen and St. Helena; while the Firth presents every facility for BOATING, SAILING, and FISHING.

The Hotel contains Dining Saloon, Drawing-Room, Billiard-Room, and Thirty Bedrooms, with numerous Private Sitting-Rooms.

HOT and COLD SEA WATER BATHS have been erected within the Hotel grounds by Messrs Doulton & Co., London, Manchester and Paisley. The sea water is pumped direct from the open ocean at high tide into large tanks and heated by steam, and Needle Spray and Plunge Baths can be had at any time. The Baths are under the Superintendence of a qualified Bath Attendant. BOWLING GREEN. LAWN TENNIS COURT.

Tariffs are on very moderate terms, Families being specially dealt with.

The Establishment is under the Personal Management of

DONALD CAMERON, Proprietor.

Loch Maree Hotel

ROSS-SHIRE.
(Lately Her Majesty's West Highland Residence.)

THIS HOTEL, beautifully situated in the centre of the Loch Maree District, and overlooking the Loch, is now leased by Mr THOS. STEWART McALLISTER, INVERNESS, and under first-class management.

N.B.—A COACH awaits at Gairloch the arrival of Mac-Brayne's Steamers during the season to convey Passengers to Loch Maree—eight miles distant

Visitors can have twenty square miles of Free Fishing in Loch Maree; also fishing on several other small Lochs quite close to the Hotel.

Boats and Tackle supplied free from the Hotel. Hill Ponies kept for hire. Post and Telegraph Office adjoining the Hotel.

Posting in all its Branches.